HOME AT LAST CHANCE

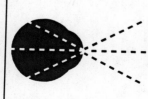

This Large Print Book carries the
Seal of Approval of N.A.V.H.

HOME AT LAST CHANCE

HOPE RAMSAY

KENNEBEC LARGE PRINT
A part of Gale, Cengage Learning

GALE
CENGAGE Learning®

Detroit • New York • San Francisco • New Haven, Conn • Waterville, Maine • London

GALE
CENGAGE Learning

LIBRARY OF CONGRESS CATALOGING-IN-PUBLICATION DATA

Ramsay, Hope.
    Home at last chance / by Hope Ramsay. — Large print ed.
        p. cm. — (Kennebec large print superior collection)
    ISBN-13: 978-1-4104-4328-1 (pbk.)
    ISBN-10: 1-4104-4328-0 (pbk.)
        1. City and town life—South Carolina—Fiction. 2. Large type books.
I. Title.
PS3618.A4775H66 2011
813'.6—dc23   2011033478

Published in 2011 by arrangement with Grand Central Publishing, a division of Hachette Book Group, Inc.

Printed in the United States of America
1 2 3 4 5   15 14 13 12 11
FD332

For my husband, Bryan,
whose love of stock car racing is
everywhere in this book.

ACKNOWLEDGMENTS

Thank you to my fabulous critique partners: Robin Kaye, Carla Kempert, and Lavinia Kent for their continuing help, guidance, and inspiration. I'd also like to acknowledge my wonderful editor, Alex Logan, for making me dig deeper and go further with this story than I thought possible. Many thanks also to Jan Nash for sharing her lovely story about prayer blankets. I am also indebted to Camomile Hixon for losing her unicorn and making me think about the nature of magic. And finally, I'd like to acknowledge the music of singer-songwriter David Wilcox. His song "Language of the Heart" was a touchstone for this book.

CHAPTER 1

Tulane Rhodes leaned forward in his seat and scowled at Sarah Murray out of a pair of greeny-gray eyes. "You painted my car sissy pink and put a bunny on its hood. How do you expect me to feel?" he snarled.

Sarah breathed in the scent of leather upholstery and corporate money. The National Brands Learjet had been placed at her disposal. She had about an hour — the time it took to fly from Martinsville, Virginia, to Columbia, South Carolina — in which to take charge of this angry man. She wasn't sure she could do it even if she had a hundred years, but she was going to give it her best shot. Her career depended upon it.

She squared her shoulders inside her black power suit. "Pink is the official color of the Cottontail Disposable Diaper brand," Sarah said. Her mother would be proud of her calm, controlled tone. Mother always said a proper Boston lady didn't raise her voice, but used quiet logic instead. Sarah really didn't want to be her mother, but right now, it was the best strategy she could muster.

Sarah continued ticking off points on her fingers. "Also, the car in question doesn't *belong* to you. It belongs to Jim Ferguson Racing. And I'm sure I don't have to point out that Mr. Ferguson is not happy with you right now. National Brands paid Mr. Ferguson millions of dollars for the privilege of painting that car pink. As part of the sponsorship deal, you — as Mr. Ferguson's driver — have a responsibility to show up at personal appearances. If you had shown up at your appearances last week, National Brands wouldn't have felt the need to send me here to do your advance work."

"To bully me, you mean," Tulane said as he settled back into his seat and crossed his arms over his chest. His biceps twitched. He was angry.

And huge. Tulane Rhodes filled the reclining seat with six feet and two hundred pounds of South Carolina good ol' boy. He possessed all the classic markers of his kind — a broad drawl and buzz-cut hair that framed an angular face with too many sun-induced laugh lines and crow's-feet. A well-worn Alabama T-shirt stretched across his broad shoulders. And a battered Atlanta

Braves baseball cap topped off the ensemble. Maybe if Tulane had worn a blue blazer or a Nike golf shirt with khakis, he might have overcome the stereotype. But he hadn't, and he didn't.

Sarah was in trouble. This man was dangerous, and angry, and likely to run her over at 200 miles an hour if he ever found out that she was the reason he was driving a pink stock car. He was also wickedly handsome, had a reputation for being a bad boy, and those green eyes of his had the unsettling effect of making her feel as if her panties were on fire.

She needed to concentrate on the task at hand, but she had no idea where to begin. So she borrowed a page from Grandmother Howland's handbook. She gave Tulane Rhodes *the Look*.

When given with the proper stare and just the right lift of an eyebrow, the Look could turn someone to stone in about one second flat. Grandmother Howland, who had been a devoted librarian and churchwoman, could lift her eyebrow perfectly and command silence, just like that.

"I am *not* a bully, Mr. Rhodes. I expect you to be an adult about this," Sarah said in a soft voice that she tried to invest with all the proper venom of her grandmother.

Tulane cracked the smallest of smiles. Lines bunched up around his eyes while his lower lip stretched into a sexy curve that displayed a couple of dimples. The mental image of Grandmother faded.

"Ma'am, pardon my asking, but you got something stuck up that butt of yours?"

"I beg your pardon?" The Look vanished.

"Well, you were grimacing, you know? You looked like you had gas pains or something. I guess it was just a passing thing, huh?" His smile broadened.

The man was onto her. Her black suit hadn't hidden her good-girl nature, apparently. Sarah had no other weapons at her beck and call so she forged ahead, just like Grandmother would have done.

"I would appreciate it if you would refrain from using such vulgar language. I must remind you that you will be the spokesperson for Cottontail Disposable Diapers, a family product with a wholesome image," Sarah said.

"Well, I'm not the wholesome family man you're looking for." Tulane broke eye contact and ducked down to stare out the window to his left. The jet had just taxied to the end of the runway, and the engines revved in anticipation of takeoff. The glare from the window highlighted the pulsing tendons in his jaw.

He shifted his gaze. "I know diddly about diapers. On the other hand, I did read something about National Brands making some real fine rubbers. You want to paint my car with a logo for condoms, I'm right there with you. I'm willing to talk about safe sex any day of the week. In fact, I try to practice safe sex *every* day of the week. But diapers? Uh-uh. Way I figure it, a diaper bunny is about the shittiest thing you could put on Jim Ferguson's Cup car."

Sarah could feel her cheeks coloring at Tulane's use of profanity. When was she going to get over this? She was twenty-five years old, a graduate of Harvard University, and she wanted to be like Deidre Montgomery, National Brands' vice president of marketing — a woman totally fluent in business profanity. How could Sarah ever achieve success in business if she couldn't get over her strict upbringing?

"Don't sputter, now," Tulane said, as if he could read her most intimate thoughts. "I hate it when a woman starts sputtering in outrage. It always reminds me of Miz Lillian Bray, the chairwoman of the Christ Church Ladies Auxiliary back home in Last Chance, South Carolina. You cuss in front of her and you're liable to end up serving endless hours as an altar boy." He looked out the window again. The Learjet was rolling, and the engines pressed Sarah back into her seat. With a roar, the little jet sped down the runway, rotated nose up, and surged into the sky. The ground dropped beneath them, providing a view of the spring-green vistas of the Virginia countryside.

Sarah studied the man for a long moment, trying to imagine him as an altar boy. She failed. Her experiences with altar boys had been far-reaching and entirely unsatisfying.

"Mr. Rhodes, I think it would be helpful if you considered me to be just like Miss Lillian. Just remember that my reports back to headquarters will make or break your career." Oh boy, she was so lame — like she really had that kind of authority or power. He was in trouble, but not that much trouble.

He gave her a smarmy look that started at her chest, came up to her face, and went back down, as if he realized she had overreached. She should have resented that gaze, but it made her feel oddly titillated and strangely alive. She didn't think any man had ever looked at her quite like that, as if she were a fat slice of Boston cream pie.

"If you don't mind my saying so," Tulane

said, "you are a whole lot younger than Lillian Bray. And, for the record, you sure don't have her skill when it comes to the Look either."

Sarah opened her mouth and shut it again. How on earth did he know about the Look?

"You were about to say something?"

Just how had this conversation taken this strange turn? "Mr. Rhodes, I need you to remember you are now a spokesperson for Cottontail Disposable Diapers. You have to be a role model. Why don't we spend our time more profitably by going through our schedule for the next couple of days?"

He settled back into the brown leather seat and tipped his baseball hat down over his eyes. "Honey, you can yammer all you want, but I was up late last night going over car setups with my crew chief, and I thought I'd get a little shut-eye before you have me officiating at diaper-changing contests."

"Mr. Rhodes, those events are designed to build traffic at the store."

Tulane opened one eye and angled his head. "Oh, really? I thought it was just for the fun of it."

"Sorry."

"Uh-huh. Look, lady, I don't want to be here. I don't want to go to Value Mart and put on a pink shirt with a bunny logo and sign autographs for people who are laughing at me. I'm only here because ya'll bullied Jim Ferguson and he told me to be here or else. So you could do me a huge favor and just hush up." His head slapped back on the seat, and his eye shut.

That was it — Sarah's career was officially over.

Tulane tried not to concentrate too hard on the high-pitched white noise of the jet engines. Their revs were not quite matched, and that sent a little harmonic buzz through the cabin that made his skin crawl.

He hated flying. He could never admit this or the entire world would laugh at him. A man who drove cars 200 miles an hour should not be afraid of flying. He took a deep breath, trying to counter his fear.

Maybe he should worry about losing his ride. That was a real and tangible fear. He was deep in Jim Ferguson's doghouse, and if he didn't straighten up and fly right, he might be out of a job.

The plane hit a serious bump in the sky, and every nerve ending in his body fried. He concentrated on relaxing the tense muscles in his jaw and thought about the little bitty woman National Brands had sent down to take charge of him. Sarah Murray was a bona fide nice girl. All by its lonesome, this made her immediately irresistible.

And she was easy on the eye. Some pretty impressive curves lurked under that black suit. She had killer eyes, too, of a shade not quite brown and not quite green. Her eyes kind of scrunched up when she smiled, and her freckled face was adorable when she blushed. Someone up in New York either had a sense of humor or knew exactly the kind of nursemaid to send in his direction. He really couldn't be nasty to a nice girl like that.

The plane buffeted sideways. Tulane opened his eyes. Sarah was studying him with a calculating look on her face. He needed to act fast, before she figured out he was a sissy when it came to planes. That would be too much to bear. He usually bloodied the noses of the bullies who crossed his path, but he was going to have to charm this woman.

He hauled in a big breath. "I reckon I owe you an apology."

He didn't sound real sincere, but she smiled up at him with a toothy grin that hit him like the g-forces on turn two at Bristol

Speedway. The plane skipped around the sky.

"So I couldn't help but notice that you come from up north." Oh brother. How the heck was he supposed to get around this little bitty obstacle with a line like that? His body flushed hot.

"I've lived in Boston most of my life. I moved to New York right after graduation from Harvard to take the job with National Brands."

"So did your folks come over on the *Mayflower* or something?" he asked.

Sarah's eyes flashed with annoyance. "Everyone asks that question. As a matter of fact, my mother's family *did* come over on the *Mayflower.*"

"And your daddy's family, too?" With his luck, her daddy was a governor or something. That would make her not only a cute bully, but a well-connected one.

"Dad's from Wyoming."

"Really?"

She nodded. The plane bumped. Tulane clutched the armrests. She noticed, but said nothing. *Good.*

"And what about you, Mr. Rhodes?"

He relaxed his death grip and reached for his Southern charm. "Well, I reckon you know all about me, ma'am."

"I know you grew up in a small town in South Carolina with a peculiar name. Your mother is a hairdresser and your father is a mechanic?"

He tried not to cringe. He wasn't about to make his daddy a national laughingstock by telling the truth about him. He'd been protecting Daddy's honor all his life, so he'd lied through his teeth in that bogus bio. He needed to change the subject. Now.

"So tell me," Tulane said, "how'd a nice girl like you get into the business of advancing celebrity athletes like me?"

"Mr. Rhodes, I hardly think —"

"Better fasten up back there," came the disembodied voice of the pilot. "We're going to have to weave our way through a few thunderstorms."

Just then, the plane took another hit from turbulent air. The clouds outside the window were turning an unsettling shade of gray. Tulane battled his fear by tightening his seatbelt.

He turned back toward Sarah. She didn't seem to be all that worried about falling out of the sky or being struck by lightning.

She leaned forward, as if nothing untoward was happening. "What I was about to say is that I hardly think driving a stock car makes you an athlete. An entertainer perhaps. Certainly a daredevil, but not an athlete."

"Trust me, it's a sport," he said through his locked teeth.

"It's entertainment. And besides, you just go around in circles for five hundred miles, so it's not very entertaining entertainment. That probably explains why it's the fastest-growing phenomenon in the entertainment industry."

"Look here, you name me one other sport where a man goes out and risks his life every time he performs." *And every time he has to fly to another city.*

She smirked. "Bull riding."

"What?"

"Bull riding. Not only do bull riders have to hang on to a raging bull, but they take their lives in their hands every time they enter the ring."

"Yeah, well, I reckon you'd never catch a bull rider in pink."

Her eyes widened, like she knew some great big secret. "You might be surprised what bull riders wear."

"And just exactly what do *you* know about bull riding?"

"My father rode bulls for a living. He was pretty good at it, too. I saw some pictures of him all dressed up in fringe and sequins —

purple ones."

"You're kidding me, right?"

"Why would I kid you about that?"

A flash came from outside the fuselage, followed by a crack of thunder, and it felt as if God were trying to strike one of them dead. "Shit," Tulane said aloud.

The red crawled up Sarah's neck, but otherwise she seemed unperturbed by the thunderstorm.

"How did a bull rider produce such a prissy little daughter?" Tulane asked.

"You think I'm prissy?" Sarah sat even straighter in her chair and looked down her nose. She resembled a twelve-year-old trying to be outraged.

"Yes, ma'am," he drawled, forgetting about the black cloud beyond the window.

Her eyes sparked with ire. "I am a lady, Mr. Rhodes, not a priss. I realize this distinction is probably lost on a person such as yourself."

"You don't like being prissy, do you?"

"I'm not prissy. I'm a businesswoman. I have a job to do, and I'd appreciate it if you would —"

"Like hell," he said.

The blush staining her neck started to crawl up her cheeks.

"See? I say the word 'hell' and you light

up like a neon Budweiser sign. Honey, *hell* isn't even a really bad cuss word. NASCAR wouldn't even dock me points or fine me if I said that word in a TV interview."

"I don't think it's necessary for us to have a full discourse on profanity, Mr. Rhodes."

"If you want to learn how to cuss, I can sure teach you how. Believe it or not, I have been fully briefed on the Federal Communications Commission's list of seven dirty words that are never to be said over the airwaves. Would you like me to help you learn them? We could start with the filthiest one on the list. By the way, it's f—"

"Don't say it, please." Sarah closed her eyes, but her face glowed. She didn't appear to be angry. She looked turned on and hot. Tulane suddenly knew exactly how to handle this particular nice girl that the folks in New York had sent to keep him in line.

"Okay, I won't say that word, although it almost escaped my lips a while ago when that lightning hit."

"I'm not surprised." She opened her eyes and gazed up at him. Yup, she was like every nice girl he'd ever met. A naughty spirit lurked deep inside her, yearning to be free. And wasn't it fun to play dirty with a nice girl?

"Okay, forget the FCC," Tulane said with

a smirk. "Let's start with something easier, like taking the name of the Lord in vain. People these days hardly think that's cussing."

"I'm surprised you would want to chance such a thing, given the way you've been clutching the arms of your seat."

Uh-oh. He didn't like that. If she ever told anyone that he was afraid of heights, he'd be laughed at from one end of America to the other. What in the world was he going to do about that?

One answer came immediately to mind as he studied her nice-girl pearls and pumps. It would be easy to compromise her integrity.

He launched his attack. "I have no idea what you're talking about. But why don't we just move to the really easy cuss words, like 'hell'? No one considers that a cuss word anymore. C'mon, girl, just say it once for me."

Sarah angled her chin up and something naughty ignited in her eyes. Tulane breathed a little easier. This might be fun.

"The hell I will," she said, and then her face turned beet red.

And just at that moment, a ray of sunshine came cascading through the window, lighting up her red hair like fire and making her look like a demonic angel. Tulane's pulse rate climbed, but for the moment it had nothing to do with his fear of flying.

CHAPTER 2

Sarah kept counting way past twenty as she paced back and forth across the gray linoleum of the Columbia Metropolitan Airport's General Aviation Terminal. The heels of her not-so-sensible pumps clicked against the floor like a ticking time bomb. She pressed her cell phone to one ear while she kept one eye on that infuriating man.

Tulane Rhodes sprawled in an athletic fashion across several of the terminal's plastic seats. He'd squared the baseball cap on his head, and the brim shaded those come-hither eyes of his. He was clearly happier on the ground than in the air. She wondered how she might actually use that little tidbit of inside information to control him.

Like that was ever going to happen.

Steve Phelps's assistant came on the line and gave her the bad news: There had been a screwup, and their scheduled limousine pickup had been inadvertently canceled.

Sarah knew that this screwup had been intentional, on purpose, and fomented by Steve, so that Sarah would fail to get Tulane to his personal appearance on time.

Steve wanted her gone from National Brands as quickly as possible. This explained why Steve, who was in charge of the NASCAR program, had ordered her out of the research department and onto the corporate jet.

This assignment might be beyond Sarah's experience, but she was not going to fail. "Oh hell," she muttered as she ended the call with Steve's less-than-helpful assistant.

As if on cue, Tulane licked his long index finger and drew an imaginary chalk line in the air. "That was real nice, honey, but in situations like this you probably want to really let it fly, you know?" Tulane said from his relaxed position on the bench. "There's nothing like yelling the f-word right out loud when things get screwed up." He launched an impossibly sexy smile that didn't show any teeth. "Go on. Do it. It might be real fun."

He was right, of course, but she couldn't let her lips form that word or say it out loud. She hated herself for that inability. So many of her problems would be solved if she could learn how to be like Deidre or some of the other women at National Brands. Maybe if she were that sort of hard woman, she could hurry Tulane along to one of the rental car agencies. With the weather delay and Steve's apparent sabotage, they needed to rent a car, and fast.

Sarah took a deep, calming breath. She could manage this situation.

"Well," she said to the man draped over the bench, "if Mohammed won't go to the mountain, then I guess we'll have to get the mountain to move." She braced her hands on her hips.

"Am I Mohammed or the mountain?" he asked, tipping back the brim of his dirty baseball cap.

"The mountain. God knows you're big enough. Isn't there some kind of weight penalty for race teams with large drivers?"

"I'm just long, honey, but I don't weigh much. You stick around me, and you'll find that out, sooner or later."

The blood heated her cheeks, and that appeared to amuse him. No doubt, in grade school he'd been like Georgie Porgie, kissing all the girls and making them cry.

"If you're suggesting that you and I will become intimate, the chances of that ever happening in this lifetime are nonexistent."

Tulane clutched his chest. "Man, you are one coldhearted woman. Can't you see I'm trying my best to get on your good side? And trust me, honey, you got several real nice sides hiding under that man-tailored suit you're wearing."

"Mr. Rhodes, you" — she pointed her finger, even though it was appallingly rude — "are trying to get me in trouble. So just stop with the lewd remarks, salacious suggestions, and offers to impugn my integrity. Grab your bags and get the lead out. We've got to go rent a car."

"Wow, how many three-dollar words do you know? I'm impressed."

"Mr. Rhodes, time is flying, and if I don't get you to Orangeburg on schedule, I will get into trouble."

"Oh. Well. I don't want to get you into any trouble." He settled deeper into the chair.

She had to control her temper. She counted to ten and tried hard not to grind her teeth. "Please get your bags," she finally said quietly. "We don't have much time."

"You mean I have to get up?"

"Yes," she ground out.

"You mean I have to carry my own bags?"

"Didn't I just ask you to get your bags?" For goodness' sake, she sounded just like

Mother. How awful.

"Well, hell," Tulane drawled, "what does National Brands pay you for, anyway? I thought an advance *man* was supposed to carry baggage, sort of like a Pullman porter. I thought an advance *man* was supposed to have all the details worked out."

"Are you suggesting that we've got a problem because I'm not a man, Mr. Rhodes?"

"I sure do wish you would call me Tulane. And no, we don't have a problem because you're a woman, but jeez, I have a reputation to maintain, you know, and you seem to be impervious to my many charms."

"Pick up your bags," Sarah said in a hard tone of voice that betrayed her fury. "We're heading for the rental car shuttle. And if I hear one more whine out of you, I'll call up *USA Today* and tell them lies about you." She turned on her heels and started walking away, her shoes making a lethal sound against the tile floor.

"What kind of lies?" he asked from behind.

"I'll tell them you're a sissy who's afraid of flying, enjoys wearing pink, and is ready to come out of the closet." She turned away before he could see the color rising to her cheeks. She felt a rush of satisfaction.

Finally, she was acting the part of a tough businesswoman.

And her gambit worked. Tulane got up, picked up his duffel bag, and followed her out of the terminal.

"Please tell me that was a joke," he said as he caught up to her.

Well, wasn't that interesting? The man was actually worried about what people thought of him. Maybe she could control him, after all.

Thirty minutes later, Sarah knew that controlling Tulane was an impossibility. The man was incorrigible and immature.

And his chest was really ripped. She had watched him change his shirt and pants in the rearview mirror as she navigated a rented Camry onto the highway. He was now dressed in the official pink golf shirt bearing the logo for Cottontail Disposable Diapers.

"Honey, you can go faster," Tulane said as he leaned forward from the back seat and spoke directly into Sarah's ear. "I should have known you would drive like some kind of granny. Have you always been this up-tight?"

A delicious flush of gooseflesh prickled her skin. "In case you haven't noticed, there is heavy traffic, and the speed limit is sixty," she said.

"Just because the speed limit says sixty doesn't mean you have to keep the speed-ometer right at that mark. No one goes the speed limit if they can help it. You can pass that truck."

He pointed over her shoulder. Sarah eyed the big eighteen-wheeler. "Not on the left, I can't. The traffic is slower in that lane."

"On the right, honey. Take the high side if they won't give you the low side."

"Huh?"

"Never mind. Look, dig deep and punch the gas. It'll give you a thrill. And I have this notion that you need a few thrills in your life besides checking me out in the rearview mirror while I change clothes."

"I did no such thing, Mr. Rhodes," she said, and the blush gave away her lie.

He snorted. "Oh, yes, you most certainly did. I'm starting to think that hiding out under that black suit is a woman who'd like to live a little more dangerously. And I would be obliged if you'd call me Tulane."

"I have no wish to live dangerously, *Tulane.* I am a sensible woman." She said the words without much conviction. After all, hadn't she turned down the safe job in Boston for the marketing job in New York with National

Brands? That had not been a sensible decision, as Mother had pointed out on many, many occasions. Mother was always right.

He leaned forward a little farther until his lips were mere millimeters from her ear. He smelled like sunshine and good 'ol boy — a heady and intoxicating mix that made her a little light-headed.

"Honey," he whispered, "we got a baby race to officiate. Either you pull over and let me drive, or you put this thing in gear and pass that truck. I know you can do it. Just think of that bull-riding daddy of yours and punch the gas and feel the thrill. C'mon, baby, do it. You know you want to."

Her right foot inched forward. The engine revved, and the Camry strained forward. She checked her rearview mirror, but Tulane preempted her by checking the lane to the right. "You're clear, honey," he said. She gritted her teeth and pulled out around the truck, passing on the right.

She flexed her hands on the wheel as the full force of the car's engine pressed her into the seat.

"Okay, now pull over to the left and get around that van," Tulane directed. She stopped thinking and did what he told her to do. She crossed three lanes of traffic and passed the van on the left, where the road was less congested, her focus fixed on the road before her.

"God, this is fun," she whispered.

"All right, y'all, are you ready?" Tulane said into the microphone. He stood on the sweltering blacktop of the Value Mart in Orangeburg, South Carolina, while he strolled down a line of makeshift baby-changing tables that had been set up under a tent.

Someone in New York had to have their head examined. This was pitiful and embarrassing. He stared down the lane of changing tables manned mostly by women. This was also a symptom of something seriously wrong with his sport and his country. The corporations were taking over. They were trying to tame the good ol' boys. They were trying to appeal to women.

At least there was one guy competing. Tulane strolled over to him and sniffed his baby daughter. *Ewwweee,* that kid was ripe. Tulane shook his head and leaned in to the young man. "Son, I'd say your young 'un needs more than a new set of tires. I'd say she needs a major rear-end adjustment there, if you catch my drift. You sure you're up to this?"

The young man nodded. "I'm not about

to let a bunch of women show me up," he said.

Me neither. Tulane nodded and grinned. "You show 'em, you hear?"

Tulane turned back to the lineup of contestants. "All right, ya'll, listen up." The contestants assumed positions of readiness as he waved a green flag over his head. He felt like an idiot.

He took a fatalistic breath and began to recite his lines. "This is the final heat of this competition, and the winner gets five hundred big ones to spend in the store. Ready? One . . . two . . . three . . . Ladies — and gentleman — start your changing." He dropped the flag.

The adults set about changing their little ones using the patented Cottontail "quick-release tabs for faster pit stops" and Cottontail baby wipes in a pop-up box.

It was over in about a minute, and the young man with the stinky child had managed to win first place. Tulane felt a certain amount of male pride. He posed for photographs with the winner, holding the baby while she drooled on him. Meanwhile, the manager of the Orangeburg Value Mart fussed and fretted while Sarah lined people up for autographs.

Twenty more minutes of this humiliation

and he could relax in the air-conditioned Camry, watching Miss Priss drive like a granny all the way back to Palmetto, South Carolina, where Ferguson Racing had its headquarters. By this evening, he could get off this merry-go-round for a few hours before he had to do it all over again.

This whole setup was torture, pure and simple. He ought to make a protest under the Geneva Convention, or call out the Red Cross, or something.

Sarah, still wearing her black suit and looking hot and sweaty and good enough to eat, led him to a card table under the tent and put a Sharpie in his left hand and a bottle of water in his right. She turned and began hustling the line of autograph seekers forward. She was competent and well organized, he would give her that.

He also found himself staring at the rounded contours of her butt. Imagine all those curves . . . and brains to go with them. The nice ones were always smart, weren't they? He studied Sarah's round little bottom and felt his body heat rise.

Tulane inhaled and held his breath for a moment. The venue smelled like popcorn and sunburned blacktop. He let the breath out and focused on putting Sarah and all his troubles with his sponsor out of his mind. He needed to keep his temper and remember that he was here among race fans. He wanted to improve his reputation. He needed to make Jim Ferguson happy.

He started signing stuff. He'd been at it for about fifteen minutes when a flash of something bright in the corner of his eye made him look up.

"Oh sh . . . oot," Tulane muttered. His day had just gotten a whole lot more complicated.

He turned away from the line of autograph seekers and toward Sarah, who stood beside him like the jailor she was supposed to be, even if she was stacked and well educated. She leaned down over his chair, close enough for him to get a good look down her notched-collar blouse.

"Is something wrong?" she whispered, her breath whistling in his ear.

Was something wrong? Was she kidding? He was on the brink of disaster. "See that lady crossing the parking lot? The one way over yonder?" he asked.

"The one in pink?"

"Uh-huh. Do me a favor, honey, and tackle her before she gets here."

"Tackle? I'm only five two and, really, the point is to avoid lawsuits. Do you know her?"

"She's my mother."

"Your mother?" He was so dead. She wouldn't tackle his mother. Sarah and his mother were two of a kind.

"Why do you want me to tackle your mother, Tulane?" she asked in a sweet, innocent voice.

"Look, I didn't tell Momma I was going to be here today, and Last Chance is just down the road a ways. Truth is, I was trying to avoid having to go home this evening."

"When was the last time you visited your mother or talked to her?"

He gritted his teeth. "It's been a while. You gotta help me here. Go talk to her before she embarrasses me in front of all these people." He gave her that clueless guy look every female fell for.

Except Sarah Murray, Boston-born advance person and jailor.

She continued to stare down at him with an arch look. "You ought to be ashamed of yourself."

With that deeply troubling response, she turned on her heel and strode across the melting macadam. He hoped Sarah could divert Momma before she publicly bawled him out for not visiting Uncle Pete. Visiting Pete sucked these days, on account of the fact that Tulane's uncle was very ill with lung cancer.

He pushed thoughts of Pete out of his head and, in the vacuum created, it suddenly occurred to him that he'd just sent his corporate jailer over there to talk with his momma. And Momma was going to tell Sarah everything, including all the stuff Tulane hadn't put in his official NASCAR Sprint Cup biography.

Oh great. He was done for.

Based on Tulane's appearance this morning, Sarah wouldn't have been surprised if his mother had turned out like a Jeff Foxworthy redneck joke: fat, dumpy, and dressed like trailer trash.

But Ruby Rhodes didn't fit that bill. She stood only an inch or so taller than Sarah, with a girlish figure and a cap of curly black hair that spilled over the brim of a pink golf visor. Her green eyes had been tastefully made up, and her peaches-and-cream complexion said she had either a beauty regimen that included retinol or a plastic surgeon hiding out somewhere.

She didn't look old enough to be Tulane's mother. Her sleeveless pink shirt had been hand-appliquéd with the words "Tulane's #1 Fan," done up in striped pink seersucker that matched her pedal pushers. The shirt, like the woman, might have just come off a country club golf course.

Sarah intercepted her before she could reach the shade of the tents. The sun beamed down on Sarah's shoulders. Her suit trapped heat like a convection oven.

"Mrs. Rhodes," Sarah said in her best professional voice, "Tulane asked me to escort you to the store, where you can wait for him in the air-conditioning."

Tulane's mother stopped and took a long moment to size Sarah up. "Who died?" she asked.

"I beg pardon?"

"Sugar, in that black suit, you look like you're either on your way to, or just come from, a funeral. Didn't anyone ever tell you that black is not your color?"

"No, ma'am. I'm . . . uh . . ." Sarah ran out of words. Her stomach felt suddenly queasy. The Value Mart hot dog she'd consumed twenty minutes ago rested there like cement.

"It's hot as Hades out here, sugar," Tulane's mother continued. "And black is a poor choice for this part of the country. You aren't from around here, are you?"

"No, ma'am. I'm from Boston, originally."

"Well, that explains it. You know, if I were you, I'd definitely try green. It would bring out the color of your eyes and complement the highlights in your hair. Is that a natural color?"

"Yes, ma'am. Why don't we step inside the store and we can wait for Tulane?"

"Oh, no thanks. I'm used to the hot. Born and raised not twenty miles from here. I can manage. And I see him right over yonder and —"

"Mrs. Rhodes, Tulane —"

"Oh, call me Ruby, sugar. And you are?"

"I'm Sarah Murray. I'm with National Brands."

Ruby blinked a few times. "Well, if you're with National Brands, why are you wearing black?"

Because black is a power color, and I thought it would help me keep your son in line. Instead it was doing a good job of slow-cooking her.

"I mean," Ruby continued, while Sarah stood there sweating through the armpits of her hundred-dollar silk blouse, "shouldn't you be wearing pink?"

Was that the Southern variety of sarcasm? It was delivered in a friendly tone, like Ruby Rhodes might be giving fashion advice and not expressing her opinion of the Cottontail Disposable Diaper pink car advertising campaign. It was hard to decide, what with the sweat running down Sarah's back, and the sun beating on her head, and the heat radiating up through the soles of her closed-toe shoes.

"Uh, thanks, I'll keep that in mind," Sarah said.

"You do that, because pink — especially in a deep rose color — would be good for you."

"Thanks. Now, if you'd like to step over —"

"Oh no, you can go back to work or whatever you were doing. I'll just wait right over yonder for Tulane." She pointed to the tent where the autograph seekers were lined up.

"Ma'am, your son asked me to —"

She gave Sarah the Look. Ruby Rhodes had definitely mastered it, because it froze Sarah in midsentence.

"He sent you here to take care of me, didn't he?"

"Well, yes, ma'am," Sarah said cautiously. "He wanted to make sure you were comfortable."

"No, sugar, he wanted to make sure I didn't go over there and embarrass him. And really, I ought to do that, because he deserves it, but I have more manners than that."

"Yes, ma'am." Sarah felt light-headed. She needed to get the woman out of the sun and into the store where they could both cool off. She longed to take Ruby by the arm and drag her toward the beckoning doors of the big-box retailer.

But it was against corporate rules for her to touch or manhandle anyone. Management had insisted that every employee attend a sensitivity training session on how to avoid lawsuits. So she stood there, envying Ruby's sun visor, cotton shirt, and sandals.

"He deserves a lecture," Ruby continued. "Do you know he didn't call last week on my birthday? And then," the woman said, putting her hands on her hips, "I read in the *Orangeburg Times and Democrat* just this morning that he's going to be up here signing autographs, and he didn't even bother to tell me. Now, I ask you, if you were his mother, wouldn't you want to give him a piece of your mind? The boy lives over in Florence and never comes home to visit, even though it's not a very long drive."

"Ma'am, I promise you can give him a piece of your mind. In fact, he probably deserves a piece of your mind. Just wait until he finishes signing autographs. Now, if you would just come with me —"

Sarah took a step toward the store doors,

and the world tipped sideways.

Ruby reached out a steadying hand, and Sarah latched on to it like it might be a lifeline. "I don't feel well," she murmured, right before her brain shut off and she pitched forward, into the arms of the small but capable Ruby Rhodes of Last Chance, South Carolina.

CHAPTER 3

Sarah hardly weighed much, for all her curvy shape. Tulane carried Sarah in his arms. She wasn't unconscious anymore. She cracked one hazel eye.

"I fainted, didn't I?"

"Yes, ma'am, but don't worry, as usual Momma's got everything under control." Tulane wondered if Sarah heard the sarcasm in his voice.

He carried Sarah toward Momma's Ford Econovan, where Ruby stood, shaking her head in disgust. Tulane wasn't sure whether Momma was annoyed because of Sarah's stupidity in wearing black on a steamy day, or whether she was on the warpath because he had forgotten all about her birthday. Momma slid the door open on the van. Ruby had already turned on the motor, and the AC was roaring.

He laid Sarah out on the back bench seat and turned toward his mother. "I'll drive.

You get some Gatorade in her," he said.

Ruby stepped up into the back of the van and bent over Sarah. Tulane closed the sliding door and climbed into the driver's seat.

"Bless your heart," Ruby said from the back seat in her best motherly voice, "here's some Gatorade. It'll fix you up good as new." Tulane watched in the rearview mirror as Ruby lifted up Sarah's head and tipped the bottle of sport drink. Sarah drank. Her color began to improve.

Thank God. Maybe she wouldn't die of sunstroke. Maybe he wouldn't have that on his head.

"Think we need to take her to the emergency room?" he asked.

"We can take her over to see Doc Cooper if she isn't feeling better by the time we get to Last Chance," Momma said.

He should have known that was coming. But he couldn't let his National Brands nursemaid ever see Last Chance, South Carolina. He had to extract himself from this situation.

"Momma, I —"

"We're going home, Tulane, where I can keep an eye on her to make sure she's okay." Momma said this in her no-nonsense voice. Tulane knew he was done for.

He had two choices. He could argue with

Momma and let Sarah see his temper fully unleashed, or he could shut up and drive. All in all, given that he was in the doghouse with his sponsor and car owner because of his temper, he decided discretion was the better part of valor. But keeping his cool was hard.

And, boy howdy, once Sarah figured out his secrets, he was going to have to keep her from spilling them to the world. How was he going to do that without also pissing off his sponsor and potentially losing his ride with Ferguson Racing?

He was caught in a vise manned by two little bitty women and the vastness of corporate America.

"Momma, I really think —"

"Son, you are coming home and that's the end of it. And while you're there, you can visit your uncle Pete. He's not doing so well, and you've hurt him by staying away."

Guilt and sadness constricted his chest. He hadn't been visiting the folks precisely because he didn't want to see Pete. It was selfish, but seeing Pete bald and feeble did something unpleasant to Tulane's insides.

"Momma, we have luggage in the rental, and —"

"That's no problem," Ruby rejoined. "We'll just go get it and then head home.

46

I'm thinking Miriam has extra rooms in that house of hers. I'm sure she wouldn't mind putting Sarah up for the night. I'll just give her a buzz on the cell phone, and we'll have it all arranged. Don't you worry. Sarah's going to be fine, and no one will blame you for anything."

"Blame me? But —"

"Hush up." Momma pulled out her phone and started dialing. The arrangements were made inside of three minutes.

By the time they had picked up the luggage from the rental car and were headed south on Route 321, Sarah had recovered and was sitting up.

"Thanks, Mrs. Rhodes," Sarah said. "I'm so sorry that I —"

"Now, that's all right. It happens. And you being from up north and wearing black didn't help. I'm going to take you home and feed you supper. We can get to know each other, and then Tulane's daddy will drive you back up here tomorrow morning, early enough for you to get the rental car and make your appointments in Florence and Palmetto."

Momma turned and glared at Tulane's reflection in the rearview mirror. "Because we all know how important it is to meet one's obligations. Don't we?"

"Yes, Momma." It was over. Tulane had lost. He always lost when he went toe to toe with Momma.

"Really, Mrs. Rhodes, I'm feeling much —" Sarah started to say before Momma cut her off.

"Don't you worry about a thing. You know, I would be so happy to give you some advice on color choices. You are definitely an autumn. Now drink your Gatorade."

Sarah drank.

"So you're from Boston?" Momma asked Sarah a moment later. Tulane stifled a groan.

"Yes."

"With that hair and your name, you must be a nice Irish Catholic girl?"

"Momma! Stop! You can't go around —"

"Hush, Tulane. Just drive. We're getting to know each other."

"No, ma'am, I'm a Presbyterian," Sarah said.

"Oh, well, isn't that nice? A Protestant girl. We're Episcopalians. I'm afraid we don't have a Presbyterian church in Last Chance. But we do have a Baptist and a Methodist and an AME, of course. That would be the largest congregation, the AME."

"I guess it would," Sarah replied, as if this

48

conversation weren't utterly bizarre. No doubt there were people in Boston who had similar conversations with strangers, and Sarah came from those people. That or she was just stringing Momma along so she could get the full picture on just how strange his kin were.

Tulane glanced at her in the rearview mirror. The garish red color was fading from her face, and her freckles were popping out. Boy, she was cute.

"So, did your family come over on the *Mayflower*?" Momma asked.

Tulane gripped the wheel and gritted his teeth.

"Yes, ma'am," Sarah said, and Momma straightened right up in her seat like she'd been hit with a cattle prod.

Oh brother! It was a lead-pipe cinch that the Last Chance church ladies would all know about Sarah's background before suppertime. Every single one of those old biddies would want to meet the little Presbyterian from Boston whose forebears came over on the *Mayflower.* And then, after that, they would start introducing her to the eligible men in Allenberg County, which, unfortunately, included himself.

"Her daddy's a bull rider from Wyoming," Tulane said out loud. That ought to cool

Momma's ardor. A bull rider wasn't nearly as high-toned as forebears who came over on the *Mayflower.*

"A bull rider, really?" Momma said, turning in her seat to give Sarah another measuring glance.

"Dad was born in Wyoming and grew up on a horse farm," Sarah said. "It was natural that he would ride rodeo."

"Well, I'll be. We have a nice young man named Dash who grew up on a horse farm in Texas before he came to live in Last Chance. We'll have to introduce you."

Tulane glanced in the rearview again. "Honey," he said to Sarah, "don't you let the Christ Church Ladies Auxiliary try to match you up with Dash Randall. That boy is the baddest boy in Allenberg County."

"Really? And what does that make you?" Sarah shot back with a little gleam in her eye.

"The second baddest," he said, forcing a grin to his face.

Their eyes met in the mirror, and his heart rate spiked.

Uncle Pete looked feeble. He'd always been bald on top, but now his head was a big pink dome covered by skin so pale and translucent that Tulane could see the veins.

Tulane hated seeing Pete like this, reclining in his living room when he ought to be down at the hardware store. Tulane hated the lineup of medicine in white bottles that stood on the buffet in the dining room. He hated sitting here in the matching recliner, trying to find some positive sign in his uncle's pale and sunken face.

He needed something to hold on to. Pete had always been his anchor. Back when he'd been thirteen and in deep, deep trouble, Pete had pulled him from the brink.

"So," Pete said in a whispery voice. "Your momma dragged you home, huh?"

Tulane squirmed in his chair. How was he supposed to answer that question? It felt like someone was pulling a string attached to his belly button. He was scared that if he said anything his voice might waver.

"Well, I'm glad you came, anyway. There's something I need to talk to you about."

Tulane turned and really inspected Pete for the first time since entering the room. He had to grit his teeth. His uncle was at death's door. "If you're going to start talking about the pink car, Pete, I'd just as soon not."

"Son, I don't know why you're letting the color of your car get to you. Last weekend, you didn't drive smart. I could see that on the TV."

"Yeah, well, it's not as easy as it was when it was just you and me and Bubba working on a car. I've got a team manager, a crew chief, and an engineer who looks down his narrow little nose at me on account of I only have a high school education and he's a college boy."

"And you're letting that get to you?"

Tulane shrugged.

"Son, you are the driver of a Cup car. You have reached the highest place you can in your profession. You need to grow up."

Tulane closed his eyes. This was not a new refrain. Everyone said he needed to grow up. He wasn't entirely sure what folks meant by that.

"If you mean I have to sit back and let my jerk of an engineer do stupid things and hold my tongue about it, well then, I've learned how to be really mature."

"That's not what I mean."

"Then what?"

"You man up, and you tell your engineer that you have a different opinion."

"Ha! They don't listen to me, Pete. They are like bullies on a playground — my engineer, my sponsor, all of them. I'm just the driver, and a rookie at that. I'm supposed to do what they say and keep my mouth shut. That's what they think being grown-up means. I hate to complain, but you know that old story about being careful what you wish for?"

"Jeez, Tulane. What? Are you afraid to succeed?"

Tulane stared at his uncle. "What the hell does that mean, anyway? People throw that around like it means something. I'm afraid to fail. Okay, I said it. Happy?"

"No, I'm not happy. And I do believe that a man can be afraid to succeed. You have a chance of a lifetime; don't screw it up."

"Look," Tulane said. "I can't stay too long. Momma's entertaining my advance person, so —"

"Advance person?"

"Yeah, well, she's more like a nursemaid. Although quite frankly, she's not terribly competent."

Pete cracked an eye. "Nursemaid?"

"Yeah, a cute one, too, with freckles and a Boston accent. Her family came over on the *Mayflower.*"

Pete snorted. "Boy, you are in some serious trouble."

"Yeah, I know."

"Well, it serves you right." Pete sat up in his chair, and the recliner moved with him. "You listen to me, Tulane. You have talent.

53

And you will be a huge success if you would just get out of your own way. Pride is one of those things that can ruin a man. You just remember that, you hear?"

"You're not the one who has to wear pink."

"You win races, and nobody's going to think twice what you're wearing. You quit messing around and show those people what you know and what you can do on the track. I'm getting tired of watching you lose. And even more tired of watching you behave like a jerk. I taught you better."

Pete's body might be wasting away, but the spark was still in his eyes. Pete loved to win. To Pete, winning was everything.

Pete continued in his hoarse voice, "You want to stop folks from laughing at you? Then you buckle down and behave like a serious driver."

Tulane nodded. Pete was right, of course.

"Okay." Pete leaned back in his chair. "Now you go on home, and you treat your sponsor's people with respect, you hear me? And you work on winning races." Pete turned and stared hard at him. "You do that for me." He nodded once and then brought his head back to rest on the chair's high back.

Pete closed his eyes. His lecture had

clearly taken every ounce of strength he possessed. Tulane sat there for several minutes, feeling emotions he didn't want to explore or even name, until his uncle fell asleep.

Ruby and Elbert Rhodes lived in a single-story white clapboard house with a wrap-around porch. A flower border of early-blooming lilies ringed the foundation, while an old wisteria twisted up the porch trellis and gave the house the air of a Tuscan retreat. A row of rocking chairs with chintz cushions made Ruby's house the model for a sappy Hallmark greeting card.

Sarah took off her suit jacket and rocked in one of those rockers, while an old-fashioned porch fan whispered from above. Ruby headed for her kitchen to work on supper, and Tulane took off in his brother's pickup to run errands, which included visiting his sick uncle and hauling her luggage over to the neighbor's house.

Being left alone allowed Sarah to think about the mess she'd made of her career. She might have gotten Tulane to his personal appearance on time, but fainting had to be pretty high up on the unprofessional scale.

No doubt Steve Phelps would hear about it, and it would make his day. It wasn't a

55

crime to faint, but Steve would find a way to make it seem like a crime, because Steve wanted her gone.

He had good reason to want her gone, too. The downward spiral in Sarah's brief career had started when she had foolishly believed that Steve would give her credit for writing the Cuppa Java marketing plan. But he hadn't. Instead, he'd pretended that his meteoric rise within the marketing department had been earned on his own merits.

That had hacked Sarah off. Her brilliant plan for getting even was to write a supremely stupid marketing memo about a pink car and baby-changing races and put Steve's name on it. Deidre was supposed to take one look at that memo and realize what a poseur Steve really was.

But instead, Deidre had taken the memo seriously.

Now Steve was in charge of the pink car program and Sarah had been sent here to do an impossible job, and to come face-to-face with the implications of the memo she had written.

This proved one thing for certain: Sarah sucked at revenge, just like she sucked at everything else a modern businesswoman needed to excel at.

Steve was going to find a way to get her

fired. It was only a matter of time.

Her dark thoughts were interrupted some time later by a little voice that asked, "Are you really a Pilgrim?"

Sarah opened her eyes and found herself staring at a little girl in a pink sundress with something that might be ketchup smeared on its yoke. She wore a pair of Little Mermaid sandals that exposed grubby toes. Most of her honey-colored hair had escaped her pink ponytail elastic so that it framed her face in a slightly sweaty tangle. She gave Sarah a sly smile. Her top front teeth were missing and the new ones — too big for her face — were just making their first appearance.

"Hello," Sarah said.

"Are you? 'Cause Granny says you came on the *Mayflower*. Didn't the Pilgrims come on the *Mayflower*?"

Sarah blinked a few times. She must have dozed off. She felt groggy. "Uh, yes, the Pilgrims came on the *Mayflower*. But that was a long, long time ago. I didn't personally come to America that way. I was born here."

The little girl cocked her head, studying Sarah closely. "My name's Haley, what's yours?"

"Sarah."

The girl swayed there for a moment, screwing the toe of her sandal into the floorboards, as if weighing whether to continue. "Are you Uncle Tulane's girlfriend?"

Sarah almost choked.

"Are you?" the girl asked before Sarah could stop sputtering. " 'Cause I heard Granny on the phone saying that even though you have no fashion sense and are a Pilgrim, she thought you might be perfect, except for the fact that your daddy is from Wyoming. Is Wyoming up north?"

"Uh, no. And perfect for what?"

Haley shrugged. "Don't know, 'cause I only heard Granny's side of the conversation. She was talking to Miriam Randall. Where's Wyoming?"

"Out west."

"So you're not his girlfriend?"

"No. Tulane and I work together."

" 'Kay. So, do you have a boyfriend? Are you married to anyone else?"

Sarah wasn't sure where the little girl's mind was moving, but she didn't like the direction. "Nope."

"Really?" The girl's eyes grew round. Clearly the little girl was too young to understand that a match between a northern Presbyterian and a Southern Episcopalian would be viewed in some circles in both Massachusetts and South Carolina as marrying outside the faith.

"You wanna meet my daddy?"

Oh, so that was her game. Daddy must be divorced.

"Well, I —"

"Daddy's the chief of police," Haley said, then leaned in like a conspirator. "He's a widower, you know." She leaned back and nodded in a way that suggested she'd been peeping at keyholes and listening to her grandmother gossip with the other ladies in town. Clearly, there was a move afoot to find someone for the widowed chief of police. Probably without much success given the fact that Last Chance, South Carolina, appeared to be a place where eligible females younger than sixty were scarce.

Nevertheless, the fact that Tulane Rhodes, bad-boy stock car driver, had a policeman brother was pretty interesting news. His bio had failed to mention that very marketable fact. She wondered if Tulane's brother was photogenic.

"So the chief of police is your uncle Tulane's brother?" Sarah asked, trying to confirm the family relationships.

"Yes'm. And he's a widower 'cause my

momma is with Jesus up in Heaven. She died in a car wreck. Kinda like the wreck Uncle Tulane was in last weekend. Did you see him wreck? I saw it on TV."

Clearly little Haley wasn't much troubled by the fact that her mother was in the arms of the Savior or that her uncle cheated death every Sunday. "I didn't see Tulane wreck his car," Sarah said. She didn't explain that she hadn't seen this event because she had never in her life watched a stock car race. The fact that she had written a marketing memo about stock car racing had nothing to do with the sport and everything to do with advertising and good market research.

Oh yeah, and revenge against Steve for stealing her ideas on the Cuppa Java campaign. Of course, her revenge had backfired, proving that Mother was right: Sarah didn't have much talent for the cutthroat business world.

"I'm glad Uncle Tulane had a car seat, otherwise he might be with Jesus now, too," Haley said.

The little girl said the words "car seat," and suddenly Sarah's mind went off on a wild tangent. Her mind did that sometimes. "Car seat?" she said aloud.

"Yeah, you know, like babies ride in," Haley replied. "Granny said Uncle Tulane wasn't hurt 'cause he has a special car seat. She said it was like the car seat I had when that no-account drunk wrecked Momma's car."

Sarah's heart squeezed in her chest. Good grief, Haley had survived the accident that took her mother's life. The accident must have happened a while ago. Haley had no memory of it.

Haley was also about as photogenic as a kid could get, even with her hair a mess and her dress stained. In fact, her grubbiness was completely adorable and real. Sarah felt suddenly queasy — the sort of queasy that gripped her when she was about to make a leap of logic and find a wickedly good advertising idea.

Haley nattered on. " 'Course, I didn't have a car seat when Woody West, Jane's boyfriend, crashed Granny's car into Jesus down at Golfing for God. I got a big bump on my head that time. Daddy thinks I started hallinating when that happened, but he's wrong about that."

Golfing for God? What on earth? Sarah was abruptly brought back to the conversation. Had she missed something important? "What?"

"You know about hallinating, don't you?" Haley said, and then launched into an

61

explanation. "It's when someone sees things that aren't there. But I really do see the Sorrowful Angel."

"Oh, I see." But Sarah didn't see at all.

Suddenly, Tulane was there on the porch with them. He swept down on the little girl, rescuing Sarah from the nonsensical conversation. He grabbed Haley by the hips and backside and boosted her up into the air. Sarah had been so intent on the ideas forming in her head that she hadn't noticed Tulane's return.

Tulane twirled the little girl around on his shoulders and tossed her up into the air in a homemade thrill ride. He looked so utterly at ease playing with Haley. The image of Tulane with a child had seemed out of place this morning, but now it didn't seem out of place at all. He was good with the little girl, and he had been surprisingly good with the babies and toddlers at the baby-changing event. All of which would be necessary for this idea that was starting to gel in her mind.

Just then, a tan police vehicle pulled up to the curb, and Haley wiggled out of Tulane's grasp.

"Hey, Daddy," she yelled as she ran down the porch steps, her wild hair bouncing. A large man in a buff-colored uniform unfolded himself from the driver's side. He stepped onto the curb and picked Haley up for a somewhat less exuberant hug.

Tulane's brother was taller and wider through the chest. But other than that, you'd have to be blind to miss the family resemblance.

Haley's father set the little girl down on the lawn and headed up the path with that same loose-jointed gait that marked his younger brother. This man seemed more serious than Tulane and much more dangerous — packing a latent power along with his handgun. He gave little away in his glance, shaded by the brim of his uniform Stetson.

Tulane introduced Sarah to his brother, Stone. She shook the policeman's hand and said a few inane words of greeting. Inside of a minute, Stone excused himself and stepped into the house with Haley bobbing in his wake, talking a mile a minute like a little chatterbox.

Stone Rhodes had a name that fit. But he was amazingly photogenic, which made him perfect for the idea that had just struck Sarah from out of the blue.

"So," Tulane said, once his older brother was out of earshot and Sarah had returned to her rocking chair. "I'll bet Haley told you all about her momma being with Jesus in Heaven, didn't she?" He picked up a long-necked Bud that he'd rested on the porch railing and sat himself down in the rocking chair next to Sarah.

"Yes, she did. And I —"

"Did she tell you about Golfing for God?" His voice sounded pinched.

Sarah cocked her head. "Yes, she said something odd about a car crashing into Jesus. It sounded like one of those bad jokes about God and Jesus golfing with Saint Peter."

The corners of Tulane's mouth turned down. "I wish it were a joke, honey."

"You want to explain?"

"No."

"Okay," she said, but her curiosity had been thoroughly aroused.

He picked up his beer and leaned back in his seat. He took a long swallow, his Adam's apple bobbing. Then he rested the bottle on the rocker's broad armrest while he rocked. Sarah found herself studying the hand that held the bottle: long-fingered, broad-palmed, with short square nails. His hand simultaneously conveyed strength and gentleness, power and dexterity. Her mind flashed on those hands caressing more than just a bottle. Her body flushed with the thought.

This was dangerous. She needed to focus on her job and saving it. She took a deep breath and let it out slowly. When her heart rate slowed, she spoke. "Are you going to tell my bosses about how I humiliated myself?"

He angled a glance at her. "No. Not if you keep my secrets."

She looked away. "I suppose I should thank you. But I figure they're going to find out I fainted anyway."

"Yup, I reckon so. And I figure you're going to find out all about Golfing for God. So maybe I should just tell you and have done with it."

"What is Golfing for God? A charity or something?"

He let go of a bark of laughter. "I only wish. No, Golfing for God is an eighteen-hole miniature golf course just south of town. It's a running joke in Last Chance. It's filled up with fiberglass statues of everything from Eve to Goliath. And there's a life-sized ark."

"Really?"

"Yeah, really."

"So why is that a problem? It sounds like fun. Can we go play a round after dinner? I'd like to see a putt-putt dedicated to God."

Tulane stared at her as if she had dropped in to visit from Venus. "You're kidding, right?"

"No, why would I kid about that?" She met his stare, glare to glare, and she counted it as a victory when he finally looked away, out beyond the wisteria.

He took a long pull on the beer and then turned back toward her. "Unfortunately, the place was damaged by a thunderstorm back in October. My mother's car was hijacked during that storm by my sister-in-law's moron ex-boyfriend. Haley was in the car when it was hijacked. The idiot hijacker crashed the car into a fiberglass statue of Jesus in the parking lot of Golfing for God. Jesus is all smashed up, and the place is out of commission. And that's not the worst of it. See, Haley took a pretty good blow to the head, and . . ." His voice trailed off.

"And?"

"Well, the thing is, she says she sees angels."

"I see."

Tulane took another long sip of beer and continued, "Haley and her angel, not to mention Golfing for God, are off-limits. You understand me?"

"Yes, I think I do."

Tulane shook his head. "No, I don't think

you or the people in New York really *do* understand. See, since I got the ride last year with Ferguson Racing, it's like the world wants to know my life story and, quite frankly, I'm not interested in telling certain parts of it. I just want to drive cars and win races and have people take me seriously for my driving. So I would be obliged if you would forget about Haley and Golfing for God."

"Okay, I'll try. But the thing is, she said something a minute ago that got me thinking."

"What part of 'forget about Haley' did you not understand?" He leaned forward in his chair and glowered at her.

She held up her hand. "Please don't get angry. Just listen, okay? Have you ever thought about using your position to support car seat safety? With your brother a policeman, it would . . ." She stopped midsentence. Tulane wasn't happy.

"Have you ever done this before?" he asked.

"Done what, visited South Carolina? No, I'm afraid this is my first time. I'm a South Carolina virgin."

His cheeks colored, but she chose not to make any comment about it. *Virgin* was a perfectly fine word, but Tulane evidently found it titillating, which said a great deal about his maturity.

"No, what I meant to ask is, well, who else have you advanced in your career at National Brands?"

Uh-oh.

"I can see by the look on your face that you are an advance-man virgin, too. And by that last comment, I'd have to say you are seriously deluded about stock car racing fans. Car seat safety? Are you kidding?"

She brought her sweaty hands together. "Okay. You're right," she said. "I've never advanced anyone before. I'm mostly a researcher for the marketing and advertising departments. But, speaking as a market researcher, I've just come up with a good idea that will get you out of officiating at baby-changing races. Do you want to hear it?"

She hoped he did, because she needed to stop the baby-changing thing. That had been one of her worst ideas ever.

Tulane cocked his head. "You're a researcher? You mean, like a librarian?"

Something snapped inside her. This might be the last chance she would have to save her job and make something of herself. So, she gathered herself up and glared back at Tulane Rhodes. "Give me five minutes and

I'll explain why car seats might be the solution to your problems." *And hers, too.*

He nodded his head. She took that for a green light and started to talk a mile a minute. She figured if she had only five minutes, she would either make her point or crash and burn.

Haley Rhodes pulled on her granny's shirttail. "Hey, Granny, did you know Miss Sarah isn't really a Pilgrim? She's a librarian."

Granny was working in the kitchen, draining butter beans into the sink, but she paused and frowned down at Haley. "Haley Ann Rhodes, how many times have I told you that it's impolite to eavesdrop on folks?"

"Yes'm, I know, but I wasn't eavesdropping, 'xactly. I was just playing in the living room, and Uncle Tulane and Miss Sarah were on the porch, and I just happened to hear them talking. And she told Uncle Tulane that she was a librarian."

"Well, that doesn't sound right. She works for the company that sponsors your uncle's car."

"I *know* that. She was talking about how she worked in the library and did research on ladies with babies who buy diapers and other stuff like cribs and cradles and car seats."

"Did she now." Granny opened the oven and pulled out her pot roast. The smell was mouthwatering.

"Yeah. And she said pink was a good color because the diaper bunny is colored pink. I reckon Uncle Tulane shouldn't feel so bad about the color of his car. After all, Barbie has a pink car. And doesn't Mrs. Henrietta Charles over in Allenberg have a pink car that she got selling Mary Kay?"

"Yes, but Mrs. Charles doesn't have any babies, and your uncle is a man, Haley."

"Well, Sarah also said Uncle Tulane could help people with their car seats."

Granny frowned down. "Help them with car seats?"

"Yes'm. She said that people would be interested in the fact that my momma was with Jesus, but that I was saved by a car seat. Uncle Tulane said he wasn't ever going to talk about how a car seat saved my life, but after Miss Sarah talked for a while, he finally agreed that doing car seat safety checks would be better than having a race to see how fast diapers could be changed."

"Well that is an interesting idea, but I don't think you can help."

"But, Granny, Miss Sarah talked really,

really fast and she talked Uncle Tulane right into it. I know that on account of the fact that he used his phone to call someone in New York about it — someone she called the Dragon Lady."

Granny squatted down to be on Haley's level. "Dragon Lady?"

"That's what Miss Sarah called her. But she's not a real dragon, Granny. I heard Miss Sarah call her by another name I can't remember."

"Are you sure you heard that?"

"Yes'm. But Uncle Tulane said I was off-limits on account of the fact I can see the Sorrowful Angel. What did that mean?"

"It means, young lady, that you should mind your own business." Granny stood up. "Now go tell your daddy and sister that supper's nearly ready."

Haley took one step toward the door and then turned. "But Granny, what if I *want* to help Uncle Tulane teach people about car seats?"

Haley glanced toward the corner of the kitchen near the broom closet. The Sorrowful Angel was there, only she wasn't very sad right now. The angel never spoke, but Haley had gotten the knack of figuring out what the angel was thinking. The angel had listened to the conversation between Uncle

Tulane and the lady from New York just as hard as Haley had. The angel had dried her tears and nodded her head, as if she thought the idea was a real good one.

That had to be a sign.

"Haley, now is not the time to discuss this," Granny said. "I think it might be a very nice thing for Uncle Tulane to use his position to promote the use of car seats, but I don't think it would be right for you to be involved. And I know your daddy wouldn't like the idea. Not one bit. Now you go outside and tell your daddy and your sister that supper will be ready in about ten minutes."

Haley turned and headed out to the backyard, pretending to mind Granny. The angel followed with a gleam in her sorrowful eyes.

Granny prob'ly thought Haley was going to forget about the car seats. But Granny was wrong.

Deidre Montgomery pressed her fingers against her temples. Tulane Rhodes could be impressively articulate for a redneck. And he'd just handed her an answer to two questions that had been plaguing her for some time.

The first question was prosaic: What to do

about Steve Phelps? The man was a huge problem. He was stupid, but the Board thought he walked on water. How he had ever managed to come up with the Cuppa Java campaign was a mystery. Deidre was sure he didn't dream up that campaign all by himself. But she didn't yet know who had helped him.

The pink car memo was a different situation. That idiot idea had Steve's name written all over it. Deidre had allowed the repainting of the No. 57 Sprint Cup Ford to go forward, with the conviction that the Board would soon discover the truth about Steve Phelps.

Unfortunately, the pink car was selling diapers like mad.

Deidre was going to have to take the program away from Steve, or her own position at National Brands would be jeopardized.

Tulane Rhodes had just given her the means to regain control.

The second question — well, it was one of those existential questions that she had been asking herself for more than a decade.

She pushed herself up from her chair and walked across the deep carpet toward her credenza. She had purchased the cabinet when she made vice president and was given this corner office on the thirtieth floor of the National Brands Madison Avenue headquarters. It had been handcrafted by a cabinetmaker. She had waited almost a year for him to finish it.

That thought always gave her a modicum of inner pleasure. For an impatient woman, she could be patient when she wanted to. Andrew had known this about her. Andrew had known all her secrets and all her weaknesses, and he had loved her anyway.

Thinking about Andrew always made her feel hollow inside, like she might be on the verge of tears. But she never cried.

She unlocked the top drawer and drew out a photograph in a sterling silver frame. If she were a braver woman, or one not so given to self-indulgent guilt, she might have allowed this photo to sit on her desk, along with the photo of Andrew. But she was not brave or guilt-free.

Deidre studied Kelly's smiling face: just two years old, the image of her father, with her curly blonde hair and cornflower blue eyes. If she had lived, she would be seventeen now, and planning for college.

Deidre could rationally explain that Kelly's and Andrew's deaths had been caused by a drunk who had already paid the ultimate price for his mistake. Guilt would not bring them back. There was no revenge to be had.

But for years, no one could solve the riddle as to why Deidre had walked away with only a couple of broken ribs. As a supremely rational woman, she had spent the last fifteen years searching for an answer to that question.

Her current high-powered corporate life would not have been possible without the central tragedy of Kelly's and Andrew's deaths. It was normal to ask why. But the answer to that question had always worried her, as if their deaths had somehow cleared the path for what she had become.

She would gladly trade her current life if she could go back in time and make sure Kelly's car seat was compatible with the station wagon's seatbelt system.

She couldn't go back. But suddenly, from out of the blue, Tulane Rhodes had handed her one answer to the impossible questions she asked every day. He had given her a way to go forward and make sense of something that would never be sensible.

She put Kelly's photo back in the credenza and locked it. She took three or four deep breaths, composing herself.

When she was ready, she drew herself up, straightened the seams in her Armani skirt like a knight checking his armor, and headed out in the direction of the CEO's office. She had a few corporate dragons to slay, a car seat program to launch, and, after that, she needed to rescue the young market researcher Steve Phelps had insisted on sending down to South Carolina.

What was Steve up to? Sarah Murray had no business advancing any National Brands spokesperson, least of all the difficult but oddly articulate Tulane Rhodes. Sarah belonged in the research department, and Deidre aimed to put her back where she belonged.

CHAPTER 4

Ruby and Elbert's dining room was large, with a blue floral wallpaper pattern set off by white crown and chair moldings. The room was on the formal side, but the people in it — especially Elbert Rhodes — were not.

Tulane's father, dressed in black with a gray goatee and a long braid, would have fit right in with a pack of biker boys. He stared at Sarah with a pair of pale wolf eyes, and she had the uncanny feeling he could see right through her.

Ruby sat at the other end of the table, looking like a *Southern Living* fashion plate. To say that Ruby and Elbert were a pair of odd bookends was to understate things by a mile.

Sarah was directed to a seat sandwiched between Stone's older daughter, Lizzy, on her right, and Tulane on her left. Stone and Haley sat across the table.

Spread before them on an everyday table-cloth was a cornucopia of food in steaming platters: pot roast, black-eyed peas and rice, lima beans, and something green and gooey that had to be okra.

Elbert said grace, and then Ruby started passing around bowls so the family could help themselves. Tulane tucked right into the peas and rice and pot roast.

When he handed the okra off to Sarah, everyone at the table paused and glanced up at her as if waiting to see what the woman from up north might do.

"Okra is one of Uncle Tulane's favorites," Lizzy said with a teenage sneer. "Isn't it, Uncle Tulane?"

"Uh-huh," Tulane said mechanically as he conveyed a big forkful of the stuff from his plate to his mouth.

Sarah stared down at the disgusting vegetable, gritted her teeth, and spooned out a little serving onto the pretty blue willow-ware. It immediately left a trail of slime on her plate.

An uneasy silence settled over the table, punctuated only by the sounds of silverware scraping on china. The Rhodes family was single-minded about their eating.

Sarah stared at the food on her plate and wished she were somewhere else, like at the hotel in Florence, South Carolina, where she was supposed to have spent the night. Why oh why had she chosen to wear the black suit? And why had she mouthed off about the stupid car seat idea? And why had she written that stupid pink car memo? All her problems traced back to that one single decision — where she had broken all the rules.

She was so going to lose her job when she got back to New York. Unless, of course, she could score some points with Tulane Rhodes, who, let's face it, was never really going to be fired no matter how badly he behaved, because he was a talented stock car driver.

She stared down at the okra in its puddle of ooze. Here was the acid test, like some challenge on *Fear Factor*. If she ate this awful stuff, it might win her a few points with the man sitting to her left.

So she snapped her spine straight, braced herself, and daintily conveyed a little bit of the okra from her plate to her mouth. She managed to choke it down and had to admit that while its texture was an odd combination of fuzzy and slimy, it had an interesting taste.

Tulane chuckled from his place to her left. "Honey, you don't have to eat the okra if you don't want to."

Sarah looked up. The spark of humor in his verdigris eyes made something hot and wicked ignite in her midsection.

Elbert took that moment to clear his throat. "So, Sarah," he said. "I need to clear something up with you."

"Yes?" She braced herself, expecting to get an earful of complaint about the pink car.

"I'll bet you read Tulane's official biography where it says I'm a mechanic, didn't you?" Elbert said.

Sarah clamped her lips closed and nodded, afraid to say anything more.

Beside her, Tulane slammed his tea glass down on the table so hard it made the food dishes jump. "Daddy, don't —"

Elbert stared at Tulane. "You hush up. To be honest, I'm disappointed in you." Elbert turned his head and gave Sarah a winning smile. "I don't suppose you saw the old putt-putt place outside of town?"

"Um, no. But Haley said something about it. Golfing for God?" She stifled the urge to duck under the table. World War III was about to erupt any minute.

"That's the one. You need to know that that's what I do for a living. Well, that's what I did for a living before the lightning strike hit the place and caused the explosion."

She frowned. "You play putt-putt golf?"

Elbert shook his head. "No, ma'am. I *own* Golfing for God. And I ran the place until we had to close it down last October. See, my daddy built it back in the 1950s. There are angels who live on that land, and they've been whispering to the Rhodes family for generations."

Angels and miniature golf. Wow. She could understand why Tulane had lied about his father and didn't want his niece to be a poster child for car seat safety. "Really?" She tried to sound polite in order to mask the utter surprise of this revelation.

"Yes, ma'am," Elbert said as he leaned his elbows on the table. "Golfing for God had been serving the people of Allenberg County for years until last October. Did Tulane tell you about the explosion out there?"

"It wasn't an explosion," Haley said earnestly. "The Sorrowful Angel had to stop the bad men from hurting me, and your angels helped." She turned toward her grandfather. "The angel is really, really sorry about what happened, Granddaddy."

It was Stone's turn to slam his tea glass down. True to his nature, though, he only glared at his father. He didn't say a word.

Elbert ignored Stone and smiled down at

his grandchild. "I know, darlin', and it wasn't all her fault." Elbert's benign and adoring gaze lasted only a moment. He turned on Tulane. "Son, are you ashamed of me?"

Sarah glanced sideways. Tulane's face and ears went red. The tendons in his cheeks and jaw bunched for a moment as if he were gritting his teeth. "Daddy," he finally answered in a tone that suggested he was trying to keep his temper, "don't you think it's about time you retired? I could buy you and Momma a nice house someplace, like Palm Springs, on a real golf course."

"You know, Jimmy Marshall has been after me for weeks now. He thinks I should sell out, too. But even though I'm at a loss as to how to get Golfing for God back in business, I still don't want to move to Florida."

"But Daddy, even before the explosion, not too many people were visiting Golfing for God. It doesn't make much sense to —"

"That's not true," Ruby said. "Ever since the golf course got listed on roadsideamerica .com last year, we've been getting a steady stream of visitors. In fact, the Professional Miniature Golf Association has been in contact with your daddy about the possibility of hosting an association championship."

"Really?" The question popped right out

of Sarah's mouth before her brain caught up with it. She was getting another one of those gut feelings that usually ended up with a good idea.

"Really," Ruby replied, glancing at Sarah with a little half-smile. "I believe a thing like that would be good for businesses in Last Chance. I guess you would understand all that, being a businesswoman yourself."

Sarah felt a sudden flush of pride. Ruby thought she was a businesswoman. The moment of pride lasted until Tulane turned toward her and glared. He was really angry this time.

"This is none of your business," he said.

Sarah sealed her lips. But her mind kept working on the idea. A PMGA championship held at a place called Golfing for God had some pretty amazing potential appeal. She figured there were dozens of politicians and ministers who might want to attend a thing like that.

"Sarah, stop it." Tulane's voice sounded sharp.

"Stop what?"

"Thinking."

"Thinking?"

"Yeah, thinking. I can tell something is running through that devious corporate mind of yours. Like how to connect me,

Cottontail Disposable Diapers, Golfing for God, the PMGA, and car seat safety into one mega-big advertising and marketing campaign. I'm not interested."

"But —"

"Not interested." He pushed back from the table and stood up. He had not finished eating.

"Momma, that was good. I forgot how much I enjoy your cooking. Now, if ya'll would excuse us, I'm going to take Sarah over to Miriam's."

Sarah stood up, too, knowing that it was probably best to get Tulane out of there before he and his father got into a donnybrook. She followed him through the front room and out onto the porch. "I guess you aren't about to explain what just happened in there, huh?" she asked.

"Nope. We're shelving this conversation permanently. You've learned every last one of my secrets." His body was drawn taut like a bow. He was furious and embarrassed. She felt for him. Parents could be so embarrassing sometimes.

"I'm not going to tell people about your father, okay? Believe it or not, I actually understand."

He stepped down off the porch and headed toward a beat-up Ford pickup that he'd borrowed from his brother. His shoulders were straight, and every muscle in his body seemed tight.

"I'll give you my solemn promise. Okay?" she said to his back.

"I'd like to believe you," Tulane said as he reached the truck and opened the passenger-side door. He turned toward her.

"I'm trustworthy, really I am," Sarah said, and her inner Puritan whispered, *Most of the time.* Luckily her inner Puritan didn't say that out loud.

Tulane stopped and gave her a measuring look. "Okay," he said. "If you're so trustworthy, then swear that you won't tell the world about Golfing for God. And when you swear, I want you to cross your heart and then spit on your hand." By the gleam in his eye, he seriously expected her to do this.

"Spit on my hand? No way. I'll cross my heart, and that's the limit."

"It ain't any good without spit." His eyes flashed with a deadly combination of amusement and something else she couldn't quite decipher.

"Well, as you have pointed out any number of times today, I am a lady, and ladies do not expectorate."

He chortled. "Another three-dollar word.

Are you going to swear or not?"

She held up her right hand. "I swear I will not tell anyone about Golfing for God. And even if you do something about car seats, I will keep Haley's accident and problems to myself." She crossed her heart. She did not spit on her hand.

"It ain't legal without spit."

He waited.

She demurred.

After about thirty seconds of silence, he shook his head. "C'mon, let's go do something more fun, like get a drink down at Dottie's."

"I thought you were taking me to Mrs. Randall's house. And besides, I don't drink much."

"Why does that not surprise me?" He gestured toward the open truck door.

She walked past him and stepped up into the cab. The man scared her a little, but she couldn't deny the fact that every time she found herself in his presence, she lit up like a firefly. The idea of having a drink with him sounded like an adventure, the kind Mother would not approve of.

He closed the door and leaned in to speak through the open doorway. "If you don't want to get a drink, that's okay."

The little glow inside her died. He didn't

see her as the type to go out drinking, did he? He expected her to be prim and proper. Well, to heck with that.

"I could use a drink," she said firmly.

A slow, dangerous smile crossed his face.

Sarah approached the margarita cautiously, like a little sparrow approaching a crust of bread. It amused Tulane in ways he didn't wish to explore too deeply, any more than he wanted to explore the fact that she now knew the entire truth about his crazy family.

They sat at a table at Dot's Spot, Last Chance's one-and-only nightspot. It was comfy at Dot's. There was sawdust on the floor, boiled peanuts to snack on, alcoholic beverages of all kinds, and real rednecks who liked to talk bass fishing.

There was also usually live music, provided by the Wild Horses, the local country-and-western band. But not today. The band had been getting gigs all over the place recently because Tulane's brother Clay was sitting in on the fiddle. And his new wife, Jane, was singing lead.

Tulane reckoned it was a lucky thing the Wild Horses were up in Columbia at the Bluebell Lounge, because that way Sarah could avoid meeting Clay. It was a lead-pipe cinch that if Clay ever had a moment to talk with Sarah, his brother would tell her all about that time Tulane had accidently set fire to Mr. Nelson's cornfield.

Clay just loved to tell that story.

What was he going to do about Sarah Murray? She knew way too much about him now. Maybe he could get something to hang over her head. But that was unlikely, given that she was the epitome of a nice girl. Getting her into trouble would be immature. Besides, after his visit with Uncle Pete, he really wanted to behave himself. He wanted to man up and be mature.

And he wanted to win a race before Pete died.

Tulane took a long pull on his beer and forced that unpleasant thought into the back of his brain. He had no idea what to do about Sarah, or Uncle Pete, or his stupid pink car. He was tired of thinking about those problems. So he decided that he would just enjoy the moment.

He launched a smile in Sarah's direction. "So, tell me the truth. You've never had a margarita before, have you?"

She angled her hazel eyes up at him. "Actually, I'm not that pathetic. I've had one or two."

"And how old did you say you were?"

"Twenty-five." She whispered the words, as if she were ashamed. He tried to ignore the sudden urge to protect her. She couldn't really be as naïve as she sounded, could she?

"Honey, you've had four years to practice drinking margaritas legally. And more than that, if you were like any average college kid with a fake ID. So telling me that you've drunk margaritas once or twice makes you practically a margarita virgin, too."

"There is no such thing as being a little bit virgin," she said, something naughty sparking in her eyes. "Either you are or you're not."

"Well, that's good, because I wouldn't want to be corrupting the morals of a nice girl like you." Much.

Her mouth stretched into a sexy-as-sin grin. "Wouldn't you just. And I'm not nice. I refuse to be nice. *Nice* is an insipid adjective."

He let himself smile, knowing for a certainty that there were some smiles women found irresistible. "Boy howdy, you do have a three-dollar-a-word vocabulary, don't you? But don't you worry. I do understand it. And if I weren't trying to be grown-up and responsible, I might even try to help you get over being nice. I have this feeling that with practice, you might find you have a talent for sin."

She giggled — no doubt as a result of the alcohol she had just imbibed. She squirmed in her seat as she took in all of Dot's Spot with a pair of wide, girlish eyes. Then her gaze returned to his, and she smiled up at him. He picked up his beer and downed it in several swallows.

Someone punched up a George Strait two-step number, and Sarah started tapping her toe to the music. Every time her toe moved, her knee brushed up against his, setting off little electric shocks.

"That's it," he said, pushing up from the table. "It's time for you to learn to two-step."

"Huh? But I don't know how to dance."

"Figures, you being a virgin and all." This should be good.

Tulane snagged her hand, registering her birdlike bones and the soft flesh of her palms. She was so tiny and so utterly female that it felt as if someone had just squeezed his gonads.

He pulled her out onto the dance floor and turned her around to face him. Her head barely reached the bottom of his chin. He snaked his right hand around to the back of her waist, his palm warmed with her body heat. He suddenly felt as awkward as a fifteen-year-old.

"Okay," he said, leaning down and talking into her ear above the music. "All you have to do is remember that this is like walking. You start back on your right foot and just alternate right and left."

"Uh-huh. Right." Her voice sounded tight. Good, he wanted to keep his nurse-maid a little off balance.

"Okay," he whispered, trying to focus on the dance and not his raging hormones. "It's six beats and four steps. One, two, three, hold, four, hold. Got that?"

"Uh, no, not really."

"Okay, don't worry. I got you. I'm leading, and I'm in control. You just follow me. Start on your right foot."

He waited for the beat to roll around and then he gave her a little nudge backward. She stumbled a couple of times and stepped on his toes once. But in about three minutes, the girl was two-stepping like someone born in Texas. She had a talent for this that seriously outstripped her abilities to talk a mile a minute and wheedle information from his family.

He pulled her close enough to get his nose down into that glorious crown of red hair and smell her earthy scent. A moment later, just as they were beginning to get a rhythm going, someone tapped on his shoulder.

"Mind if I cut in?"

Tulane turned to find a seriously inebriated Bubba Lockheart standing behind him. Bubba, who had once been Pete's main mechanic, outweighed Tulane by a good eighty pounds. He was dressed for work in a greasy blue shirt with his name — Bubba, not Frank or Francis — embroidered right above the right shirt pocket.

Bubba was drunk as a skunk, a turn of affairs that had become something of a habit with the boy recently.

"No, Bubba, you can't cut in. You're drunk and dirty."

Bubba's brow lowered. "Aw, c'mon, Tulane, there ain't no other women in here."

"Well, this one is with me, and she isn't interested in getting grease on her black suit."

"Um, maybe we should just leave, okay?" Sarah said, pulling Tulane in the general direction of the door. "We don't want any lawsuits, remember? That would be bad for the Cottontail Disposable Diaper image."

And wasn't that just like his little nursemaid? Not that Bubba would ever think about suing anyone he picked a bar fight with. But, just the same, it was nice to know that Sarah Murray, librarian, was in Tulane's corner.

"Yeah, Tulane, you wouldn't want to be caught dead fighting, especially wearing pink." This came from Roy Burdett, who worked the day shift down at the poultry plant out on Route 321. Roy was in his mid-fifties, with a red face, a Country Pride Chicken hat perched on his head, and a nasty disposition that had been fed by his nagging wife and more than a couple of beers.

Tulane consciously unclenched his fists and worked at controlling his temper. Maybe he should have taken off the pink shirt before walking into this place. He would never hear the end of this. Especially if he let Sarah yank his chain.

On the other hand, if he got into a brawl with his sponsor's nursemaid standing right there, it wouldn't be good. Jim Ferguson would be angry and disappointed. National Brands would be outraged. And just about everyone else would nod their heads and say that it was just Tulane being Tulane.

But, most important, Pete would be disappointed. Pete wanted him to grow up and be a man. And sometimes a real man had to walk away from a fight. It was counter-intuitive, but Tulane knew that having a brawl right now would be stupid.

So he choked back his pride, and he smiled his best smile, and tried not to get angry. He was going to walk away from this fight and make Pete proud of him.

"Roy, Bubba, I don't want to fight with anyone. I just want to teach this Boston girl how to two-step. Now, if y'all would just back off, we can avoid a sticky situation."

He turned his back on Bubba, intent on continuing his dancing lesson with Sarah.

Unfortunately Bubba wasn't interested in making anyone proud of him. Bubba was, in fact, too drunk to be thinking rationally. So the big, greasy mechanic shoved Tulane in the back and sent him careening into the jukebox.

Tulane stopped thinking when that happened. His natural instincts took over. He turned and rammed his fist right into Bubba's nose. Bubba hit the floor, whimpering like a wuss.

That was a huge mistake, because Roy Burdett wasn't about to stand by and watch his drinking buddy get punched. Roy stood up and came at Tulane with blood in his eye. Tulane braced himself for Roy's charge.

That's when little bitty Sarah picked up a chair and blindsided Roy right upside the head.

Roy went down without a sound.

"Nice shot, girlfriend," Dot Cox said from her spot behind the bar. The proprietor of Dot's Spot was on the long side of fifty, and her flame-red hair came straight out of a bottle. Trashy from the tassels on her neon-green western shirt right down to her snakeskin cowboy boots, Dottie Cox was the antithesis of every one of the old biddies in the Ladies Auxiliary.

Which made her okay with Tulane.

"Reckon I better call the EMTs. Ya'll may want to make a quick getaway before Stone gets here. 'Cause you know every time I call the EMTs, Stone hears about it." She smiled and batted her false eyelashes at Tulane. "It sure is nice to have you home, Tulane. It's been boring around here with you gone."

Dottie flicked her gaze to Sarah and then back. "Y'all are in some high cotton now, aren't you?"

"Oh, Dottie, meet Sarah Murray. Sarah works for my sponsor. And, as you can see, she has a wicked way with a chair when she's backed into a corner."

Dottie turned toward Sarah. "You the one put him in a pink car?"

Sarah stood there like a one-eyed cat watching a bird. Tulane wasn't entirely sure how to read the sudden tension radiating from Sarah's straight, puritanical spine.

Did Sarah feel guilty about the pink car?

Or was she just now realizing she had knocked Roy Burdett unconscious?

"No," she finally said, shaking off whatever it was that had frozen her in place.

Tulane grabbed her by the arm of her black suit. "Honey, it's time to get out of here. We've broken enough rules for one night, and while I know that rule breaking can be fun, the point is to not ever get caught."

A few minutes later, Sarah found herself riding shotgun in the old Ford pickup. She rested her head on the seat back and tried to figure out whether she was embarrassed, frightened, or merely turned on by the sudden adrenaline rush.

"I reckon we're even-steven now. I swear I won't tell anyone about the bar fight or you fainting, if you won't tell about all that stuff you heard at dinner," Tulane said, the dashboard lights illuminating his handsome profile.

"You're serious about this?"

"Sure I am. Besides, I owe you one for taking out Roy tonight."

"I'm so embarrassed —"

"Embarrassed? Honey, you got a real talent there. I reckon you're a bar-fight virgin, too?"

"Uh, yeah, I guess. My father and mother would be mortified by what I just did. Not to mention my boss."

"Ah, the Dragon Lady — Deidre Montgomery. So, it's a deal then. Mum's the word on both sides."

"Good grief, I've made a total hash of this assignment, haven't I?"

"Uh, no, you just saved me from getting a black eye. And, truth to tell, you probably saved yourself from getting grease all over that nice black suit. But, see here, there's just one thing. Even though I swear on a stack of Bibles that I will never tell Deidre Montgomery or Jim Ferguson about what happened tonight, you gotta understand that everyone in Last Chance is going to know what you did before the night is out. It could go either way with the Ladies Auxiliary."

"Either way?"

"Yes, ma'am. Either they'll think you're a floozy and a tramp, or they'll think you were justified in taking Roy out, seeing as he's a married man and was drunk. The ladies take a dim view of drunks in our town.

"Now the way I see it, you are probably

going to get a pass from the Ladies Auxiliary on account of the fact that every one of them already knows you are a descendant of Pilgrims and you were only at Dottie's because I took you there."

She managed a little laugh. "That's funny."

"You think I'm funny?"

"Yeah, I do. And I know you don't like being laughed at, which is probably why you make a big joke out of everything. But what just happened isn't a joke. I could have hurt that man. I don't know what I was thinking, really."

"Take my word for it, there's nothing to be embarrassed about. We were defending ourselves. We didn't pick the fight. We were sober, more or less, and Bubba and Roy were acting like a couple of bullies. I believe in putting bullies where they belong. Don't you?"

"Uh, I don't know. I don't usually get involved with bullies. My goodness, Tulane, I had almost finished my margarita, so I wasn't exactly —"

"That one drink wasn't enough to classify you as being wasted. Besides, I told Dot to make it weak."

"You did?"

"Yes, ma'am. I didn't want to be blamed

for getting you drunk. You being a librarian and all."

"Well, thanks for the vote of confidence." She was suddenly annoyed with him. She hated being treated like she was incompetent. Even if she *was*.

"I promise you, this will not get back to your bosses," Tulane said. "And the way I see it, if you promise to keep your mouth shut, and I promise to keep my mouth shut, neither one of us will get into any trouble."

"What if he sues?"

Tulane snorted. "Neither of those boys will remember a thing tomorrow morning. And, trust me, this isn't the first time they've been hauled off to Doc Cooper after a night at Dottie's."

He turned the truck into a gravel driveway overhung with Spanish-moss-draped trees. A moment later, a large Queen Anne Victorian came into view. It was run-down, like something out of a ghost story. The yard and the foundation plants needed a good trimming, having grown up almost to the level of the porch railing. The only illumination came from a single porch light.

Tulane set the brake and killed the engine. "Well, we're here at Miriam Randall's house. C'mon, I'll introduce you to the old gal."

Tulane got out of the driver's side, circled around the truck, and opened the door for her. He gave her his hand and helped her down from the high cab as if he were a gentleman.

Which he was not. But, holy moly, his hands felt incredible — rough and warm and dry and big and manly. Heat sizzled through Sarah's core. It was a miracle her clothing didn't spontaneously combust. She needed to cool it. Tulane was off-limits, and it would be professional suicide to develop a crush on the guy.

They headed toward the house just as the front door opened, spilling light out onto the yard. A small figure stood silhouetted in the doorframe.

"Tulane Rhodes, is that you?"

"Yes, ma'am," Tulane said, using the polite voice one used when speaking with a church lady.

Sarah recognized that voice. She had mastered it at a young age, since she had been surrounded by church ladies who had watched every step she ever made. Maybe she and the big, bad good ol' boy had more in common than either of them might have thought when they first met.

They walked up the porch steps. "Miz Miriam Randall, this is Sarah Murray, who works for National Brands."

"It's nice to meet you," the old lady said. "I gather ya'll stopped by Dot's Spot on your way here."

Sarah's mouth went dry, and her words of greeting died in her throat. *Goodness, what now?*

"We did, Miz Miriam," Tulane said into the sudden silence, as if he understood Sarah's inability to speak. "I hope you weren't expecting us earlier."

The old woman grunted. "I was. And you should be ashamed of yourself, taking a person like Sarah to that wicked place. I'm just so glad she studied self-defense." Miriam smiled at Sarah. "Ya'll come on in."

Sarah choked on a nervous laugh. Miriam shuffled back from the door, leaning on a cane.

"Ma'am, if you don't mind, I need to get along home," Tulane said. "We've got to be up at the crack of dawn. So I'll just leave Sarah in your hands." He stepped back, retreating like the British at the Battle of Lexington.

"I'll pick you up at six o'clock on the dot," he said to Sarah as he climbed into the truck and fired it up.

"Come on in, Sarah," Miriam Randall said. "I've already heard a lot about you."

Well, that was obvious. Sarah had no choice but to follow Miriam into a sizable front parlor, stuffed with Victorian settees upholstered in red velvet and striped damask silk. A baby grand piano stood in the corner between the bay window and the pink marble fireplace. Hardbound books and potted plants crowded together on a bookshelf that stood against the far wall. The place smelled of lavender and resembled a set from *Arsenic and Old Lace.*

Miriam Randall wore her stark white hair in a set of crown braids and might have been the model for one of Norman Rockwell's grandmothers, except for the red Keds slip-ons and the rhinestone-encrusted eyeglasses.

Miriam sat down in one of the red velvet chairs and gestured toward the settee, her dark brown eyes sparkling behind the fifties-style eyeglasses. Sarah sat down and noticed the tray on the coffee table filled with a Royal Doulton tea service, featuring blue borders and old-fashioned tea roses. Ah yes, Miriam had been waiting for her in true church-lady fashion.

"So," Miriam said, presenting a cup of tea, "Ruby says you're from Boston, and your forebears came over on the *Mayflower.*"

"Yes, ma'am. And one of my ancestors

fought in the Revolution." She neglected, of course, to point out that she also had a few hotheaded abolitionists in her family tree, as well as an ancestor who served with General Sherman in the Civil War. No sense stirring up trouble.

"My, isn't that nice. And you're a Presbyterian."

"Yes, ma'am." Sarah nodded and held her teacup just like Grandmother Howland had taught her. Miriam had met her match. The old biddy had no idea just how stuck up her mother's family was. All Sarah had to do was pretend Miriam was her grandmother. Heaven only knew how many Saturday afternoons she had been expected to have tea with Grandmother. And Heaven help her if she spilled a drop or didn't sit up straight.

"I wanted to thank you for putting me up tonight. I'm afraid I made a fool of myself today in my black suit," she said. Humility was always a polite way to start.

Miriam smiled like she was thinking about what had just happened at Dot's Spot. "Well, sometimes things work out for the best, you know. The Lord has a plan for us all."

"I'm sure He does have a plan," she said agreeably.

"Absolutely. You should never doubt. And speaking of the Lord's plan, if you want to take my advice, the Lord wants you to keep an eye out for a man of faith who has his priorities in the right order."

Huh?

Miriam snickered like a demented schoolgirl. "I know what you're thinking, Sarah. You think I'm giving you banal Christian advice. But I'm speaking literally here." Miriam stopped and slurped her tea. Then put the cup down with a pair of hands that were rock steady, despite her advanced years and obvious senility.

Miriam settled back into her velvet chair and blinked at Sarah from behind her coke-bottle glasses. For a moment, she resembled Mr. Magoo with rhinestones.

Sarah coughed and put her cup down in its saucer. She continued to hold the saucer the way Grandmother had taught her. "Mrs. Randall, really, I'm not looking —"

"But of course you are. Everyone who hasn't found their soul mate is always searching. The Lord made us to go through life two by two. That's just a plain fact."

"Yes, but I don't need —"

"Of course you need help. It's hard to find the right one. Either there aren't enough eligible ones, or there are too many. And

it's so easy to make a mistake. So when I
—"

"Really, Mrs. Randall, I don't want to be
—"

"It's all right. I understand. But see, the thing is, you should be searching for a man of faith."

"You mean like a minister?" Sarah's voice cracked in alarm. *A minister? Was Miriam crazy? Not ever. Not if he were the last man on earth. No, no, no, no.* She wasn't going to become her own mother.

"Oh, well, he might be a minister," Miriam said in a rational tone of voice. "I hadn't really thought about that. Maybe a deacon? It's not really important." She waved her hand in dismissal.

"But you said something about a man of God, and I —"

"Oh, no, I said a man of *faith.* And besides, don't take me literally, child. That would be a mistake."

She had no plan to take anything Miriam said literally, or even seriously. "Faith?" She failed to keep the skepticism out of her voice.

"Oh, yes. You should be searching for a man who values the important things. A good man. A man who knows how to follow the straight and narrow. A man who values love before money. A man who knows what's important in life."

Who didn't want a man like that? But men like that did not really exist, proving that Miriam was a nut job.

"Mrs. Randall, I'm not ready to settle down. There are some things I need to do first, but I'm sure when I'm ready, I'd like to find a man like that."

Miriam laughed and rocked a little in her chair. "Of course you aren't ready to settle down. No one really is, are they? But then God has a way of putting the right one in your path. But recognizing him can sometimes be tough, so let me give you a little advice. Be careful not to judge the book by its cover."

Sarah involuntarily flashed on the long line of seminary students who had graced Mother and Dad's dining table over the last few years. Not a one of them was blessed in the appearance department. If she didn't know better, she would swear that Mrs. Randall had consulted with Mother, and the two of them were ganging up on her.

She was never going to settle for a dull, boring, straight-and-narrow minister of the Word. Ever. Mother and Mrs. Randall and the world needed to quit pushing guys like that at her.

106

Sarah smiled sweetly, laying on the charm as she returned her cup to her saucer. "I will keep what you say in mind, Mrs. Randall."

And run like heck in the opposite direction.

CHAPTER 5

Hettie Marshall got out of her Audi TT and leaned against its polished fender as she lit a cigarette. She kept half an eye trained on the alley by the Cut 'n Curl, just in case someone came by. She hated to think of the gossip that might ensue if anyone ever found out she had this hidden vice.

She took a deep drag and felt the muscles in her neck and shoulders ease.

Normally she would have gone out to the potting shed to indulge this secret habit, but she hadn't had time this morning. Henry Dixon, of Dixon Investigations, had called her right before she left for her weekly hair appointment. Mr. Dixon said he had something interesting to share with her.

That was bad news. Hettie had been praying that her husband, Jimmy Marshall, the owner of Country Pride Chicken, wasn't doing anything even remotely interesting. She wondered, as she dropped the cigarette and stubbed it out with her Isaac Mizrahi pumps, what she might do about Jimmy and his interesting pastimes, whatever they might be.

Her meeting with Mr. Dixon wasn't until 4:30 that afternoon. She would be a wreck by that time.

She popped a wintergreen Lifesaver in her mouth and headed toward the Cut 'n Curl. The odor of hot coffee and hairspray welcomed her as she pushed through the beauty shop's doorway. The conversation halted the moment she stepped into the room.

That little pause was an affirmation of sorts. A lonely affirmation. Hettie had worked hard to maintain a distance between herself and the other women of Last Chance. It was required for a woman of her station.

Hettie was, after all, the Queen Bee of Last Chance, South Carolina, a member of the DAR, and a Southern aristocrat right down to her bones.

Queen Bee was an unofficial title, of course, never spoken to her face. The title carried little power, in reality. In truth, Lillian Bray was the bully everyone kowtowed to. Miriam Randall was the woman everyone listened to. And Ruby Rhodes was the woman everyone wanted as a best friend.

Hettie would have liked Ruby as a friend, too, but that was not possible. Not with Ruby's husband being the kind of man he was. Sometimes it was a bitch being the Queen Bee of this little town.

"Hey, Hettie," Ruby Rhodes greeted her, a big smile on the hairdresser's face. As always, Ruby was tastefully dressed in an ensemble that was probably purchased at Target. Hettie's outfit had been purchased at Bergdorf's in New York three months ago. And yet, Ruby looked more at home in her clothes.

For that matter, Ruby looked more at home in her skin. Hettie wondered how the woman managed when she was married to a man everyone thought was one step away from the crazy farm.

"Oh, Hettie, you won't believe it, we think we've found the perfect wife for the minister," Millie Polk said from her place at the manicure station where Jane, Ruby's new daughter-in-law, was artfully applying polish.

Hettie kept a neutral smile plastered on her face. The members of the auxiliary were single-minded in their determination to make an honest man out of William Ellis. She thought maybe they should let Bill alone to figure things out for himself. But of course, no congregation wanted their minister to be a confirmed bachelor. A thing like that could lead to gossip.

And Lord knew, this town had a talented crop of gossips.

"Who is it this time?" Hettie asked as she followed Ruby to the shampoo area at the back of the shop.

"My son's nursemaid," Ruby said with a melodramatic roll of her eyes.

"Who?"

Ruby draped a plastic sheet around Hettie's shoulders and tilted the chair back. She started shampooing Hettie's hair. "Her name's Sarah, and she works for National Brands. They sent her down from New York to make sure Tulane stays in line."

"How did you meet her?"

Ruby continued to work up a lather as she related a long story about a black wool suit, a baby-changing race, and fisticuffs at Dot's Spot.

"And Lillian thinks this woman is perfect for Bill? Lillian must be slipping." Hettie sat up as Ruby wrapped her hair in a towel.

"Well, I reckon she's willing to overlook the fight at the bar, given the fact that my son was involved and we all know how trouble follows that boy."

"Also, Sarah's kin came over on the *May-flower*," Millie added enthusiastically as Hettie and Ruby returned to the salon's main room. "That's a plus in a minister's wife, don't you think?"

"Definitely," Hettie said politely as she took her seat. Ruby began to comb out her hair, her hands moving with competence. Ruby was a gem, in more ways than one. Who would believe that a little place like Last Chance would have a beautician with such talent? Ruby saved Hettie from having to drive all the way to Columbia every week.

Honestly, if Ruby had wanted to set up a shop in New York, she would have become rich and famous.

"And then," Millie continued, "there's what Miriam had to say about that Boston girl. I declare, Miriam really has done it this time."

Hettie's stomach flip-flopped and she ground her back teeth together.

"Really, Millie, you don't believe that stuff Miriam hands out, do you?" Hettie looked at Millie in the mirror. The wife of Last Chance's main banker looked back.

"Hettie, we all know your views on Miriam Randall, but the rest of us have faith in her," Millie said.

Hettie looked away. She was not going to

dignify Millie's comment with a response. After all, she was the woman who had dared to flaunt Miriam's advice ten years ago and marry Jimmy Marshall, even though he was not her soul mate. Jimmy was the man Mama had picked for her.

And Mama trumped Miriam every time.

Ruby began to work on Hettie's ash-blonde tresses, making minuscule adjustments to the cut. They sat there in silence for the longest time, Hettie not daring to open her mouth for fear that she might show way too much curiosity about Miriam's latest matrimonial prediction.

But Ruby, bless her heart, had the sense to know that Hettie had no interest in gossiping about Bill Ellis or some Yankee girl from Boston. The idea was preposterous, in any case.

"Well, aren't you even the slightest bit curious about what Miriam had to say?" Millie asked, oblivious to the tension radiating from Hettie's core.

"No," Hettie lied.

Hettie folded her hands in her lap and squared her shoulders.

It doesn't matter one iota what Miriam has to say, she told herself.

But she didn't believe a word.

■ ■ ■ ■

The Ferguson Racing headquarters in Palmetto, South Carolina, resembled a giant bird of prey, with an angled glass façade, exposed steel beams, and a sloping, angular roof. The place intimidated Sarah as she followed Tulane across the plaza and through a veritable grove of flagpoles, each flying the colors of one of the many Ferguson racing teams.

She hadn't expected ever to see the headquarters of NASCAR's largest race team. But she and Tulane had been summoned here directly after the baby-changing races at the Florence Value Mart that afternoon.

She didn't have a good feeling about this. She was supposed to be on the corporate jet, winging her way back to New York. Instead, she followed Tulane into the first-floor conference room and came face-to-face with the fabulously platinum and perpetually annoyed Deidre Montgomery.

Today, the Dragon Lady wore a beige Carolina Herrera suit, accented by an understated but exquisite gold chain. Her outfit probably cost more than Sarah made in half a year of toiling in the National Brands research department.

Jim Ferguson, the owner of the Cottontail Disposable Diapers Ford, was there, too. He sat at the end of the conference table, looking just as craggily handsome as he did in his oil additive commercials.

The Dragon Lady stood up and shook Tulane's hand. Ferguson stood as well and nodded a greeting to Tulane. They all sat down again.

Sarah had been completely ignored in the first round of introductions, which was pretty much par for the course. She took a seat at the end of the table and folded her hands in front of her and awaited her fate.

Deidre smiled an icy smile at Tulane. "Jim and I have been talking about the car seat safety idea you mentioned to me on the phone yesterday. I called this meeting because I wanted you to know that we at National Brands think this is a very good idea, and we want to put some dollars into it."

Tulane flicked his gray-green eyes toward Sarah and then back at the Dragon Lady. "Yes, ma'am, only —"

"Jim and I have been talking, and" — she turned toward Ferguson and gave him a phony smile that the racing legend did not return — "we think it's probably a good idea to create an entirely new nonprofit

115

group to educate consumers and promote car seat safety inspections. We'll have to talk to the tax guys, of course, but —"

"There's no need to create a new organization." The words jumped out of Sarah's mouth before she remembered that Deidre didn't like being interrupted or contradicted. Especially by lackeys who had not been acknowledged upon entering the room.

Deidre stopped speaking and stared at Sarah as if she had been deposited at the table by aliens. "What?" The word came out with the force of a bullet.

Sarah clenched her hands together and tried to tamp down the nerves fluttering in her gut. "While we were killing time between events today, I googled 'car seat safety.' I got two million hits. We don't have to reinvent the wheel. We just need to connect Tulane with one of the existing programs."

Deidre's gaze took in Sarah's slightly rumpled black business suit. The Dragon Lady gave Sarah a pitying smile. "Sarah, I have something much bigger in mind." She turned back toward Ferguson. "As I was saying, we can brand the —"

"Hold on," Jim said, his blue eyes shifting to Sarah and then back to Deidre and finally to Tulane. "I think car seat safety is a great idea. But I'd really like to know if this car seat thing is going to allow us to tone down the color of the car. Or at least to reinvent the bunny on the hood. The guys in the pits have practically revolted over having to wear pink suits with snuggle bunnies on them. It's just not manly, Deidre."

"It's the color of the brand, and the bunny is our logo, Jim. We're not about to —"

"Um," Sarah ventured in timidly. "About the bunny."

"What now, Sarah?" Deidre said impatiently.

Sarah interlaced her sweaty fingers and told herself she had nothing whatsoever to lose. The only hope she had of salvaging her career and undoing the damage she had done to Tulane's was to stand up for her ideas, instead of letting other people steal them.

So she cleared her voice and forged ahead bravely. "The bunny doesn't work. All our focus group research says Tulane skews alpha. So putting a cuddle bunny on the hood of his car is, well . . . odd, to say the least. It's a turnoff to our key consumers. We ought to rethink the uniforms and drop the logo or redesign it to give it some attitude and —"

"Wait a sec. You want to redesign the logo?

What are you, nuts?" Deidre leaned forward.

"All I'm saying is that the logo would work better on a race car if it was less Beatrix Potter and more Racer Rabbit," Sarah said, referring to the beloved Saturday morning cartoon character who regularly got himself and his little green race car into tight scrapes.

Tulane and Jim looked up at her in unison. "Wow, that's brilliant," Jim said. "Why not?"

He turned toward Deidre, whose features had gotten hard. Deidre was about to go nuclear.

"Absolutely not. We have a logo and it's —" Deidre started.

"Have you ever seen a Racer Rabbit cartoon?" Jim asked.

Deidre shook her head. "I don't have children."

"Well," Jim said, "Racer Rabbit gets himself into deep trouble every Saturday, and he counts on Foxy Roxy to get him out. Foxy is a good little fox who follows the rules, and Racer is just — well, sort of like Tulane — he never met a rule he didn't want to break." Jim said this with a semi-stern glance at Tulane.

"The thing is, Deidre," Sarah continued, taking Jim's words as an invitation to expound, "*Racer Rabbit* is the top-rated kidvid show on network television for the under-five set. Cottontail Disposable Diapers does a lot of advertising on that show because mommies watch it, too."

"Is that so?" The muscles in Deidre's jaws pulsed.

Oops, maybe she had overstepped.

"Yes," Sarah said, pressing her palms together and praying that she hadn't just committed professional suicide.

"Well, we can't change the logo, okay? Now, let's get back to the discussion of car seats. I think we should —"

"Look," Tulane interrupted. "Y'all should know that the car seat idea was Sarah's, too. It's not my idea. I only suggested it because I thought it might be a way to get out of officiating at baby-changing races." He stared soberly at Deidre. "I realize that you want me to be your tame stock car driver, but those baby-changing races are humiliating. You're making me a freaking laughingstock, and I don't really like it."

"Tulane . . ." Jim's voice was stern. "That's enough."

Tulane leaned back in his chair, folding his arms over his chest. He was furious, and Sarah felt a huge rasher of guilt descend right down on her head. What on earth had she been thinking when she'd put that particular detail into her revenge memo?

Short answer: She'd been trying to embarrass Steve Phelps. But Tulane Rhodes was paying the price. Proving that revenge was never a very good plan.

Jim turned toward Sarah. "So the car seats were *your* idea?"

She nodded. "Uh, yeah."

"Where did you come up with that idea?"

Tulane gave her a warning glance.

She shrugged. "I don't know. It just came to me. And for the record, Jim, Tulane was great with the kids at the baby-changing races. But, uh, they —"

"Enough, Sarah. You weren't invited to this meeting to —" Deidre started.

"No, wait. I'm interested in what she has to say," Jim interrupted.

Deidre aimed her laser-beam look at Jim. Usually this gaze caused people to curl up and die on the spot. But Jim seemed impervious. Maybe Deidre had met her match. Sarah shifted her gaze from Deidre to Jim to Tulane and back again as she realized that no matter what she said, someone was going to be unhappy.

"Sarah?" Jim said.

"Well, um, I don't know where the idea came from. Seeing a lot of mommies with babies, probably. And, um, as I said before,

Tulane was good with the babies."

Tulane rolled his eyes. His biceps flexed. He was unhappy, and she didn't blame him.

"Could we please get this conversation back on track?" Deidre gave Sarah the laser-beam treatment. Sarah felt a little queasy.

"No," Jim said firmly. That one little word was so forceful and compelling. When Jim Ferguson spoke, everyone listened, even Deidre.

"No?" Deidre said, giving Jim another arch look, but this time the whole laser-beam thing seemed to have lost its potency.

"Deidre," Jim said with quiet authority, "if we continue down this road, it's going to end badly. So I have a suggestion to make."

"Okay." Deidre didn't sound too sure.

"I'd like you to assign Sarah to Ferguson Racing for the season as our sponsor liaison. We can use her as a go-between on this car seat safety idea, and she can coordinate your hospitality events and whatnot from here. She appears to be a very creative young woman. And I think we ought to collaborate on this idea of a license deal with Racer Rabbit. That idea is brilliant, and you'd be a fool not to think it through."

"I can't assign her as a sponsor liaison. To be honest, she should never have been sent down here to advance Tulane. She has no experience, and she's basically a research assistant in the marketing department. She doesn't have —"

"A market researcher? Really?" Jim asked. His voice sounded calm, but amused. "Well, I'll be. I guess she has a handle on the consumer end of things, doesn't she? I'd say she has a better handle on it than the rest of the folks up there in your shop." He leaned in toward Deidre. His whole demeanor was firm and in control. "Besides, Tulane has a point. Baby-changing races are humiliating in the same way as making a bunch of good-ol'-boy mechanics wear powder pink and a bunny logo is.

"Don't get me wrong. I know that contractually you have the right to paint that car. But I don't need to honor that contract for more than this year. So I'd say there is a lot of room for compromise and coordination. We could start with Sarah's ideas on car seats and Racer Rabbit."

Holy moly, Jim Ferguson was giving her credit for her ideas. That had never happened, ever. Sarah squared her shoulders. It felt really nice to be recognized for once.

A muscle ticked in Deidre's cheek, and Sarah worried that her boss might literally start breathing fire. Instead, Deidre took three or four deep breaths, then said,

"Would you gentlemen excuse us for just one moment? Sarah and I need to have a little chat."

Deidre didn't wait for anyone to answer this question. She simply stood up and nodded toward Sarah. "Come with me."

Sarah had no choice but to follow her boss out into the hallway and then into a ladies' restroom.

No sooner had the door closed behind them than Deidre turned on her. "That was some performance you just gave. Did Tulane tell you what to say?"

Deidre's words felt like a slap to the face. "No, I —"

"Don't." Deidre waived her hand impatiently. "Of course he put you up to this. He thinks he can manipulate me by manipulating you. But he's wrong. He and Ferguson probably set the whole thing up. And he's already gotten you into big trouble. You *do* realize that."

Sarah tried to decide if she minded being in trouble. For once in her life, she didn't think so, even though she wasn't entirely sure how Tulane had gotten her into trouble. It seemed clear that any trouble was entirely of her own making and involved a very stupid memo about a pink car.

Deidre shook her head. "I'm going to have

to make you the liaison to Ferguson Racing or run the risk of further alienating Jim Ferguson. I can't afford to do that right now. I need his cooperation on this car seat idea. This project is very important to me, Sarah. And that means you're going to have to relocate here."

"You're going to do what Ferguson asked? You're going to make me leave New York?"

"Not permanently. Just for a few months. I'm sorry. I know it's awful here. I tried to find a Starbucks and they don't have them anywhere. But I'm going to have to do it. Jim can be a pain in the ass sometimes, and it's your job to make him happy."

It struck Sarah right at that moment that moving to South Carolina was a good way to get out of the library and far, far away from Steve Phelps.

That sealed the deal right there.

"Okay," she said with more enthusiasm than was probably wise.

"You'll do it? Really?"

She nodded.

"Good. Now, let me make myself clear. Your job is *not* to express your thoughts on the color of the car, the design of the uniforms, the corporate logo, or the organization of the car seat safety campaign."

Sarah found herself nodding, because at

that point it seemed the best thing to do if she didn't want to mess up what had just happened.

"And one more thing," Deidre said, wagging a finger at her. "While you're in South Carolina, I want you to compile a complete dossier on Tulane Rhodes. I want to know everything about him — secret ex-wives, bastard kids he doesn't want to talk about, DUI convictions. You understand? That bio of his is a complete fabrication, and I'm not going to have some complete jerk, or worse yet a reprobate, as the spokesperson for *my* car seat safety campaign. Is that clear?"

"Yes," she said. Oh boy, this was bad. Sarah had promised Tulane that she would keep his secrets. She couldn't break that promise, even if she hadn't spit on it. Promises were something a person kept, no matter what.

Deidre raised her eyebrow in a truly amazing facsimile of Grandmother Howland. "I want every detail of Tulane Rhodes's life, and I want it on my desk by the middle of next week. You have a talent for research. Use it. Are we clear?"

"Yes," Sarah managed to choke out from her clenched teeth.

"Good," Deidre said as she turned and examined herself in the bathroom mirror.

"I'll expect regular reports. And I don't want you to rest until you have uncovered all his secrets. We need to find a way to pressure Jim into firing him. He's all wrong as a spokesperson for my campaign. So I need the dirt and I need it quickly. Hopefully, Tulane Rhodes will misbehave and make our jobs a whole lot easier."

Five days later, Sarah sat in the little office Ferguson Racing had given her in their vast complex of garages and meeting rooms. She stared out her single window at the view of a large parking lot filled with pickup trucks and team haulers. The last few days had been a whirlwind. She'd left her apartment in Brooklyn; found an extended-stay hotel in Florence, South Carolina; rented a car; and ensconced herself here in redneck land. She felt like Custer scouting out the Indians.

If the folks here knew that her main job description was to mess things up in order to get Tulane fired, they might not be very charitable. What on earth was she supposed to do?

Her moral dilemma became obvious when Tulane strolled into her office and sat his long, lean body down in her single office chair. He wore a gray striped golf shirt and a pair of blue jeans so faded that the knees were starting to unravel. He smiled that little smile of his and put a stack of papers on her desk. Then he gave her a singularly wicked look and said, "Welcome to Dixie, honey."

"Uh, thanks." She folded her hands together, hoping that he wouldn't notice the way they were sweating. He filled up her tiny office and made her realize that her new job was fraught with all kinds of occupational hazards.

Why did he have to be so handsome? He walked into a room, and her hormones immediately perked up and started paying attention.

"So I just came from Jim's office, and he told me that I have to be nice to you. He also says that anyone as smart as you are when it comes to marketing could probably unsnarl all of this stuff." He pointed to the stack of papers.

"What's this?"

He shrugged. "A lot of e-mails and crap from people who want a little piece of me. Jim says I need to go through this stuff and figure out which offers I want to take. He says it would be good for my career. Only trouble is, I have no head for this crap."

She pulled a piece of paper off the stack. It was from a toy manufacturer who wanted to work with Tulane on a toy pink car with a snuggle-bunny driver. Obviously, any toy like that would have to get National Brands' approval and probably a license fee for the use of the trademark.

"All right, I'll go through this paperwork for you and weed out the good ideas from the bad ones."

"I'd be obliged." He paused a moment and then leaned forward a little in his chair. "I reckon having you here will make it easier to keep an eye on you, just in case you get any ideas of spilling the beans on my secrets."

"Um, about that topic, Tulane, there's something I need to tell you."

"Uh-huh?"

"See, um, well, Deidre wants to know your entire life story, and I'm supposed to give it to her by the end of today. She wants to make sure you're an acceptable spokesperson for car seat safety. She's looking for someone with more of a mom-and-apple-pie kind of reputation, you know."

He crossed his arms and leaned back. "So, you're going to try to fix things for me by telling her all about Haley, aren't you?"

She shook her head. "No, I'm not. I promised you that I wouldn't. But I think it would help your cause if you'd release me from that promise. I think Deidre needs to know the truth."

"Hell, no." The twinkle left his eyes, replaced by something hard.

She nodded. "Okay. I understand. But you should know that if I don't tell her something, she's going to . . ." Crap, how could she explain what Deidre was planning to do? It was so unfair.

"Going to what?"

She swallowed. "See, she's on a tear about the car seat thing. When I suggested car seats, I had no idea she would adopt the idea like a woman possessed. But she's really hot to trot on this, and that's a problem."

"Is it? It's going to get me out of baby-changing races, isn't it?"

"Uh, maybe, but not if she decides you're unacceptable as a spokesperson for car seat safety, it won't."

"What?"

Sarah pressed her hands together. "See, she wants to make sure you have pure motives."

"Pure motives? You've got to be kidding me."

She shrugged. "She's not sure you're the right image for the campaign."

"The right image? Honey, my only job is

winning races and showing up where you and Jim tell me to go. My job is not to project an image. Does Jim know this?"

She shook her head. "No. I thought I would discuss this with you first, since I gave you my promise. I could hardly have an honest conversation with Jim without telling all your secrets. Which reminds me, doesn't he know about your family?"

"Yeah, he knows about Daddy running a mini-golf place. But I never told him about the angels. I'm not telling anyone about them."

"I guess I understand. But —"

"Look, Sarah, I'm going to hold you to your promise. You can tell Deidre whatever you want about my background, just so long as you don't tell her the truth about Daddy or Haley and the whole angel thing. I don't want the world laughing at my family."

"Tulane, I'm not sure Deidre would laugh. I mean, if you explained about Haley and her mother, then —"

"I'm not having this conversation." He stood up and walked to the door. "You fix it, you hear? You tell her anything you like just so long as you protect Haley from that woman. And while you're at it, why don't you fix my image, too. The way everyone is talking about you, you're a freaking miracle

130

worker."

He turned on his heel and left her sitting there with a headache.

Her cell phone chose that moment to ring. She checked the caller ID. Mother.

Boy, when it rained, it poured. And Mother had this uncanny ability to call every time Sarah's conscience tweaked. It was like Mother and Jiminy Cricket were joined at the hip or something.

Sarah pressed the talk button. "Hello, Mother."

Mother's soft but cultured voice came over the line. "So are you settled? I haven't heard from you since Friday and I was starting to worry."

"Yes, I'm settled. National Brands put me up in one of those fully furnished extended-stay hotels. And I discovered that they actually do have Starbucks here. So I'm fine. Really."

Silence beat for a long moment. "Sweetie, I talked to Dean Albert this morning, and the opening in the fundraising department is still —"

"Mother, we've been over this. I don't —"

"But it's a perfect job for you. You could use everything you learned about marketing. You'd be working to help poor people and troubled teens instead of using your talents to sell diapers. I thought I raised you to have a conscience."

Oh brother, she was laying it on. Guilt percolated up through Sarah's middle. What would Mother say if she knew the whole truth — about the pink car memo, and the lies, and the morally ambiguous promise she'd made to Tulane?

Mother would be horrified.

Good reason to stay here in South Carolina.

Mother continued to list all the reasons why Sarah should give up her career, move home, and do good deeds.

"Mother, this new job is a big opportunity for me, okay?" Sarah replied when Mother paused for a moment in her tirade.

"Sarah, I know you think it's a big opportunity, but have you thought deeply about what the Lord wants you to do with your life? I only worry because . . ."

Mother continued her sermonizing while Sarah leaned forward and studied the marketing numbers that marched across the display of her laptop. She had to do something quick or Tulane might be out of a job.

What had he said before he left? Oh, yeah, that she needed to change his image.

Sarah quit paying attention to her mother, especially since Mother was saying stuff

Sarah had heard a million times before.

The numbers started speaking to her in their own language. And what they had to say was truly amazing.

"Are you listening?" Mother asked.

"Yes, Mother," Sarah answered mechanically as she frowned down into her computer screen.

Mother sighed audibly on the other end of the line. "Sarah, I really don't like the sort of person you are becoming. I'm sorry to be so negative, but there it is. I'm your mother, and I'm entitled to an opinion. There is more to life than selling diapers."

Mother *was* right about that, but holy moly, Tulane's pink car was selling boatloads of them.

How could that be? The memo had been a joke.

But the numbers didn't lie. The numbers said that Tulane's name recognition with consumers had been steadily climbing, despite the fact that he had failed to finish in two races. In fact, the best he'd managed so far in his rookie season was a twenty-ninth place finish.

"Well? Aren't you going to say anything in your own defense?" Mother asked.

"Um, Mother, I'm really busy right now. Maybe we can talk another time?"

"You haven't been listening."

"I *have* been listening. And I've heard it before. You want me to come home to Boston and take the job with the Urban Ministries of Massachusetts. You think that using my talents to sell things is a waste of spirit. I know. I've heard. But selling things is something I'm really good at. And everyone wants to do what they are good at. I mean, God wouldn't have given me this talent if He didn't mean for me to use it."

"Well, that's nonsense. If you were good at breaking and entering, I doubt that the Lord would want you to do *that*."

That was Mother, always with the snappy comeback filled with a moral lesson. "There isn't anything wrong with selling things. It's not the same as breaking and entering."

"Just so long as you don't sell your soul."

"I have to go. I have work to do."

Like lying to Deidre about Tulane? her inner Puritan asked. *Like ruining people's lives because of a little revenge that went awry?*

Darn. Her inner Puritan was worse than Mother and actually sounded like Jiminy Cricket. "Good-bye," Sarah said and pressed the disconnect button before Mother and her inner Puritan could gang up to make her feel like a spiritual loser.

She turned her attention back to the

marketing report on her computer. She shook her head in disbelief. Her stupid pink car memo wasn't so stupid after all.

A plan began to evolve in her mind. She could save Tulane's career and, in the process, make him an incredibly wealthy man. She turned away from the computer and pulled out the messy stack of papers Tulane had left on her desk.

She started reading, and she didn't move from her office for the rest of the day. By quitting time, she'd written Deidre a memo, but it wasn't the dossier on Tulane that Deidre had asked for.

It was, in fact, the memo Deidre had forbidden her to write, but she'd written it anyway, because Deidre would recognize a good idea . . . and probably steal it.

CHAPTER 6

Despite its Scottish name, Tavish McStaggers was the epitome of the Southern roadhouse. Neon beer signs festooned its tinted glass windows and lit up a dim and smoky interior. The smoke hanging over the oak bar, pinball machines, and pool table reminded Sarah that she was no longer in New York City. This was tobacco country. They didn't believe in making smokers go outside to do their thing.

It was Wednesday evening, and she'd been invited to an impromptu dinner with the members of the No. 57 Cottontail Disposable Diaper Ford. Sarah was a little nervous about this meeting, but she figured that meeting the members of Tulane's team was part of her new job description.

Fifteen people sat around a table at the back of the restaurant, including Tulane and Doc Jackson, the crew chief; Sam Sterling, the team's manager; and Sam's wife, Lori, who was the logistics coordinator.

Tulane, Doc, and Sam sat around one end of the table. Sarah took a seat at the opposite end, next to Ken Lewicki, the team engineer.

The remaining team members could only be described as a bunch of good ol' boys, with crew cuts, tattoos, and a prodigious amount of facial hair. Some of these big, hairy men were members of the pit crew — the ones National Brands dressed in pink every Sunday. Now, jeans and Harley-Davidson T-shirts seemed to be the uniform of choice.

These men inspected Sarah like she had just come to visit from a foreign country. Which was probably true, since four days ago she had been living in Brooklyn. How on earth had she ended up in this alien territory? Short answer: misguided revenge; two days in Last Chance, South Carolina, learning Tulane's secrets; and the strange machinations of Jim Ferguson's mind.

A waitress came by, and Sarah ordered a diet Coke.

"Not much of a drinker, huh?" Ken Lewicki said when the waitress left. He lifted his own soft drink in a toast.

Well, that made him unique, because everyone else seemed to be drinking beer.

She mentally slapped herself for ordering the soft drink. She really needed to learn how to be a better social drinker.

Unlike most of the men at the table, Ken was clean-shaven with spiky bronze hair, a square chin, a perfectly straight nose, and clear blue eyes. He didn't have one trace of a Southern accent.

"You're not from the South, are you?" Sarah said.

He laughed. "Haven't you heard? Stock car racing is now a nationwide fad. I'm from Lansing, Michigan. And, if I'm not mistaken, you're from someplace in New England."

"Boston."

"So how do you like the South?" he asked.

"I haven't been here long enough to form an opinion," she replied carefully.

He chuckled then and started talking all about his own experiences negotiating the alien culture of the South. The man seemed oblivious to the fact that the other people sitting nearby found his remarks incredibly loud and insensitive.

Kenny also didn't know when to stop talking. Sarah started to space on his conversation as he waffled on about this and that and the other thing. While her mind wandered, she glanced around the table at the rest of the team. Eventually her gaze landed on Tulane, who was deep in conversation with his crew chief.

Like just about everyone at the table, he was talking in a language she couldn't follow, but that didn't seem to matter as she studied the way he held his knife and fork, the way he chewed his food, the way his mouth quirked at the corner when he laughed.

Her insides reacted immediately, and it wasn't just because he and Deidre had put her in a moral bind. Oh no, this was a much more visceral feeling. She'd felt it the minute he'd waltzed his jeans-swathed backside into her office this morning. She was seriously attracted to this guy.

He was everything alien and dangerous — the very antithesis of the sort of man Mother would approve of. And certainly not the guy Miriam Randall had told her to be searching for. His unsuitability drew her like a flame draws a moth.

Tulane looked up at that moment and caught her stare. A slow smile spread across his lips, folding his cheeks into rows of laugh lines, his eyes dancing seductively. He appeared ready to forget the conversation they'd had earlier in the day.

She smiled back as heat crawled up her face.

"So," Tulane said in a voice that carried all the way down to her end of the table. "Who's for pool?" He held her stare, and then asked, "Sarah?"

Her stomach dropped three inches, but she couldn't look away. "I . . . uh . . . don't know how to play pool."

His grin widened. "Of course you don't. Would you like to learn?"

That brought her up short. Was he trying to lead her astray so he would have leverage over her? After all, the guy had already taught her how to swear, pass on the right, and survive a bar fight. Now there was a seductive thought.

"Sure. I'm game," she found herself saying.

He stood up. "Okay, then, let's get you a cue stick."

She pushed back from the table and followed him toward the front of the building and the pool table.

Tulane pulled a couple of cue sticks down from a rack on the wall.

"Uh, do they have any short ones?" she asked.

He shook his head. "Honey, this isn't like some things, where length matters. A cue stick comes in just one size." He handed her a stick that was almost as tall as she was.

"Oh." She wondered what things he might be thinking about. He said "things," and her mind moved directly to the gutter.

He pulled down a triangular frame, then started pulling balls out from under the table and placing them on the green felt top. "Now," he said, investing his voice with a certain professorial manner, "the balls come in two kinds, solids and stripes. That's important."

He collected the balls into the triangle and arranged them. "This is called racking the balls."

"Sounds painful."

"I'm shocked. Where did a nice girl like you learn such things?"

"From you."

His smile broadened. "I reckon you did. I reckon I have some talent in this teaching department." He paused a moment as he positioned the triangle over a little white dot in the middle of the table and then removed the frame.

"Now, normally we'd flip to see who gets the chance to break, but I'm going to let you have the honors. We'll chalk it up to you being a pool virgin and me being an experienced teacher, okay?"

He picked up a white ball and held it up. "This is a cue ball. It's the only one you're allowed to hit with your stick. It's also the one you don't want to put in any pockets."

"Uh-huh."

He placed it over the white dot at the end of the table opposite the group of balls. "Okay. Now, take a position at the end of the table and line up your stick with the cue ball."

She moved to the end of the table and leaned over the table like she'd seen people do in the movies. The posture felt awkward. "Like this?"

He stood at the other end of the table, his gaze dipping down and then back up. One of his dimples made a sudden, wicked appearance. A little flush of excitement inched down her spine. He was getting a bird's-eye view of her bra. It was new. She had bought it on a whim because it pushed up her assets and did things for her cleavage. Tulane appeared to have noticed.

He hesitated, obviously enjoying the view, and then he cleared his throat. "Uh, well, no."

She straightened up. "No? What am I doing wrong?"

He headed around the table in her direction. "Uh, just about everything."

"Really?"

"Uh-huh. Look here, I want you to stand with your legs perpendicular to the table and your feet about shoulder-width apart. Balance your weight on both feet."

She did as she was told. "Like this?"

"Uh, well . . ." He moved around the table until he was standing behind her. In the next instant, he grabbed her by the hips and positioned her body at the edge of the table. The palms of his hands felt unbelievably warm through the fabric of her pants. He let go. Disappointment settled into her stomach.

"Like that," he said, and his breath feathered across her cheek.

"Okay, what's next?" she asked, her voice sounding unusually husky.

"Are you right- or left-handed?"

"Right."

He leaned forward and grabbed her right hand and placed it way back on the stick, near its butt end. His motion had the effect of bringing the front of his body into contact with the back of hers. She was overwhelmed with his citrus scent, and the rounded contours of his thighs, and other bits of his equipment pressed up against the cleft in her bottom. Her heart slammed against her rib cage.

He backed up. "Okay," he said, his voice sounding a little pinched. "Put your left hand palm down on the table about seven inches from the cue ball."

She bent over, with Tulane right behind her. The man had to have a really good view of her bottom. She didn't want to think about all that wide expanse of behind, and panty lines, too.

"Okay, now, lift your thumb and lay the shaft of the cue in the crease between your thumb and the side of your hand."

Goodness. Her entire nervous system went a little haywire the minute he said the word "shaft."

"Now slide the stick back and forth in the crease. It should slide smoothly and evenly."

She did it. "Ah. It's pretty smooth," she said, her voice squeaky.

"Good. You've made an excellent bridge."

"Bridge?"

"That's what they call that little crease there where you've got the stick."

"Oh. Okay." Thank goodness they didn't call it something salacious, otherwise she might turn into ash right on the spot.

"Okay, honey, the trick to making a good shot is to slide the stick back and forth in the slot a couple of times and then, when

144

you're ready, you pull back and strike the cue ball at its center. You got that?"

"Uh-huh." She managed not to strangle on the words. It occurred to her that *slot* was a whole lot more salacious than bridge.

"Let 'er rip," he said.

She did as instructed, striking the cue ball solidly. It rolled over the felt and smacked the other group of balls with enough force to scatter them in all four directions. One of the colored balls dropped with a *thud* into a corner pocket.

"Good break," Tulane said. He pulled the six ball from beneath the table and held it up for her to see.

An intense flush of pride washed through her and must have shown on her face, because Tulane gave her a brilliant smile.

He nodded, his eyes dancing with merriment. "Since you sank a ball with your break, you get to go again. And since you pocketed a solid, your objective now is to get all the solid balls into the pockets, *except* for the eight ball. That comes later." He went on to briefly outline the rest of the rules of the game.

She missed her next shot, and most of the rest of them, too. It came as no surprise that Tulane won the game. She would have been disappointed in him if he had let her win. Still, he purposely missed shots so she could have a chance to play. And somehow that seemed to underscore the fact that for a big, bad, good ol' boy, Tulane was actually quite sensitive. She was terrible at this game, but Tulane didn't seem to notice.

When the game was over, she realized the members of the No. 57 Ford team were drinking beer and lounging around on barstools, watching intently. She wondered what they might be thinking.

Tulane grinned at the crew. "Anyone else up for a game?"

Ken stood up. "Sure."

"I was hoping to goad you into it." There was an odd, tense look on Tulane's face. "Best three out of five?"

Ken nodded coolly. "What are the stakes?"

Tulane dug in the pocket of his jeans and pulled out a messy wad of bills. He counted them. "Twenty-five?"

Ken shook his head. "That all?"

Tulane shrugged. "Didn't get to the bank. You ought to spot me a few, just to be neighborly."

"Not on your life. Okay. Twenty-five." Ken dug into his chinos and pulled out a money clip. He pulled out a crisp twenty and a five. They laid their money on a table nearby, pinning it down with Tulane's beer.

Tulane and Kenny's games were not exactly friendly. There was something of the playground in the way they circled one another, like a couple of thirteen-year-olds trying to figure out who was the top boy on the field.

Sarah sat down on a high stool at the bar and ordered another Coke. Lori came down and sat beside her.

Ken won the coin toss and broke first. "Oops," Lori whispered.

Sarah turned toward her. "Oops?"

"Not good for Tulane," Lori said.

Ken proceeded to run the table. Tulane didn't even get a shot. The engineer played like a machine. He didn't seem worried, and he never missed.

Tulane broke the second game. He also ran the table, but he took a lot longer setting up his shots. Tulane had to work hard to keep up with Ken.

In the end, Ken won the twenty-five dollars in five games. He sauntered over to where she and Lori sat and leaned on his cue. He paused, as if expecting Sarah to make obeisance to him, as if he were the victor of a joust, and she the lady who was supposed to hand out laurel wreaths to the victors.

It was pretty arrogant of him. She didn't

147

think skill at playing pool meant much in the great scheme of things.

"Do you regularly beat Tulane?" she found herself asking.

He smiled as if this question was precisely the one he wanted her to ask. "Well, I probably have a few games up on him." He was trying to sound humble. He failed.

Lori snorted. "Honey, Tulane and Ken play pool all the time. It's become a regular spectator sport. I'd say Kenny has a slight edge, though."

Ken shrugged. "I can't help it if the guy insists. I'm not hustling him."

Tulane shrugged. "Just passing the time and building up team spirit." He turned around and placed his cue stick in the rack.

Sarah knew darn well that Tulane didn't play with Kenny just to pass the time. Tulane didn't like Kenny Lewicki. And Ken didn't have much respect for Tulane. That game had been all about testosterone. But for some reason, Tulane chose not to fight Kenny. He chose to compete against him in a venue where Kenny had the edge.

Maybe it wasn't about testosterone at all. Maybe Tulane was just trying to get Kenny on his side, because the two of them didn't seem to be the best of teammates. The two men couldn't have been more different if they tried.

At that moment, Tulane reached into his jeans and pulled out another wad of bills that belied his earlier comment about not making it to the bank. " 'Course, I never bet more than I can afford to lose." He winked at Sarah. "Honey, that's one of those rules that you need to remember if you ever decide to take up hustling pool for a living."

He pulled out three hundred-dollar bills and handed them to Lori. "Dinner's on me. It's the least I can do, considering how lousy I drove on Sunday. Now, if ya'll don't mind, my back is still killing me. That turn-two wall was kind of hard when I smacked it on Sunday."

He gave a little farewell wave to the crew, then turned and walked out the door, giving Sarah a great view of his Wrangler-clad behind.

CHAPTER 7

Deidre Montgomery lined up several documents on her desk. At the far right was the memo Sarah had sent a few days ago about Racer Rabbit and Tulane Rhodes's marketing appeal. Beside it stood a pile of research reports also authored by Sarah.

Next to that pile stood the famous Cuppa Java memo bearing Steve Phelps's name. Steve had used this memo to catch the attention of the chairman of the Board. Its brilliant plan for marketing a new line of gourmet coffee-makers had contributed significantly to National Brands' first-quarter results. And that, in turn, had made Steve Phelps a danger to Deidre's career.

At the end of the line of memos sat the famous pink car memo, also bearing Steve Phelps's name. Deidre had found this memo on her desk last January. It outlined a silly plan for putting a bunny on the hood of a NASCAR Sprint Cup car.

Deidre turned to Sheila Dvorak, the senior director of marketing and her right-hand assistant and enforcer. "So, what's your take?"

Sheila smiled. "My take is that every single one of these memos was written by the same person. So the main question is: How the hell did someone with Sarah's talent end up in research?"

"Beats me. But I'll take the rap," Deidre said. "I guess I was too preoccupied with Steve Phelps's little games to actually notice Sarah. She has a way of fading into the background."

Sheila nodded, but her helmet of frosted and sprayed hair stayed stationary. "*Now* I understand why the staff is whining about Sarah being detailed to Ferguson Racing. You think she's been writing everyone's memos?"

"No," Deidre said, leaning back and steepling her fingers. "I think she's been helping people, which is her job. But Steve went one step further — he put his name on the Cuppa Java memo, but Sarah wrote it. I'd stake my life on it. But why would she write a memo for Steve when she hasn't done that for anyone else?"

Sheila rolled her eyes. "You don't really want me to answer that question. It was rhetorical, right? I'll bet the guy saw it on her desk and stole it. That would be consistent with his usual mode of operation."

Deidre leaned forward and picked up the original pink car memo bearing Steve's name. "So this was supposed to be her revenge?"

Sheila smiled like a fox. "Yeah, it's pretty pathetic. But this is sweet little Sarah we're talking about. And besides, you took the bait. Her revenge might have worked, too, but Steve sent Sarah to South Carolina and you got talked into letting her stay there. That, and the fact that Tulane Rhodes looks adorable in pink."

"Well, it's all working out all right, though," Deidre said as she picked up Sarah's newest memo. It suggested that National Brands keep Tulane in the pink car for the entirety of this racing season, while the company negotiated a licensing deal with Penny Farthing Productions, the owners of the Racer Rabbit cartoon character. Sarah had outlined all the parameters of an acceptable deal, as well as the organizational structure for a car seat safety program. Her theory on keeping Tulane in the pink car was pretty simple — a good ol' boy in a pink car was news, and Tulane was sexy enough to make the rounds of nonsports talk shows, promoting Cottontail Disposable Diapers as he went.

Deidre had specifically told her *not* to write these memos, but now, studying them and realizing their competence, Deidre was happy Sarah had decided not to follow the rules.

She wasn't going to underestimate Sarah again.

Deidre waved the new memo around. "I'm going to bury Steve Phelps with this."

Sheila stared down her long nose. "Deidre, that's not entirely fair to Sarah, is it?"

Deidre shrugged. "Sarah's a big girl. It's obvious she knows how to play dirty, even though she looks like an angel. Besides, I'm thinking she wants my help in getting rid of Steve. That's why she put the first memo on my desk and sent me this one, even though I told her not to write any more memos."

Deidre leaned forward. "I want you to get the media people on this right away. I want Tulane Rhodes on any talk shows you can book for the next couple of weeks. Get the art department to start working up concepts for a new paint job — tell them to watch Racer Rabbit for ideas."

"Are you certain Tulane Rhodes is the right man for this Racer Rabbit thing? I mean, we still don't know why he's hot to trot on car seats. That bio of his is bogus, and in case you've forgotten, Sarah hasn't provided the dossier you asked for. It's almost like she's dodging you."

"You think she's covering for him?"

"Maybe. I just have this feeling she's up to something," Sheila said.

"Well, we've got some time. We can't make any driver changes until next racing season. In the meantime, Sarah's got a point about Rhodes's sex appeal. Putting a bad boy with a reputation in a pink bunny suit is news, Sheila. And it's selling diapers like mad."

Sheila nodded and chuckled. "Who would have thought?"

"You know, it's a rare thing when you get to do well by doing good."

"If you count stealing Sarah's ideas as doing good."

Deidre shrugged. "Can't be helped. We need Sarah where she is, out of the way in the boonies of South Carolina."

Tulane dropped the green flag and the contestants hopped to it, changing their babies like a pack of demented fools. He was standing under another big tent at another Value Mart shopping center somewhere in South Carolina. He had lost track of where, exactly. The last few weeks had started to blur in his mind.

Having a sponsor liaison had not fixed much in Tulane's life. In fact, National Brands was driving him crazy. They had arranged for him to appear on a half-dozen talk shows. He'd had to talk about how it *felt* to be riding around in a pink car wearing a pink driver's suit.

Right, like National Brands wanted him to say one of the words the FCC had banned on national television.

The attention was embarrassing. It was bad enough being a thirty-year-old rookie, when all the other new drivers were in their teens or twenties. But to have guys snicker behind his back just steamed him.

Jim told him to be patient. But Jim didn't have to put on a pink bunny suit week in and week out. It wouldn't be so bad if his team were winning races. But they weren't. Heck, they weren't even finishing races. Morale was lower than low. And the whole sponsor thing had become one huge, never-ending distraction.

Of course, Sarah was a distraction that Tulane didn't mind all that much. He was having a good laugh teaching the little Pilgrim stuff she didn't know about. Take poker, for instance. Sarah wasn't good at it, but she had this uncanny ability to bluff that

155

had more to do with her not knowing that a pair of deuces was a bad hand than with any ability to lie, cheat, or deceive.

He had been thinking that it was time to casually raise the stakes by suggesting they gamble for pieces of clothing instead of pennies or matches.

Naw, he couldn't do a thing like that. Getting Sarah naked would be a stupid and dangerous thing to do, even if it would be a lot of fun. Besides, she had unsnarled a lot of complications in his life, even if she hadn't gotten him out of a pink suit. She'd gone through all the sponsorship crap that had come his way and had made a number of shrewd and lucrative suggestions.

Sarah put a Sharpie in his hand, and he started signing stuff.

Another half-hour of this and he could relax in the limousine and continue his poker lessons with Sarah. It was the only bright spot in his otherwise crappy day.

After coordinating twenty-five of these horrible events, Sarah had learned not to wear black. Today, she had donned a Cottontail logo shirt and a pair of khakis. The outfit wasn't precisely flattering — her backside should bear a sign across it saying "Wide Load" — but the natural fabric had the benefit of being better suited to the ruthless heat and humidity of the South. And besides, khakis and golf shirts were the uniform around Ferguson Racing.

The heat percolated up from the blacktop right into the soles of her loafers as she headed across the parking lot at the Charleston Value Mart with some bottled water for Tulane. The poor man had been standing out there in the heat for almost an hour, showing a great deal of patience, given the circumstances.

"Excuse me, ma'am, do you work for Tulane?"

The voice came from behind her and was spoken in a deep drawl that had the same soft quality as Tulane's.

She turned to find a large man bearing down on her. He wore a black T-shirt, faded Wranglers, and a buff-colored Stetson. He was huge — taller than Tulane and broader across the shoulders.

She stared up into a shadowed face that sported a trimmed goatee and a pair of gray eyes. A dark gem, probably a sapphire, winked at her from his left earlobe.

He tipped his hat, briefly exposing dark brown hair pulled back into a long ponytail. He probably had a Harley stashed somewhere because he resembled a wicked bad biker boy in the flesh, precisely the kind who sometimes showed up and caused trouble. Biker boys seemed to think that stock car drivers should eschew the color pink.

"Ma'am?" he said, tipping his hat.

Sarah went immediately on guard and scanned the parking lot over his shoulder, searching for the Value Mart security.

"Can I help you with something?"

His mouth softened just a little, and déjà vu hit her. The guy reminded her of someone, probably some country-and-western singer like Trace Adkins or Tim McGraw.

"I need to talk with Tulane privately," he said.

Yup, he was trouble with a capital T that stood for way too much testosterone.

"Um, I'm afraid speaking with Tulane right now isn't possible. If you'd like —"

"Just tell him I'm here. He'll see me. I'll be waiting in the shade over yonder." He pointed toward the storefront, which cast a shadow across the parking lot.

The man certainly talked in short sentences, didn't he? She watched him saunter off in the direction of the store with a loose-jointed walk that was part swagger.

She turned back and crossed the blistering blacktop. The line of autograph seekers had diminished. She checked her watch.

They were right on schedule. Five minutes and she could get Tulane into an air-conditioned limo and they could practice playing poker on the way back to the Ferguson Racing complex.

She was lousy at poker, but playing it with Tulane was fun because the stakes were low and Tulane didn't care about winning. That was odd, because when it came to racing cars, Tulane was all about winning. And when he didn't win — which was pretty much every Sunday — it put him in a really bad mood.

She handed Tulane a water bottle, which he opened and crushed in several long swallows, and then he turned back to the line of autograph seekers. He could be incredibly charming when he wanted to be. She had never seen him treat a race fan — especially a young fan — with anything other than the utmost respect and courtesy.

She didn't bother him with her concerns about the man in the cowboy hat. Instead, she leaned over to the security guard standing beside Tulane. She pointed to the man, who leaned against the store's cinderblock façade with one foot cocked, in cowboy fashion. "I wonder if you could check that guy out. He's got trouble written all over him. Says he knows Tulane and wants to talk with him, but you know how some of these guys are, ready to pick a fight."

The guard, a paunchy man with receding hair and bad teeth, assessed the situation and then pulled a walkie-talkie out of his belt. He started talking loudly and officiously in true Barney Fife fashion. Everyone could hear what he was saying, including the fans. Goodness, the man was a moron.

The last three ladies in line let their gazes wander nervously in the direction of the store. Tulane looked up, too. The man standing in the shade tipped his hat again. Tulane's shoulders tensed, but he didn't say anything that might alarm the fans. He simply smiled up at the ladies and quickly finished signing the last few autographs.

When he was finished, Tulane pushed up from the table and turned toward Barney, the security guard. "Call off your dogs. The man over there is my older brother."

Sarah's stomach dropped to her ankles as Tulane gave her one of his annoyed eye rolls. "Sarah, this ain't New York, you know. We don't have drive-by shootings out here in the boonies, unless it's pheasant season. Next time, ask before you call out the cavalry. That's Clay, the brother you didn't meet before."

He shook his head in disgust, then turned and sauntered in Clay's direction. Now she realized why the cowboy had seemed so familiar and perhaps so dangerous. Clay was bigger than Tulane. But like his other brothers, Clay had the same build, the same walk, and the same deep, soulful Southern drawl. And his eyes were very much like Elbert's — the palest shade of gray.

"Uncle Pete's dead," Clay said in a low voice. "He collapsed this morning. Momma sent me to come get you. The funeral's going to be on Saturday. Aunt Arlene and Momma pushed it up so you could attend."

Tulane and Clay stood in a little scrap of shade cast by the Value Mart. It was hotter than hell out there, but suddenly Tulane felt icy to the point of numbness. He needed to get out of this heat. He needed to go someplace private so he wouldn't make an a-hole out of himself right there in public.

Pete was dead.

"Shit." Tulane stared up at the blue Carolina sky searching for something that he couldn't even name. His eyes started to water up. Sarah was standing right there, eavesdropping like she always did. He really didn't want that woman to see him cry like some kind of sissy. That would be the height of humiliation.

"Tulane," Clay said and took him by the shoulder — a steady, familiar, brotherly touch. It didn't make the ache in his heart go away. "Momma's at home waiting on you. She's pretty upset, and —" Clay's voice pinched. Pete was Momma's only brother, and Pete had been a surrogate father for Clay as well. Pete had been everything Daddy was not.

Tulane studied his brother's pale eyes, stained at the moment with a goodly amount of red. Clay had done some crying recently, by the looks of things.

"Crap. I've got all these arrangements made for me. I'm supposed to race in the truck race on Friday and —"

"I can fix everything," Sarah said, pulling her BlackBerry out of her pocket. "Let me get on it."

Bless her heart, the woman understood. She had that phone attached to her ear inside of five seconds. She started talking a mile a minute, just like a little Yankee, and something inside his chest eased a bit.

It sure was impressive the way Sarah could manage things, and Tulane felt a surge of gratitude toward her, not only for doing the arranging for him, but because she understood why going home was important.

He was suddenly mighty glad she was there, even if she *was* getting a bird's-eye view of the unwanted tears in his eyes.

One minute Sarah was standing on the blacktop at the Value Mart, and the next moment she found herself in the back seat of Clay Rhodes's minivan, sandwiched between a fiddle and a guitar case. Despite the soccer-mom qualities of the well-used Windstar, Clay Rhodes drove that thing like *he* was the stock car driver and not Tulane. He headed north at a speed that didn't faze Tulane, but had Sarah hanging on to the strap handle above the back door with her right hand and her BlackBerry with her left.

She faced her fear and discovered a talent for working her smartphone one-handed. She got Tulane out of all the races he was scheduled to run on both Friday and Saturday, as well as the hospitality tent appearances for National Brands and a number of his smaller sponsors. She even fixed it with Jim Ferguson so that a private jet would be waiting for Tulane Saturday night at the Allenberg Municipal Airport to take him directly to Charlotte, where the weekend's racing events were taking place. A replacement driver would qualify the No. 57 Ford on Saturday. Tulane would still race Sunday afternoon.

It wasn't until the green watermelon stripes of Last Chance's water tower came into view that it occurred to Sarah that she should have gotten into the limo at the Charleston Value Mart and headed back to Florence, instead of riding in the back seat all the way to Last Chance.

Of course, she had gone into crisis mode the moment she had realized the situation, and Tulane had kept her preoccupied for most of the ride as he issued directives to her like the celebrity he was supposed to be. She had handled the crisis beautifully, like a real experienced advance person, and not the virgin she had been a few weeks ago.

Except that she had advanced herself to Last Chance, South Carolina — a place with one stoplight and not much more. She had no luggage, no car, and her Black Berry's battery was just about dead.

She wondered if there was somewhere nearby where she could rent a car. It was a good two-hour drive back to Florence.

Clay pulled the van to the curb a half block down the street from Ruby and Elbert's house. Tulane and Clay got out of the van and started striding up the sidewalk, both of them tense through the shoulders, both bearing that hollow-cheeked appearance men get when they grieve and don't want to break down and show it.

Neither of them paid any attention to her as she hopped down from the back and struggled with the slightly sticky sliding door of the old Windstar. Her dying phone rang as she hurried after the big men, who were eating up the distance between the van and the house on their long, good-ol'-boy legs.

She checked the display — Deidre Montgomery.

Oh great, just what she needed. Last Chance might be in the middle of nowhere, but unfortunately it still had cell phone service.

She accepted the call. "Hello, Deidre."

"I heard about the death in Tulane's family. Are you still with him?"

Sarah should have known that Deidre would hear about today's events sooner rather than later.

"Uh, yeah, I'm here."

"Here, where?"

"In Last Chance, South Carolina."

"Where?"

"Last Chance. It's Tulane's hometown."

"You're kidding, right?" Deidre said.

"No, that's the name of the town."

"How quaint," Deidre said in her snide

New York tone.

Sarah didn't bother to explain that Last Chance was not even remotely quaint. *Quirky* was a much better adjective. "Yes, it's very quaint. It has a water tower painted to resemble a watermelon," she said.

Deidre sniggered. "Nice work, kid. Now, I want you to stick to Tulane like superglue the next couple of days. Just tell him National Brands is making you available 24/7 to handle anything he needs in his hour of grief. There's a hotel there, right?"

Sarah didn't want to explain that the only lodging nearby was a place called the Peach Blossom Motor Court, which, if Mrs. Randall was to be believed, sold rooms only by the hour.

"Uh, yeah," she said. "There's a hotel."

"Good. I want you to put on that Boston charm and worm your way into his whole family scene. You know the drill, help them brew coffee and bake cookies and that sort of thing. And you can use the National Brands expense account to purchase catering or whatever for the funeral. It's on us . . ." She paused dramatically. "And I want a full report on Monday. And don't think I won't notice if you don't send a report. I asked you for a full rundown on Tulane three weeks ago. I'm still waiting."

"About that, Deidre, I —"

"It's fine, Sarah; with the current marketing plan in place, we don't need to find a replacement until next year."

"A replacement?"

"Well, that will depend entirely on the report you file on Monday, won't it?"

"A report on what?"

"On everything. His parents, his siblings. I want to know who we're dealing with. If he's going to be a spokesperson for car seat safety, he's got to be squeaky clean, you understand? I figure a funeral is just the sort of time when the family shit is liable to hit the fan. You know what I mean?"

Heat crawled up Sarah's face, but maybe it wasn't because of Deidre's casual profanity. The woman was a witch. She wanted Sarah to spy on Tulane and his family during a funeral? Did the woman have no heart?

"Um, Deidre, there's been a death in the family, don't you think —"

"Sarah, grow up. We need to make sure this guy is the right spokesman. And it's not just National Brands that needs to know all the little details. I've been talking with the producers of *Racer Rabbit*. If we do that deal, Tulane has to be worthy of the endorsement. I've been researching possible replacements. Augie Tallon might be available."

Sarah's stomach clutched. Deidre had stolen all the ideas she had put into that memo she'd written three weeks ago. National Brands was putting all her ideas into motion, and not a single person had given her any credit.

"Augie Tallon would be an amazing representative for our brand. He's considerably smoother than Tulane," Deidre said into Sarah's ear.

"But —"

"Don't be a fool, Sarah. If you want to help Tulane, then you need to dig up the entire backstory. Who hates who. All the bad things he did as a kid and a teenager. The girls he knocked up and deserted. You know, all that stuff."

Sarah had reached Elbert and Ruby's front yard, trailing after Tulane and Clay by several yards. Fortunately, her phone began to emit a low-battery warning. "Uh, that's a lot of stuff, isn't it?"

"Yes, it is. But I know you can do it. And Sarah, the way you handle yourself in this could make or break your career. Don't disappoint me."

Sarah knew precisely how to translate those words. Deidre was eager to keep her around so she could continue to steal her ideas. That made Deidre no different from Steve. Did everyone in business have to be so sharp and driven and dishonest?

"I've got to go," she said, trying hard not to let her disgust show in her voice. The idea of using the death of a beloved family member to violate Tulane's privacy made Sarah nauseated. She wasn't going to do it.

"We'll talk on Monday," Deidre said into her ear. "And remember, I want every little detail." Deidre rang off without actually saying good-bye.

Sarah followed Clay and Tulane up the front porch steps and into the house. At least thirty people had descended on Ruby Rhodes and her sister-in-law, Arlene Whitaker, widow of the late Peter Whitaker, owner and operator of Lovett's Hardware for the last thirty-some-odd years. And since everyone in Last Chance had shopped at Lovett's at one time or another, more people were expected.

Sarah almost heard Mother's voice echoing in her ears the moment she entered Ruby's parlor and registered the sheer number of people there. There were some things that one didn't do, and spying on a grieving family and their friends was one of them. Sarah wasn't going to do that, no matter what happened to her.

Tulane and his brother went straight to their mother and the grieving widow, bestowing manly hugs as they went. Grief pinched Tulane's face.

It was time to get out of Dodge.

Sarah hugged the living room wall and made her way around the clot of people as unobtrusively as possible. She headed toward the kitchen, where she figured she could plug her —

No, wait, she couldn't plug her cell phone in. She had left her briefcase in the limo at the Charleston Value Mart, and her cell phone charger was in the briefcase.

What an idiot.

She headed toward the kitchen anyway. There was probably a phone in the kitchen. She needed to call someone at Ferguson Racing and arrange for a car to come down with some appropriate clothes for Tulane. The car could pick her up and take her back to Florence.

She finally made it to the kitchen, only to discover that the Last Chance church ladies had already staked out this territory. She should have expected this, because really, nothing brings out church ladies like a funeral. Sarah herself had been dragged to countless funerals by her mother, and put to work brewing coffee, making sandwiches, and whatever else was necessary to feed the multitudes that always descended.

She knew the drill. She was not a funeral virgin, unfortunately.

The Last Chance church ladies had arrived with the energy and zeal of missionaries bent on saving heathen souls. They had come bearing casseroles, Jell-O molds, and banana pudding. Deidre was going to be disappointed. There didn't seem to be any need for professional catering — assuming there were actually caterers in Last Chance.

In the middle of the chaos in the kitchen, like some preternatural hurricane's eye, sat Miriam Randall, dressed in a blindingly bright purple-plaid pantsuit. Little Haley Rhodes sat on her lap.

Haley's hair was coming out of its ponytail holder, and her face was smeared with what appeared to be chocolate. Nevertheless, the indoctrination of the next generation was well under way. Haley was helping to drop chocolate chip cookie dough onto baking sheets.

Sarah cast her gaze around the room, searching for a telephone. She found it, bolted to one of Ruby Rhodes's sunny yellow walls.

Unfortunately, someone who resembled

Ruby's younger clone had beaten her to it, and in grand style, too. The Ruby lookalike had the landline pressed to her right ear, and a cell phone pressed to her left. She was masterfully handling two conversations at once.

She did this juggling of conversations wearing an immaculately tailored gray summer-weight worsted suit with a cream-colored silk blouse of the same luster as the pearls at her throat and ears. Her nails were perfect, her makeup flawless, and she gave the appearance of a woman who had never sweated a drop in her life — the sort of woman who could actually wear tropical-weight worsted suits in the Carolina sun-shine and remain fully and actively con-scious.

Why couldn't Sarah be like that? Formi-dable. Imposing. In control.

The woman looked up, and their gazes locked across Ruby's linoleum floor. Her green gaze traveled from Sarah's windblown hair, across the silly bunny logo on her golf shirt, down to her baggy khakis, and ended with her slip-on boat shoes, which were ap-propriate footwear for Grandfather's sail-boat, but not at a funeral.

The woman said something into the land-line and then something into her cell phone, and hung up on both conversations simultaneously, all while continuing to study Sarah as if she had been blown in by an unwanted wind.

"Are you with Tulane?" she asked without any preamble.

"Oh, Aunt Rocky, that's Miss Sarah," Haley said from her place on Miriam's lap. "You know, the one who fainted that time." Haley smiled her Bucky Beaver smile. "Hi, Miss Sarah."

"Hi, Haley." Sarah nodded toward the little girl and the ancient church lady. Then she turned back toward Aunt Rocky, who must be the little sister Tulane had mentioned. Rocky Rhodes was stifling a little half-smile. She seemed more delighted than she ought to be, considering that someone had died. "I'm Caroline," she said, holding out her hand.

"Caroline?"

"Yes. I go by that name these days."

"But she's really Aunt Rocky," Haley said as she continued to drop cookies on the baking sheet.

Sarah wondered if the real reason Tulane wanted to keep Haley out of the limelight was that Haley knew everything about everyone and had no filter on her mouth.

Sarah ignored the precocious child and

shook Rocky's hand. The woman had a firm, businesslike grip. Rocky probably had a firm, businesslike grip on everything in her life, including her career.

"I'm Sarah Murray," she said. "I'm Tulane's sponsor liaison. I was with him when we got the news. I traveled up here in Clay's van while I worked on getting Tulane out of his various weekend obligations. Now my cell's dead, and I don't have a charger. I was wondering if I could use the phone, so I can arrange for some clothes to be brought down for Tulane."

Rocky gave her a pixie smile, full of mischief, and stepped aside, clearing a path to the phone. "Phone's all yours. But there's no need to call for a car. I can take you up to Florence, if you need."

"Oh, that won't be necessary. I don't want to put you out. I'll just get someone to send a car and then I'll just ride back. Oh, and do you know who's handling the funeral arrangements? National Brands wants to help any way we can, maybe with flowers for the service."

"Do you now? That's nice," Rocky said, a speculative gleam in her green eyes.

"Yes, we do. Do you know who —"

"You know, Momma told me all about you," Rocky interrupted.

174

"She did?" Sarah had a sinking feeling in the pit of her stomach. She could just imagine what Ruby had told Rocky — a lot of nonsense about how she had worn a black suit and fainted.

"She said you were Tulane's nursemaid, and I didn't believe her. I didn't think anyone could actually keep my brother in line, but you seem to have the knack. That's impressive." The grin on Rocky's mouth grew into a wide, beauty-queen smile.

"Uh, well, it's not —"

"I'm guessing that being his nursemaid might be pretty interesting, since my brother is so immature. I can see they've sent a sensible person to keep him in line."

"Well, um, thanks, I guess."

"C'mon, I have a car. I'll give you a lift up to Florence. To be honest with you, I wouldn't mind getting out of this madhouse before Momma and I start arguing. And besides, I could use your help."

"*My* help?"

"Momma told me you were handling all of Tulane's personal appearances. I can only assume there is a lot of planning that goes into a baby-changing race. And I can clearly see that you're in the middle of handling all the little details of my brother's life right at this moment. I know what it takes to manage details, not to mention a difficult boss. So, the way I'm thinking is that you are, pretty much, the answer to my prayers."

"I am?"

"Absolutely. I've got a crisis at the moment with my boss, Senator Warren. He's having a snit fit about some stupid Englishman who has a real estate problem that needs fixing right away. The senator doesn't really care that there's been a death in the family. He can be an insensitive SOB at times. But he *does* depend on me. So all in all, you being here is like a godsend. It means I don't have to continue to try to conduct two phone calls simultaneously."

Sarah frowned. "A godsend? Really?"

"Sarah, around here we believe in the power of prayer, and I was just praying for someone to help. And the minute the prayer left my mind, you came strolling into the kitchen. I have a huge favor to ask. I've got way too much on my plate at the moment, and none of my brothers could plan their way out of a paper sack, since they were all close to Uncle Pete. And Aunt Arlene, who might be able to do that sort of thing, is a total mess, as you might imagine. As for Momma, she just lost her only brother, and she's joined at the hip with Aunt Arlene right now. So until you walked into this room, I was thinking that I was going to have to manage this funeral all by my lonesome." Rocky smiled. "But the reinforcements have arrived, haven't they?"

"Have they?"

"Well, you did just say that National Brands wants to help any way they can. I'm going to take you up on that offer."

"You are?" Sarah could hear the jaws of the trap swinging closed. Deidre was going to love this. And Tulane was going to be angrier than one of the rodeo bulls that Dad used to ride when he was much younger, before Mother roped and tied him.

"Yes, I am. Have you ever planned a funeral before?" Rocky asked.

"Uh, no. But my mother is a devout Presbyterian church lady and member of the casserole brigade."

Rocky laughed out loud and took Sarah gently by her upper arm. "Sarah, I think I like you. C'mon, let's go. You can get some clothes for yourself and Tulane and then you can help me with the arrangements."

Rocky turned toward Miriam Randall. "Miz Miriam, can you put Sarah up for the next few days? I wouldn't want to make her stay at the Peach Blossom Motor Court."

Miriam looked up at them from behind her glasses. "Of course I can put her up.

She stayed with me the last time she was here. And thank you, Sarah. I'm sure your mother would approve of your helping out." She smiled like a possessed cherub.

"Good, it's all settled, then." Rocky tugged Sarah through the kitchen door and out into the parlor, where she announced that they were taking care of everything. Then they marched out through the front door and into the Carolina heat and humidity.

Rocky didn't wilt in the heat. This didn't surprise Sarah one bit. Because Rocky was a force to be reckoned with. Just like her mother.

Haley spooned the last bit of cookie dough onto the sheet, and Miz Miriam handed it to Miz Polk, who put it in the oven.

Haley watched the Sorrowful Angel, who was sitting in her place by the broom closet. The Sorrowful Angel wasn't bawling today, but she was sad.

Everyone was sad, on account of the fact that Uncle Pete had died.

But didn't that mean Uncle Pete was up in Heaven with Jesus? Haley just couldn't quite understand what was so sad about that.

She reckoned it was just that folks would miss Uncle Pete. And she would, too. But

Uncle Pete had been really sick for a long time. He hadn't been very happy lately.

So, all in all, maybe it was better for Uncle Pete to be with Jesus now.

"Miz Miriam?" she asked.

"What, child?" Miriam gave her a little hug. The old woman's arms were kind of bony, but Haley liked the way Miz Miriam smelled. She used lavender water, and Haley decided that when she grew up she would use lavender water, too.

"Do you think I could get Miss Sarah to let me help Uncle Tulane with his idea about car seats?"

"Well . . . I think maybe you should ask your daddy first. We talked about this before, didn't we?"

Haley had already tried once to get Miz Miriam to help her on the whole car seat thing, but she'd turned out to be a whole lot like Granny and Daddy. Of course, Dr. Newsome was kind of interested. They had spent several sessions talking about car seats and how Haley felt about them, especially since a car seat had kept her safe when she and her momma had been in that car wreck.

Miz Miriam patted her knee with one age-spotted hand and then turned her eyes toward the broom closet, as if she could truly see the Sorrowful Angel. "Sugar Beet,

I don't think your angel really wants you to help Uncle Tulane with that car seat program."

"No?"

"No, child. I think she wants you to work on something much closer to home. Didn't you say she stays in your daddy's room at night?"

"Yes'm, she does. Do you think she wants me to help Daddy because Momma died, like Uncle Pete?"

Miz Miriam gave her a squeeze. "You are a wise child, Haley Rhodes."

"But how?"

"I don't know how. I truly don't. But your daddy changed after your momma died in that wreck."

"Everyone says that. Is the same thing gonna happen to Aunt Arlene? She's so sad."

"I hope not. But we'll have to be extra kind to your aunt the next few weeks. And we'll just have to keep thinking about what to do with your daddy."

Haley sat back against Miz Miriam's warmth and studied the angel for a long moment. "Miz Miriam, couldn't you find my daddy a new wife? Wouldn't that solve his problem? I'm thinking maybe that would help to get the angel back to Heaven where she belongs."

"Ooooh, child, that's a hard one. You see, near as I can tell, your momma and daddy were meant to be together. I felt that from the time they were both just small children. And, truth be told, your momma and daddy were great friends before it ever even occurred to them to fall in love."

"So when Momma went to be with Jesus, Daddy got left all alone?"

"Well, no, you and your sister are here, aren't you?"

Haley nodded, but she understood the truth. She had been listening to Dr. Newsome go on about Daddy and Momma, and she knew what the grown-ups all said.

Daddy was lonely, even though he was surrounded by people who loved him.

Even though an angel stood over him in his room every night.

That's why the angel was sorrowful.

"Miz Miriam, everyone says you have a knack for matching people up."

Miriam chuckled. "Well, that's because they're fools, Haley. Don't you believe what folks say about me. I don't make matches. I just find them. The Lord makes the matches."

"So you're saying that the Lord made a match between my momma and daddy, and now that she's with Jesus, he has to be alone until it's his time to go to Heaven?"

Miriam gave her another squeeze. "Oh, baby, I surely do hope that's not what I'm saying. But sometimes I'm afraid it is."

Haley nodded, a deep hollow place inside her chest opening up. "If that's the truth, then I guess the angel has a really big reason to be sorrowful, doesn't she?"

CHAPTER 8

Sarah and Jane, Clay's wife, sat quietly in Ruby's kitchen after having cleaned up the dishes and put away what seemed like three tons of macaroni-and-cheese casserole. Jane was knitting on a messy tangle of army-green yarn that was supposed to be a sweater for her husband. Ruby and Arlene had gone off to bed. Clay, Rocky, and Tulane had disappeared about two hours ago.

"Wherever they are, I'm sure they're crying like little kids," Jane said. She turned back to the mess in her carefully manicured hands with an expression as placid as a Madonna.

Sarah checked her watch. It was almost eleven, and she was exhausted. "Well, I guess I can walk over to Miriam's house. She gave me a key, but I'll bet the door isn't locked. Last Chance is small enough that I could find my way."

"Don't be too mad at Tulane and Rocky for abandoning you."

"I'm not mad. Just tired."

Jane dropped the knitting onto her lap and looked up, mischief sparking her brown eyes to life. "We could call the law out on them if you want."

"Why would I want to do that?"

"Because it will probably happen anyway. And maybe we can make sure Tulane doesn't get blamed this time."

"What?"

"I know it's not my place to say, seeing as I'm a new member of the family, but it seems to me that it's open season on Tulane whenever he comes back home. In this instance, I'm pretty sure Rocky is the main instigator of any trouble that's going to happen tonight. I heard her say she was getting the beer."

"Well, Tulane doesn't have to drink it, does he?"

Jane shook her head. "He's grieving. He'll drink it. And then the trouble will happen, even though he didn't go looking for it. And when the trouble happens, Stone will step right up to the plate and offer up a sermon about how Tulane needs to grow up. This is a cycle of very negative affirmations."

"Uh, that's insightful, but see, it's my job

to keep Tulane out of trouble."

Jane leaned over the tangle in her hand. "So I've heard. How's that going?"

"We haven't been sued in the last three weeks."

"Well, that's a positive sign."

Sarah pushed up from the table. "I'm going to go see if I can find Miriam's house."

"Don't do that. Stone will take you. I'll just give him a buzz."

"But —"

Before Sarah could stop Jane, she had whipped out her cell phone and reached Stone on her speed dial. "He'll be here to pick you up in a minute."

"You didn't need to do that."

"Oh, yes I did, because Stone is dealing with his grief by throwing himself into his work. He's out there patrolling the town, keeping everyone safe. And if he saw you walking alone to Miriam's, he would be furious with Tulane for making you walk home alone, and then Tulane would have his head handed to him on that score, too."

"But Tulane is not my keeper."

"Doesn't matter. Stone approves of you."

"He approves of me? Really? I've said like five words to him."

"Yeah, I think it's the whole keeping-Tulane-out-of-trouble thing. It's like the two

of you are both enforcers or something."
She gave Sarah a speculative look. "Too bad
Miriam didn't tell you to be searching for a
tall, dark guy wearing a gun."

"How did you know Miriam told me anything?"

Jane smiled. "Because you're not from
around here. Whenever someone who isn't
from Allenberg County shows up, the old
girl immediately starts with her predictions.
I only wish you were destined for Stone,
because if you ask me, the grump needs to
get laid."

Sarah's face burned.

Jane leaned back in her chair and
stretched. "But, alas, you are not destined
for Stone. The holy rollers around here have
bigger game in mind. I swear those church
ladies have been talking about you solid for
the last three weeks."

"Really?"

"Yeah. Especially after what Miriam told
you to be looking out for."

"You know what she told me?"

"Of course I do. Everyone does. They are
pretty sure you and Bill are a match made
in Heaven."

"Bill? What are you talking about?"

"C'mon, Sarah, you've been here long
enough to know that Miriam Randall is

considered some strange combination of a matchmaker and a fortune-teller. And, as near as I can tell, the woman is connected to the larger powers of the universe. I mean, it's uncanny the way she can predict the future." Jane leaned in with an avid look in her brown eyes. "So, have you met Bill yet?"

"No."

Jane smiled broadly. "Sarah, I'm sorry to tell you, but you're in serious danger of losing your heart. Probably tomorrow."

"I am?" Sarah wasn't sure how she felt about that, having never had even one satisfactory sexual encounter in her life. Losing her heart seemed like a pretty bold next step.

"The good news is that he's not your average preacher."

"Preacher?" Sarah's voice cracked, and she sank back down into one of the kitchen chairs.

Jane frowned. "I take it the idea of you and a preacher is scary?"

"You have no idea."

"How come?"

"Because I promised myself a long, long time ago that I would never, ever, ever grow up to be my mother."

Jane cocked her head. "Your father's a preacher?"

Sarah squeezed her eyes shut and then dropped her head to the table, so she could rest her forehead against the cool Formica.

Jane howled with laughter.

Sarah raised her head. "It's not funny. Please don't tell anyone. Mother is not only married to a minister, she's a librarian at a theological seminary in Boston. You have no idea what my life was like when I was in college and living in Boston. Mom trotted out a steady stream of theological students for my benefit." Sarah paused for a long moment as she rested her chin on her fists, elbows planted on the tabletop.

"You know, it's worse than that," she continued. "My grandfather was a minister, and my great-grandfather was a missionary, and, well, it goes all the way back for generations. I am *not* going to marry a minister. Period. You understand me? So please don't tell Miriam or anyone else."

Jane's face sobered. "Sarah, I promise I won't tell a soul. But the thing is, if Miriam told you that a minister is in your future, well, a minister is in your future. When he crosses your path, something wacky is going to happen to your brain, and it will all be all right. Trust me on this."

"This happened to you?"

"Yeah. Miriam told me to search for a

188

knight in shining armor — precisely the fantasy that had gotten me into very bad situations for most of my life. I wasn't really ready to hear what she had to say."

Sarah frowned. "Clay doesn't give me a real knight-in-shining-armor vibe. A bad old redneck on a motorbike, yeah, but a knight?"

"It's worse than it appears," Jane said. "Clay is a Boy Scout who is ready to rescue me at a moment's notice while simultaneously being the epitome of a sensitive, new age guy — in disguise, of course." She smiled like a woman deeply in love.

"You really adore him."

"He changed my life." Jane let go of a sappy sigh and continued, "So, I'm telling you, resistance is futile. And, for the record, you and Bill Ellis are like a match made in Heaven."

Five minutes later, Sarah found herself riding shotgun with Last Chance's chief of police in his really impressive automobile. For a small town with limited resources, the authorities had obviously spared no expense when it came to Stone Rhodes's cruiser. The thing was loaded down with computer and communication equipment that could rival any big city.

He had just made a right turn onto Palmetto Avenue when his radio burst to life with a female voice. "Hey, Stone, I got a report of trespassers down at Speed Demon."

"Shit," Stone said right into his mic.

"Yup. I'm thinking what you're thinking." The woman on the other end of the line had a low seductive voice and a broad Southern drawl.

"Thanks, Darlene. You tell Sheriff Bennett yet?"

"Nope. I reckon you got a fifteen-minute head start before things get out of hand."

"I'm on my way, darlin', thanks."

"Don't mention it, Stony. You can buy me a drink next time you're down this way." The voice practically purred.

Okay, so maybe the grumpy chief of police was getting some action on the side. Sarah figured there was a lot about the tall, dark, and handsome chief that the church ladies of Last Chance probably didn't know. Stone leaned over and flipped a switch on the dash, and his police lights started doing their thing.

He turned toward Sarah. "I reckon I'm going to need your help."

"My help?"

"Mmm. See, that was a call about a

disturbance over at the dirt track where Tulane and Pete used to run cars all summer. I figure we got us a situation where the spokesperson for Cottontail Disposable Diapers is raising hell and trespassing. We leave this situation alone, and Tulane will end up arrested by the county sheriff.

"So I'm thinking you and I have a strong mutual interest in rescuing Tulane before that happens. And, as they say, you can catch a whole lot more flies with honey than with vinegar." He gave her a little smile that revealed a whole bunch of dimples and crow's-feet. "And besides, I figure you are being paid to keep him out of trouble, and I'm just his older brother, who has been kicking his butt for years."

And with that, Stone hit the accelerator, pulled a U-turn that threw Sarah up against the door, and then took off like a speed demon himself, right down the middle of town. Sarah reached for the "oh shit" handle and didn't even blush.

She was coming to realize that all of the Rhodes men had a talent for breaking traffic laws.

Tulane took another slug of beer and swallowed it hard so it trapped the air bubbles in his esophagus. He held on to the incipient burp, and then began a slow release of it as he burped the words to the chorus of the old Tracy Byrd song "Watermelon Crawl." He got as far as "drink don't drive" before his burp gave out.

"Ha, I win," Clay said from his place atop the pit-row wall at the defunct Speed Demon Racetrack. "I got all the way to watermelon."

"Yeah, but Pete could burp the entire refrain. You guys are wimps," Rocky said in a slightly slurred voice. She sat on the hard dirt at the base of the pit wall, wearing a pair of cutoffs and a tank top, with her hair pulled back in a ponytail. She looked like the sister Tulane remembered from his childhood, not the kick-ass staffer for a U.S. senator. He didn't get to see his sister very often these days. He missed Rocky.

But not as much as he missed Pete.

He turned away from his siblings, trying not to think about Pete, which was hard here at the Speed Demon dirt track, drinking beer and burping Tracy Byrd songs.

In fact, Tulane was well aware that his sister had suggested they all meet up here for the express purpose of remembering Pete. She had even persuaded Clay to bring his bolt cutters so they could get past the padlock on the gate.

This officially meant they were trespassing.

"Hey, ya'll, is it worse for a senator's aide to get caught trespassing or for the spokesperson for Cottontail Disposable Diapers?" Tulane asked.

"Cottontail Disposable Diapers," Clay and Rocky said in unison.

Tulane turned and scowled at the two of them. "Why does it always work that way?" He gestured broadly toward Clay. "You come equipped with bolt cutters." Then he looked down at his sister. "And you dream everything up and come with a twenty-four-pack of beer. I'm just along for the ride. But I'm always the one who gets the book thrown at me."

"Usually by Uncle Pete," Rocky said. "Here's to the old guy. I'll miss the way he used to bawl you out." She raised her beer bottle and took a hearty swig. Then she wiped a little tear from her eye with the back of her beer hand.

"Well, I suppose not having Pete bawl you out is something to be grateful for, huh?" Clay said.

Rocky snorted. "Clay, you need to quit with that positive stuff. I mean, it sucks that Uncle Pete is dead, so don't go finding silver linings, okay?"

"Sure, Rocky," Clay said. "Anyway, I reckon Tulane's got a new nursemaid now. And, boy howdy, she's a lot better looking than Pete." Clay let go of a drunken laugh.

"Oooh, Tulane, does she yell at you like Pete? That would be real entertaining, because I got a feeling Sarah doesn't know any cuss words. And Pete sure did know how to cuss. In fact, I probably learned every dirty word I know from Pete," Rocky said, raising her bottle again. "I'm gonna miss him. You remember that time he nearly blew up the house when he got an idea to deep-fry a turkey for Thanksgiving? I swear I learned seven new cuss words that day."

"Yeah." Clay's voice wavered, and he snuffled a little — in an entirely manly way, of course.

Tulane turned away again. Someone really needed to do something about this situation, or they would all be bawling their eyes out. So Tulane took another swig of beer and swallowed down on the bubbles. He turned around and this time, instead of trying to sing "Watermelon Crawl," he began reciting the Lord's Prayer. He'd seen Pete burp the entire prayer from beginning to end one time. Pete was a really impressive burper.

He got as far as the word "temptation,"

194

even though Clay cracked up and ended up spewing Budweiser from both nostrils while Rocky howled with laughter.

That was more like it. No tears. He didn't want to cry. Pete wouldn't want a bunch of tears either.

"Hey, ya'll, remember the way Pete blared that watermelon song over the loudspeakers of the store every year at festival time?" he asked.

"Don't remind me. That man had a thing for that song. He even asked me if I was ready to crawl on my hands and knees and wiggle and jiggle that year I was Watermelon Queen."

Clay snorted. "I sure would have liked to see you crawling around in that dress. As it is, everyone's saw you wiggle and jiggle, girl, so I wouldn't worry none."

"Thanks. And the next time Bubba Lock-heart tries to carry me off, I hope you are the guy who talks him down. I really don't know what I would have done that time if Pete hadn't interceded. Damn, I'm gonna miss him." Rocky's voice cracked.

Clay hopped down from the wall and sat beside her, putting his big arm around her shoulder. He gave her a hug, and then she completely fell apart, leaning over on him and bawling all over his shoulder.

Damn. She was getting snot all over Clay's T-shirt, and Clay was doing his best big-brother routine.

The party was coming apart at the seams. Tulane needed to do something quick. A guy like him, who was forced to ride around in a pink car and kiss little babies at his personal appearances, did not need to cry in public. A guy like him needed to have some really stiff rules about emotional stuff like that.

He polished off his beer and headed toward Stone's old pickup, which Tulane had driven down here after taking Rocky to the Buy Low to get the beer.

This seriously weakened his argument about how he had been hanging with his siblings and was completely innocent of any premeditated trespassing. Although in his favor was the fact that Clay had driven himself and supplied the bolt cutters. So Clay bore the lion's share of the responsibility for any trespassing that might have happened.

Not that it would matter if they got caught. Clay always managed to wiggle out of any blame that might be assigned.

Tulane got in the truck and fired up the engine. Man, that old pickup sounded good. Stone knew how to take care of a motor, all right. Pete had taught him good.

Tulane pulled the truck through the gates they'd unofficially unlocked and onto the old track. Clay and Rocky had both gotten over their grief and hopped up onto the pit wall. They watched as Tulane floored that baby and headed toward turn one.

The truck handled great as he power-slid around turns one and two and headed into the straightaway. The dark dirt slid under his wheels, and even though the lights weren't on and the track had been closed up for four years, Tulane swore he could smell the funnel cakes and hear the roar of the other cars.

A million memories assailed him as he reached turn three and power-slid through it, like one of the old boys who had invented stock car racing as a by-product of bootlegging. He doubted many of today's pretty-boy drivers knew much about power-sliding a pickup through a turn on a dirt track.

He could almost hear Kenny Lewicki in the back of his head, telling him how unimportant Pete's lessons about driving and cars were. Well, damn Kenny Lewicki. And damn NASCAR. And damn National Brands. And damn Pete . . .

The tears filled his eyes and blinded him for a moment. He took the turn too fast,

and the truck spun out. His instincts —
honed over years of driving this track —
kicked in. He guided the truck to a safe stop
facing the wrong way, with the front pointed
toward the pit entrance.

Where, right at that moment, Stone's
Crown Vic police cruiser made an appearance, with lights flashing.

Dizziness assailed Tulane, and the cruiser
lights smeared in his vision. His chest felt
like a pressure cooker that had been left on
for too long. He was about to detonate. He
needed to punch something, or he might . . .

Oh, crap, he was going to lose it. He
hadn't cried since he was a little kid. He
sagged his forehead onto the steering wheel
as the first sob hit him. After that, it was all
he could do to catch his breath.

At some point in his total breakdown,
Sarah Murray, nursemaid, hopped up on
the running board, reached in through the
open window, and touched him on the
shoulder.

Something eased inside him. The girl had
a real gentle touch.

"It's all right, Tulane," she said. "Just let it
all out. You'll feel so much better."

He took her advice. He couldn't have
stopped bawling if he'd tried.

He looked up sometime later as his sorrow started to ease, and he realized that the cruiser and all of his siblings were gone. He turned toward Sarah, who stood on the running board, silhouetted against the security lights behind her. He couldn't exactly read her expression, which was okay with him, because he didn't want to see any pity in her eyes.

He had a random thought that what she'd just witnessed was going to take their professional relationship in a direction neither of them actually wanted it to go.

"Move over; I'm driving. You've definitely had too much to drink," Sarah said. She tried hard to keep her voice level. Her heart ached for Tulane. He was so sad, and he was trying so hard to hold all those feelings in.

It really wasn't fair, the way the world imposed rules on men at times like this. She had no doubt he was embarrassed that she had seen him like this.

But she promised herself that she would hold her tongue on this matter, and on all his other secrets.

Tulane scooted across the bench seat. She opened the door and climbed behind the steering wheel. The truck seemed about five sizes too big for her.

"Am I in trouble?" he asked as he sagged back against the passenger-side seat.

Sarah fumbled around until she found the mechanism for moving the seat. She hauled it forward. She could almost reach the pedals.

"No," she said as she started adjusting the mirrors. "You're not in any trouble. You can thank Stone for that."

"I can't believe he didn't give me a lecture."

She turned the ignition key, and the truck rumbled to life. "Well, I think he understands, Tulane."

"Stone? Understand? I don't think so."

"You might be surprised. He thought it might be easier for you to have me drive you back than for him to do it. Besides, there was limited room in the cruiser since your brother and sister are both drunk as skunks."

"Me, too," he said in a little-boy voice.

"I know, dear, but it's all right. Everyone understands. Just don't make it a habit, okay? Deidre wants someone squeaky clean for her car seat campaign, and breaking and entering, trespassing, and driving a truck around a dirt oval while intoxicated is probably grounds for arrest."

"You aren't going to tell her, are you?"

"No." Sarah turned the wheel and drove the vehicle toward the gate. The cruiser was waiting for her, without its bubblegum lights going. She flashed her headlights and pulled out onto a two-lane road, following Stone back to Last Chance.

She glanced over at Tulane. His eyes were closed. Her heart lurched in her chest. She had a huge crush on this guy, and seeing him cry like that only made it worse. A girl could get a notion that a man like him needed a shoulder to weep on at a time like this.

But, of course, her shoulder was off-limits. And the very fact that Stone had hauled her out here to rescue Tulane underscored her position. It was her job to take care of him. But it was a job. Nothing else.

They drove in silence for a long time, and she thought he'd passed out. But he surprised her when he said, "Thanks for helping me out today; I really appreciate it."

"All in a day's work." Her voice sounded almost professional. "When you get home, you should drink some water and take a few aspirin, and try to get some sleep. Don't worry about anything. I've got it all covered," she said.

Darn, she sounded like a mother hen. That was good, wasn't it? She was supposed to be a mother hen. Which, of course, explained why her heart was pounding, and she was fighting the urge to reach out across the bench seat and take his hand in hers.

"Tomorrow's going to be hell," he murmured.

"You want to talk about it?"

"No."

"You loved Pete a great deal, didn't you?"

He didn't say a word, but the silence in the cab became a heavy thing. Maybe Tulane wasn't entirely cried out.

They sat in silence as the lights of Last Chance came into view. When he spoke again, his voice sounded gritty. "He never saw me win."

"Really? I thought —"

"No, I mean as a NASCAR Sprint Cup driver. Pete never saw me win a race. All those years he supported me. He taught me every damn thing I know, and when I finally made it to the top . . ." His voice strangled. "Shit," he said.

"You know, I don't think less of you because you're sad, Tulane. It's not a crime to cry at a time like this."

"Maybe for some guys. But I have rules about stuff like that."

"Well, you told me once you never saw a rule you didn't want to break."

"Yeah, well, not this one."

Sarah made a right turn off Palmetto Avenue onto a street whose name she didn't know. He started talking again. "It's so unfair," he said. "All that hard work to get to the top and what happens? Ya'll paint my car pink and make me help folks change diapers. It's stupid. I feel like I let him down somehow."

He sat up and opened his eyes. "Where are we?"

"No clue, somewhere in Last Chance. I've been following Stone."

He looked around. "Let me out at the curb."

"But —"

"Just do it."

Sarah pulled the truck over and, almost immediately, the cruiser ahead of her stopped. Tulane opened the door and stepped out onto the sidewalk. "You'll find Miriam's place just down this road and to the left. I'm walking home."

He slammed the door, turned on his heel, and walked away.

She halfway expected Stone to get out of his car and insist on Tulane being driven home, but Stone was a wiser man than that.

When Tulane was five steps away, Stone flashed his lights and pulled out from the curb. Sarah pulled out behind him. She had no doubt that Stone would guide her safely to Miriam's.

She gave a quick glance in the rearview mirror. She could just see Tulane walking along the sidewalk, heading in the opposite direction. She hoped he didn't go off to Dot's Spot and drink more. But he was a grown man, and he needed to deal with this grief on his own terms.

Still, it troubled her to know that she was responsible for a large measure of his grief. When she wrote the marketing plan for the pink car, she never once thought about what it might do to the man who had to sit in it every Sunday. She never thought that it might be a distraction that would keep him from winning races or making his family proud of him.

Suddenly Sarah could almost hear one of Mother's tirades about how she was wasting her talents on things that didn't matter. Shame washed through her.

She needed to find a way to make things better for Tulane.

But how was she supposed to do that?

She had been sent to South Carolina to spy on him. Deidre wanted her to find a reason to get him fired. And the only way to convince Deidre that Tulane might be a good spokesperson for car seat safety was to break her promise to Tulane and tell Deidre about Haley. Sarah was stuck in a moral dilemma.

CHAPTER 9

Hettie Marshall checked her reflection in the vanity mirror of her Audi. Thanks to Ruby, every hair had been tamed. Her Armani silk suit evoked class without being ostentatious. Her mineral makeup hid the red around her nose and the puffy bags under her eyes. She didn't think anyone would know she had cried herself to sleep last night.

She looked like one of the porcelain dolls she collected. And hadn't her life been like those dolls — admired and protected and lived inside a glass case?

Until Mr. Dixon had delivered his report about all the interesting things Jimmy had been up to. Hettie had expected to discover that her husband was cheating on her. But Jimmy's transgressions weren't quite so simple.

Oh, no; it turned out that Hettie's husband was a crook.

The word sent a frisson of revulsion through her. She had tried so hard to live her life between the lines. She had done everything Mama had asked of her, becoming the epitome of a Southern lady, dedicating her life to her church, marrying well.

And now this.

She was at her wit's end. Divorce was not an option. Her reputation would be lost for all time. And even though her parents had passed on, both of them would disapprove.

What was a Queen Bee supposed to do in a situation like this?

In the absence of divine guidance, the answer was clear — a Queen Bee pretended nothing was wrong and put off all the unpleasantness until tomorrow.

Hettie picked up the casserole from the passenger seat and opened the car door into the heat and humidity. One of Last Chance's citizens had passed away, and Hettie was a member of the Ladies Auxiliary. The rules for proper comportment were clear and comforting.

She entered Ruby's nice little house, paid her respects to Arlene, and then headed toward the dining room, casserole in hand.

She heard Reverend Ellis's voice before she got there. The sound of it, deep and sincere, eased the tension in her chest. It was always a marvel the way his voice resonated from the pulpit on Sunday mornings. Hettie never objected to Bill's long-winded sermons. She could listen to him for hours. He was almost as good as a cigarette for calming her nerves.

She entered the dining room, prepared to give him a big smile and a heartfelt hello. But her disquiet redoubled the instant that she saw Bill engaged in a conversation with an attractive young stranger with auburn hair.

Bill and the stranger looked perfectly matched.

Hettie wasn't sure how long she stood there transfixed. Long enough, in any case, to be caught by Miriam Randall, who came in from the kitchen, bearing a tray of cookies.

"Oh, hey, Hettie, you can put your macaroni and cheese right next to Millie's squash casserole." Miriam pointed at the spot on the dining room table.

Hettie put the casserole dish down and leaned in to whisper, "Is that the woman from Boston?" Hettie nodded toward Bill and the stranger.

Miriam shoehorned the cookie tray between the banana pudding and the Jell-O mold. She looked up with a smile. "She is.

Aren't they handsome together?"

Hettie said nothing. They *were* handsome together, and Hettie didn't want to acknowledge it. Because the redhead was a whole lot younger than Hettie. Or Bill, for that matter.

Mischief danced in Miriam's dark eyes. "But then again, Sarah is as cute as a button, and this house seems to be overrun with handsome men. I declare, Ruby has certainly raised herself up some fine-looking boys." She turned her gaze toward Tulane, who was lounging by the sideboard, scowling at the minister in a strange fashion.

Hettie squared her shoulders. She needed to get a grip on herself. "So," she said, trying to fix a smile on her face, "it looks like another one of your predictions is going to come true."

Miriam chuckled. "Oh, come now, Hettie, you don't believe I can actually predict these things, do you? And besides, what did I predict? I didn't tell Sarah that she and Bill were a match made in Heaven."

"You didn't?"

"Of course not. Just because Millie, Thelma, and Lillian decided Sarah was perfect for Bill doesn't mean I predicted this."

Hettie turned and stared. "What?"

"I told her to look for a man with good values and a strong faith. You would think the world had turned on its axis the way Lillian and the rest of the gals have interpreted that bit of advice."

"But wait, that's what you told me."

"Precisely. It's my all-purpose advice on the topic of matrimony."

"Your all-purpose . . . what?"

"You don't really think the Lord has time to spend whispering in my ear all the time, do you? So, in a pinch, when He's been silent, I give the advice my momma gave me. It's good advice. Marrying a man who has family values and a strong faith saves a load of unhappiness in the end. Don't you think? It certainly worked for you, didn't it?"

Reverend Ellis, the pastor of Christ Church, smiled benignly at Sarah, revealing a pair of perfectly matched dimples. His dark hair was just a little unruly, and a lock curled down across his brow in Superman fashion. He was about the same age as Tulane.

But far more mature.

And intimidating. Although Sarah figured that was mostly because of the Roman collar that marked him as an Episcopalian priest. That and the fact that she found

210

him . . . well . . . extremely attractive. And even sexy, which was unsettling because in her mind, ministers were not supposed to be sexy.

Finding Bill Ellis attractive was almost like ceding territory in the war she'd been waging with Mother the last few years. Bill Ellis was way more attractive than any seminary student Mother had ever brought home for dinner.

But she was not interested. She was speaking with the minister only because of the long list of funeral-related tasks she needed to accomplish for Ruby and Rocky. That list was considerably longer this morning, because Rocky was hung over and more or less useless.

First thing on Sarah's expanded list was making the arrangements for the flowers in the church during the funeral services. This was not nearly as straightforward as it might seem, she was discovering.

"So," Bill said with his winning smile, "it's not that I have any objection to having lilies in the sanctuary." He leaned a little closer. He smelled really good for a man of the cloth. "You see," he continued, "Lillian Bray, who chairs the Garden Club and the Ladies' Auxiliary, can be formidable when it comes to her gladioli — especially this time of year."

Bill rolled his eyes briefly toward a large silver-haired woman in a powder-blue tent dress who stood by the sideboard, shoveling a piece of pecan pie into her face. Lillian chewed and nodded back. And so did the thin blonde standing beside her.

Holy moly. Lillian's companion was dressed to the nines in a designer suit and a Hermes handbag, which Sarah was sure she hadn't bought in Last Chance, South Carolina. The minister did a slight double take before also giving the woman a little nod. He stared for just a moment too long.

When he turned back, his face was a little ruddy.

Well, so much for William Ellis being the man of God Miriam Randall had predicted for Sarah. The guy was obviously carrying a torch for the woman in Armani silk. Which begged the question — who in Last Chance actually dressed in Armani and Hermes?

Sarah cleared her throat and concentrated on the task at hand. "Reverend Ellis," Sarah said in her best Boston polite voice, "National Brands wants to pay for the flowers in the sanctuary. The family has requested lilies. And since Pete Whitaker was the sponsor of Tulane's Super Late Model car for many, many years, donating the flowers is our way of showing respect for the man who helped Tulane develop into the talented driver he is today."

The minister gave her a professional smile. "Yes, but, you see, Lillian's gladioli are prize-winning."

"They are?"

"Oh, yes. And any flowers you put in the sanctuary on Friday will still be there for Sunday services, and you have no idea what a pain in the neck Lillian can be about flower choices when her gladioli are in bloom."

"So I've —"

"Maybe I can help," the blonde in Armani interrupted. "Hello, I'm Hettie Marshall." She offered one slim hand. "Jimmy Marshall, the owner of Country Pride Chicken, is my husband."

So, Reverend Bill had a thing for a married woman.

That was interesting.

Friday at noon, Tulane sank down into his seat in Eugene Hanks's office for the reading of Pete's will.

Tulane's head hurt, and his stomach felt uneasy, and his eyes burned. Getting shit-faced and crying himself to sleep had not been a real good idea. Letting his feelings out sucked.

Rocky sank into a seat next to his. She also looked like crap. It occurred to him that she had never been much of a drinker, and the girl had probably consumed four beers last night. She had actually slept in this morning, which was most un-Rocky-like.

"You okay?" he asked.

She shrugged. "It could be worse."

"How?"

She gave him a tired smile. "I could be trying to plan this funeral instead of letting Sarah do it. She's a wonder. Really. And did you see how Hettie Marshall took her under her wing? I'm telling you, with Sarah joined at the hip to the Queen Bee, Momma and Aunt Arlene can relax, and I don't have to have a single conversation with Bill Ellis. This is a minor miracle."

Tulane made a grumpy sound. He didn't exactly think the whole Sarah and Bill thing was a miracle. Predictable, maybe. Still, for some idiotic reason he couldn't quite articulate, seeing Bill and Sarah bonding annoyed the crap out of him.

"I saw all three of them an hour ago, heading to the church in Hettie's sports car," Rocky said.

"Don't rub it in."

Rocky gave him a little smile. "Tulane, do you have a thing for Sarah?"

"No." He said the word too quickly.

"Then you should be happy. I really think Sarah may be the one they've been searching for. I mean, she's so nice, and her family came over on the *Mayflower* and everything."

Tulane rolled his neck, fighting the tension that hadn't been released last night. He blew out a deep breath, battling all the demons that seemed to be fighting him these days. "Yeah, now if we can just keep her from blabbing all the family secrets to the people in New York. You know, Rock, I understand how Sarah has been a help, but all in all, I wish she wasn't around."

Rocky leaned over and took his hand in hers. It felt nice to have his sister's undivided attention. In a lot of ways, Rocky had always been his best friend coming up. "That was a lie. You're as glad as I am that she's here. So what if she saw you cry like a baby last night? Her being here is a good thing."

"Right, you tell me that tomorrow after ya'll get to the church and find out they painted Uncle Pete's coffin pink."

Rocky patted his hand. "Tulane, c'mon, she's nice."

"Exactly my point."

Rocky tilted her head at him and gave him her own version of the Look. It was really annoying that even his little sister could stare at him that way.

"You like her, don't you? A lot. Come to think about it, she's exactly your type. Nice as the day is long, solidly built with lots of S-curves, and all of that with brains, too."

His face got hot.

"You better watch out, or I might come to the conclusion that you're jealous of the preacher." She smiled like a demon.

He leaned in. "Rocky, I swear, if you say one word to —"

"Look, I'll make a deal with you, Tulane. You quit calling me 'Rocky,' and I won't say one word to Momma about anything." As usual, Rocky had her way with him. She always did.

"Okay, Caroline," he said.

She turned and sat straight in her seat just as Eugene Hanks, Pete's attorney, took his place behind his big mahogany desk and cleared his throat.

Around him, Tulane's brothers and sister, Momma and Daddy, Aunt Arlene, and Alex, Arlene's son by a previous marriage, settled into their chairs. The room suddenly felt unbearably cold.

"Well," Eugene said, "Pete's will is pretty simple. Ya'll can read it for yourself. I've made copies for you. But here's the gist of it. He's giving three-quarters of the hardware store to Arlene, and the other one-quarter goes to you, Clay."

Eugene looked up at Tulane's older brother with a little smile. Across the room, Cousin Alex made a choking sound.

Eugene continued. "Pete told me the last time we talked, about a week ago, that he hoped you and Jane would stay in Last Chance. He said he didn't see why you couldn't write songs here. And he told me that Arlene felt that Jane had a real talent for hair and makeup and was a godsend to Ruby down at the Cut 'n Curl. So, just in case the songwriting business goes south, he wanted you to have a piece of the store."

Clay nodded his head, his eyes filling with tears. Beside him, Jane reached out and stroked his back. Tulane had to admit that it was real nice to see Clay with a sensible, bighearted woman, finally. Clay was such a softhearted man. When they were kids, Tulane used to sometimes call him a crybaby because he was never really able to hide his emotions. Right now, Tulane wished he had the ability to let the grief go the way his older brother could.

"Well now, let's see," Eugene continued. "He's left the house to Arlene and all the savings to you as well. He left you moderately well off, Arlene."

"He was a good man," Arlene said, dabbing at her eyes. Her mascara was a mess.

"There is only one final thing." Eugene picked up a sealed envelope. "He left this letter for you, Tulane. I have no idea what's in it, but he asked me to give it to you on the day his will was read to the family."

Tulane felt suddenly numb from head to toe. He took the sealed envelope and sat down.

"So what does it say, son?" Ruby asked.

Tulane didn't really want to read the letter in public, but his family had leaned in. He was trapped. No doubt, Pete had intended for this to happen. Otherwise, he would have asked Eugene to give Tulane the letter in private.

Tulane tore the envelope open and pulled out a single piece of white computer paper. On it, in Pete's shaky handwriting, was a single paragraph.

Tulane,
I have loved you like the son I never had. I am so happy that God allowed me to live long enough to see you finally

achieve the success that you worked so hard at for so long. It was my pleasure to help you along that road, son. I wouldn't have traded a day of watching you grow up to be a man. Now, I have only one favor to ask. Don't abandon the man who gave you life. Your daddy needs your help right now, and you are the only member of his family in a position to help him. I want you to remember me by giving your daddy the money he needs to rebuild Golfing for God, just as I supported you all those years when you needed help to pursue racing as a career.

I love you,
Uncle Pete

Tulane's voice faltered, and he had to take a couple of deep breaths before he made a total sissy of himself. Around him, the room had gotten so quiet that you could hear the traffic outside on Palmetto Avenue.

He sat there, his hands shaking, his eyes watering up, and the lines of writing blurring. *What the hell.*

"Damn it." The curse came from Stone, who stood up in the back of the room. "I swear, Tulane, if you do what Uncle Pete asks, I will never speak to you again." And with that, his oldest brother — the strong, silent ex-marine who avoided losing his cool at all costs — got up and stomped from the room like the world had just come to a freaking end.

"Well, for what it's worth," Elbert said as he also got to his feet, "I don't want your charity. So you can just take your money and shove it sideways."

And Elbert, dressed today in a pair of black jeans and a black T-shirt with the words "You Think It's Hot Here?" printed on its front, turned and followed Stone out the door. Momma said a cuss word that Tulane was pretty certain she had never, ever uttered before in her entire life and that the FCC would have condemned if said over the airwaves. Momma ran after Daddy. Then, Aunt Arlene burst into tears and followed after them both, while Cousin Alex slunk from the room.

Clay stood up and slapped Tulane on the back. "Well, if you decide to help Daddy out, I won't blame you. But I sure do wish you wouldn't. It's time to put a stake in the heart of Golfing for God."

"What on earth are you talking about?" Jane said as she stood and came to Clay's side. She gave Tulane a sober look. "You do exactly what Pete told you to do. That's a

220

dying wish, and you really don't want to mess around with the universe when it comes to stuff like that. It would be really bad karma not to do what Pete asked you to do."

Jane was not exactly a Christian, which was something the family was coming to terms with. But since Jane was one of those sweet, optimistic people everyone naturally loved, she got a big pass on her particularly weird brand of spirituality.

"Besides," she continued, "Golfing for God is a special place that should be preserved. Something miraculous happened at that place the day Woody West tried to kill me. And I still feel responsible for what happened out there."

"Little gal," Clay said, "if you and me are going to settle in this town, it just might be best if we let the place go to the kudzu. I mean, you have no idea the crap our kids will take if we let that place go back into business."

"Clay, shame on you. I'm not going to listen to this nonsense. You're the Christian. Can't you see how Golfing for God is a wonderful place to teach children about the Bible?"

"Yeah, but —"

"Well, I've said all I'm going to say on the

subject." And with that, Jane turned and strode out of the office.

"Aw, c'mon, darlin' . . ." Clay called after her as he followed, his black Stetson in his hand.

"Well, that went well, didn't it?" Rocky said as she stood up. "Boy, Tulane, I sure wouldn't want to be in your shoes." She gave him a little peck on the cheek. "Gotta run; I have to call the senator. He's up in arms over some English lord who wants to buy land in South Carolina to put up a factory."

She turned and left him standing there all alone with Pete's letter in his hand. As usual, Rocky had not taken sides. That was Rocky's particular talent. She would straddle every argument and when the going got tough, she would disappear. Rocky was real good at running. Hell, she'd run so far that she'd lost her good-ol'-girl wardrobe and even changed her name.

He backhanded the tear that managed to escape his suddenly streaming eyes. He was utterly alone with this dilemma, and no matter what he did, someone would be unhappy with him.

It occurred to him right then that the least of his problems was having to race on Sunday wearing a pink bunny suit.

■ ■ ■ ■

Sarah stared down at what passed for a green salad at the Kountry Kitchen Café — iceberg lettuce, a few cherry tomatoes, and buttermilk ranch dressing.

"You should have ordered the pulled pork sandwich," Hettie said.

Sarah looked up from the less than appetizing fare in time to see Hettie cut her barbecue sandwich with a knife and fork. "I'm trying to lose some weight," Sarah said.

"Aren't we all? To tell you the truth, I don't usually indulge. But I'm in the mood today." Hettie conveyed a dainty bite to her mouth, chewed it politely, and then closed her eyes and let forth a wicked groan of pleasure.

Sarah suddenly wished she had ordered the pulled pork, too.

"I declare," Hettie said on a sigh. "Fred Carter sure does know how to make barbecue. I should come here more often."

"Well, we'd sure like to see you more often, Miz Hettie." This pronouncement came from the waitress, a curvy woman in her middle thirties with dark hair. She was waiting on a full house of men in work shirts and John Deere hats, all of whom seemed to be eating barbecue.

The waitress refilled Hettie's coffee cup, then turned toward Sarah. "I've been dying to ask you. Are ya'll that woman who works with Tulane that everyone's been talking about?"

Sarah forced a smile to her face. "Yes, I'm Sarah."

"Hey, I'm Ricki." Ricki leaned in with a little wink. "For what it's worth, honey, I think it's a hoot that Tulane's sponsors sent a woman to keep that boy in line. How you making out?"

"Fine," Sarah said in her best this-is-none-of-your-business Boston voice. Luckily, a big dude at the corner table called Ricki by name and demanded a coffee refill, so the waitress scurried away.

"Don't mind her. She's just jealous. She's got a thing for the Rhodes boys. Almost had Clay, too, but she messed it up. She's after Dash Randall now, but I don't think Dash is interested."

"Is this all you talk about here in Last Chance? I mean, Jane told me last night that I've been the subject of gossip for weeks, and I only spent one night in Last Chance before Pete's death. Isn't there anything else happening in this town?"

Hettie sat up a little straighter in her chair

and managed not to look very happy. "No, as a matter of fact, there is nothing very interesting happening in this town. So it's only natural folks are going to gossip about you, especially since Millie and Thelma have led everyone to believe that Miriam has handpicked you for Bill."

"I'm not interested in Bill," Sarah said.

"You aren't?" Hettie put her fork across her plate, and Sarah swore that she sounded relieved.

"Nope, I am most definitely not interested in Bill. I'm working on being a success in business, not someone's wife."

"Probably a good plan," Hettie said. "So, where to next?"

"You really don't have to chauffeur me around, you know. I could probably borrow Rocky's car."

"Hmm, that's true, but then I'd have to go home, and I don't want to go home. So, where to next? We've covered the funeral home, the dry cleaners, and the florist."

"Caterers?"

Hettie snorted politely. "This is a Southern funeral. Caterers are redundant."

"Okay, then, how about taking me to Golfing for God?"

Hettie startled. "Why would you want to go there?"

"To see it up close."

"It's not in business anymore, thank goodness."

"Thank goodness? Why do you feel that way?"

"Well, it's just that it's . . . well . . ." Hettie exhaled deeply, probably so she wouldn't blurt out something unpleasant. "You wouldn't understand," she finally said. "You're not from around here."

"Okay, try me. Explain to me why Tulane is so ashamed of that place."

"Golfing for God is a mini-golf place with holes depicting Bible stories. It's pitiful. It's an eyesore. It's a stereotype of what we in the South would rather not be about."

Sarah dug in her purse and pulled out a ten-dollar bill. She slapped it on the counter. "You know, everyone around here says that, but I'm just not getting it. It's a funny idea, I'll admit that, but it's also an idea that has a lot of marketing potential. Family values are hot these days, you know."

"Marketing potential? Are you crazy? What do you want to do — bring Northerners down here to laugh at us?"

Sarah shook her head. "No. I'd like to see people of all kinds coming to your town to play the course. It's quirky, I admit, but it's fun. And it could put this town on the map."

"Fun?"

"Have you ever played the course?"

A little blush colored Hettie's alabaster cheeks. "Well, of course, when I was little."

"And . . . ?"

Hettie gave a little shrug. "It was fun. When I was six. I'm older than that now. You don't need to see the golf course. Really, we would just as soon that place didn't exist."

"But I *do* need to see it. Sooner or later people are going to find out what Tulane's father does for a living. And I need to be prepared. And the best way to be prepared is to go and see the place up close and personal."

Hettie guided her little silver car into the gravel parking lot of Golfing for God. She killed the engine and gazed through the windshield. "So, here it is, in all its glory."

"Thanks for bringing me," Sarah said.

"Oh, I'm just waiting for the moment when you realize how horrific this place is."

Sarah stepped out of the car and onto the gravel in her dress shoes. She tottered over the uneven ground toward the wreckage of what had once been a large statue of Jesus.

"You know," Hettie said as she followed across the gravel in her equally impractical shoes, "have you thought that maybe Tulane is right — that this part of his life is best kept secret?"

"He doesn't have a choice. Tulane is a celebrity now. He won't be able to keep his secrets for long. Sooner or later, someone is going to figure out that his father owns this place."

"Poor Tulane, he'll be so embarrassed."

"I'm sure he will be. But maybe I can help him minimize the damage."

"How?"

"I don't know. That's why I'm here. I've got to figure out a way to make sure that when National Brands consumers learn about this, it won't affect diaper sales."

"My goodness, that's pretty cynical, isn't it?"

"I guess it is. But it's my job."

Sarah turned and inspected the path that led to the golf course. The walkway resembled a scene from a war zone. The older-growth pines lining the walk were charred. Kudzu had invaded the space, crawling over the blackened tree trunks and crowding the walkway. The aroma of burned wood hung on the air.

"Wow, what happened out here?" Sarah asked.

"They say lightning struck the propane

tank and caused the explosion that damaged the water circulation system," Hettie said as they started walking down the path. "I've heard Jimmy talking about it. My husband, and just about everyone else in town, thinks it's a blessing that this old place has finally seen its last customer."

Hettie turned and gazed down the path, her bright blue eyes softening.

"I used to love coming here with Daddy when I was a girl," Hettie said softly. And then her eyes filled with tears that she dashed away with the back of her hand.

"Dammit. I'm an emotional wreck today. Funerals always do that to me. C'mon, I'll show you the ark."

It wasn't really an ark, just a barn shaped like a big boat with a concession stand and an office.

"Elbert used to keep the petting zoo in there," Hettie explained. "Since the lightning storm, the animals have been boarded out at Dash Randall's ranch. Plenty of pasture out there for Mamie."

"Mamie?"

"The longhorn."

Sarah laughed.

"What's so funny?"

"The fact that you know the cow's name. Does everyone know her name?"

"Uh, I don't know. I see Mamie several times a week. I board a horse over at Dash's."

"Ah." There was something very likable about Hettie. Somewhere behind that brittle façade was a real person. Sarah stepped past the shuttered sales counter and headed toward the first hole.

Eve, rendered in fiberglass and wearing fig leaves, stood beside the apple tree, reaching for a bright red apple. The fruit was being offered by a serpent painted to resemble a copperhead. It was a par-four hole that required a golfer to putt the ball through the roots of the Tree of Knowledge in order to reach the hole on the other side. Beside the tee box was a little plaque bearing the words:

The serpent was more cunning than any beast of the field.

Sarah read the scripture. "That's from Genesis 3. Although, technically, Eve didn't put on her fig leaves until *after* she ate the fruit. But I suppose having a naked Eve on a putt-putt place in the middle of the Bible Belt would be too shocking, huh?"

"I'll bet Ruby just loves you to bits."

"Huh?"

"You're exactly the kind of woman I'd want looking after my son. A good woman

230

who knows her scripture is worth a lot to a mother."

"Do you have children?"

Hettie shook her head and turned away. Sarah silently followed Hettie's gaze as she surveyed the golf course. Fiberglass statues spread before her in every direction. They ranged from David and Goliath to the resurrection of Christ. It was amazing. At once both campy and surprisingly artistic. But decay had crept in. The place needed attention and repair.

Sarah closed her eyes and breathed in the scent of the pines and something else. Something old and primal. There was magic here. She could feel it.

And then it struck her, like the proverbial thunderbolt.

Golfing for God *was* magic. The kind of magic people grew up and forgot about. Like Racer Rabbit or that simple faith Haley Rhodes talked about when she said her momma was up in Heaven with Jesus.

"This is where Elbert sees his angels," she said.

"Please, don't tell me you —"

"No, I don't really see them. But I feel them here. Like a possibility. And it just occurred to me that we're all in trouble if we lose our simple faith in angels. I know you don't want to hear this, but Golfing for God matters."

"You're as crazy as Elbert."

"Maybe I am. But admit it, Hettie, when you thought about coming here as a kid a minute ago, it brought tears to your eyes. Where does it say that we have to grow up and lose the fun of a place like this?"

"But it's a joke, and not a very funny one."

"See, you've grown older and you've lost the ability to believe in miracles. You know, if you want my advice, someone in this town ought to form a committee to resurrect this place. I mean it."

Hettie looked aghast. "A committee to resurrect it?"

"Exactly. A committee of dedicated church ladies who would do a whole lot better for the town if they would quit trying to meddle in people's private lives and get to work on something worthy, like helping people remember what it feels like to have simple faith. The world could use a whole lot more of that, if you ask me."

"But I thought you wanted to help Tulane. Tulane would hate it if anyone formed a committee to save this place."

"I'm sure he would. But he needs to grow up enough to embrace the innocence. Maybe all of us do."

"What?"

"You heard me. A minute ago you said I was cynical, and you know what — you're right. There is nothing cynical about this place. Hettie, open your eyes, and see it like a six-year-old."

CHAPTER 10

Emotions were running high when Sarah returned to Ruby's house later that day. The reading of Pete's will hadn't gone well, evidently.

Arlene was weeping openly. Elbert was missing in action, reportedly off somewhere riding his Harley. Jane and Clay were out in the backyard, arguing. Cousin Alex was sulking in one of the rocking chairs out front. Rocky was AWOL but had checked in by cell phone to make sure that the funeral arrangements were on track. Stone was missing, too, but that was nothing new.

The brigade of church ladies had vanished, no doubt heading home to make supper for their own families. They had mostly cleaned up after themselves, leaving only a small stack of dirty dishes that had not fit in the dishwasher.

Ruby, like some stereotypical steel magnolia, seemed unfazed by it all. She sat in her parlor, playing Chinese checkers with her granddaughters.

Sarah had nothing better to do, so she started washing the leftover dishes, her mind wandering back to the problems she would face on Monday. Deidre wanted a full report, and there was nothing Sarah could say that would please both Deidre and Tulane. She was stuck.

"Hey."

The sound of Tulane's voice jolted Sarah out of her thoughts. His body heat registered against her backside as he took the sponge from her hands. He stood just behind her, not touching, but making her whole body react to him in the most adolescent manner.

"You've been standing there staring out the window for the last five minutes without washing a single dish. Are you eavesdropping on Jane and Clay? I think they're having their first argument as a married couple. Momma thinks it's cute. I think it's dumb."

"They're arguing about Golfing for God."

"Yeah. Stupid thing to argue about. So, what have you been up to, besides flirting with the preacher, managing Pete's funeral, and pretending to wash dishes?"

She snagged a dish towel from the rack above the sink and turned to face Tulane as she dried her hands. He stood just inches from her, and she had to cock her head back to see into his eyes. Her body began to hum the way it always did when Tulane got too close.

"To tell you the truth, I went out to see Golfing for God this afternoon with Hettie Marshall. And now that I've seen it, I'm at a loss as to why you —"

"You went out to Golfing for God? What the heck for?"

"I had to see the place."

"No, you didn't."

"Yes, I did. I have to know what I'm dealing with."

"What *you're* dealing with? How about what *I'm* dealing with." His voice rose in pitch, and a muscle ticked in his jaw. "Did you hear what happened at the lawyer's this afternoon?"

"No."

"Pete asked *me* to help Daddy rebuild Golfing for God. Can you believe it?"

"Good for him." Sarah draped the dish towel on its rack and then leaned back into the kitchen counter, crossing her arms.

"Good for him? What's that supposed to mean?"

Sarah shrugged. "Look, I never met Pete, but if he thought rebuilding Golfing for God

236

was a good idea, then I guess I agree with him."

"Why? You saw that place. It's an eyesore and a joke. Why should anyone rebuild it?"

"Well, I guess you and I see different things out there. I saw a place where kids could learn their Bible stories. I saw a place where angels just might reside."

"Huh?" Tulane's lower jaw dropped open, and he stared down at her like she was ready to be hauled away by men wearing white coats.

"Don't look at me like that, Tulane. I'm not crazy. And I'm pretty sure your father isn't crazy either. And to be honest, I don't see that Haley's angel is something to worry about. When I was her age, I believed in angels. Didn't you? I believed in a lot of things, like Santa Claus and flying reindeer. Give her a break, for goodness' sake. She's seven."

"Honey, you believing in angels and Haley seeing one are not the same things. You have no idea what my life or Haley's life has been like growing up here. So don't stand there and tell me how Golfing for God should be saved. I'm telling you, the best thing that ever happened was that lightning bolt hitting the place. Maybe if we buried Golfing for God, my family could move away from this town, and then things would be different."

"Tulane, moving away is not going to change the past. Things won't be different. Trust me on this. I have experience. Just moving away doesn't change who you are."

"You, experienced? That's a laugh. You're about as gullible as a six-year-old. That probably explains why you don't understand the whole Golfing for God problem."

"I wish you would quit doing that."

"What?"

"Calling me nice and inexperienced. I'm not as nice as you think I am. Besides, nice people usually finish last."

"Well," he said with a grin, "if you're really serious about wanting to be naughty, I can help. I mean, if you want, I could take you out this evening, and we could raise a little hell."

She blushed. "What sort of hell?" she whispered.

"Oh, I don't know. The usual kind. Last Chance, South Carolina, is a great place to raise hell. There are church ladies on every corner just waiting for a boy to slip up."

He was daring her, wasn't he? Trying to make a point about Golfing for God by suggesting that she was too childish to really understand the truth.

What would happen if she took the dare?

A whole range of emotions seized her. Excitement. Dread. Fear. Anticipation. Every cell in her body sprang to life.

"Okay," she said, raising her chin and squaring her shoulders. "I'm in."

The stunned look on Tulane's face told her she had just surprised the heck out of him.

Good.

The dashboard lit up Tulane's face in green. He focused on the road and floored the accelerator. Stone Rhodes's Ford pickup might be beat-up on the outside, but there wasn't anything wrong with the engine. It roared to life and took off, pressing Sarah back against the headrest.

A stretch of two-lane road spooled ahead of them, ruler straight but undulating over a series of three small hills like a piece of Christmas ribbon candy.

As the truck accelerated, Sarah fought her instincts and kept her eyes fixed open, taking in every terrifying moment. This was rule-breaking at its finest, because the green needle on the dash said they were going ninety by the time they hit the rise of the first hill.

The truck went airborne and gave her a

spine-tingling jolt as it hit the pavement on the downside, only to accelerate again up the next hill and down, and then the next.

Tulane hit the brakes, and the tires squealed, and she could smell burning rubber. The truck wobbled sideways. She was pretty sure it would flip over and she would die right there. But it didn't happen.

She lived to tell the tale. The truck slowed as the road curved left. Tulane glanced over at her. He said nothing. He didn't need to say anything.

He slowed the truck to a near creep and doused the headlights. A second later, he turned left onto a dark, unpaved road that rolled past a couple of brick gates bearing a sign that read Edisto Country Club.

"The country club?" she asked.

"Yes'm. No finer place for breaking the rules and raising hell than the country club."

"Are we going to play golf?"

"This ain't that kind of country club."

"Then what kind is it?"

"The kind that doesn't allow any of Elbert Rhodes's kids as members. And since you already know about Golfing for God and the whole angel scenario, I reckon you have a handle on why."

"I see. So this is about social justice, then?"

He laughed out loud. "Lord a' mercy, you are funny. No, ma'am, this is about trespassing."

"Uh, after last night I would have thought that you would be —"

"Honey, we are out breaking the rules and raising hell. Do you want me to stop?"

She shook her head no.

The road widened, and Tulane pulled the truck into a gravel parking area. Moonlight gleamed on the tin roofs of a row of bungalows to the left and sparkled in a body of water to the right.

Tulane killed the engine. "That," he said, pointing to the water, "is the Edisto River. It's the longest blackwater river in America. And this country club is an old-fashioned Southern swimming hole — a place where the high and mighty of Allenberg County stay cool on hot summer days."

"Oh." The bottom of her stomach dropped to her knees. If they were here this late in the evening, it could mean only one thing: Tulane intended to go swimming. And neither of them had swimsuits, unless, of course, you counted their birthday suits.

He chuckled in the darkness. "You up for a swim?"

"You're talking about skinny-dipping, aren't you?"

"Yes'm, I surely am. I dare you to take off your clothes and get wet."

"You dare me?" She was in so much trouble, because she *wanted* to take off her clothes.

"C'mon," he said, opening the truck door. "Let's take a walk up to the pier."

Sarah got out of the truck and followed Tulane up a narrow concrete pathway to a dock that jutted into the river. The Edisto was only about fifty feet wide at this juncture. Moonlight glinted off its black surface, like little silver fish dancing in darkness. The air hung heavy and damp, laden with the scent of copper. A forest of unfamiliar trees stood at the water's edge like dark sentries, their branches trailing long beards of Spanish moss.

This was sultry and alien and seductive. Something wicked awakened inside her, beating to the rhythm of her heart and the blended song of the tree frogs and crickets.

They walked out onto the pier, their footsteps sounding hollow on the wooden planks. Tulane turned for a moment, his head cocked and eyes unreadable in the darkness. He wavered for an instant as if considering his next move. She silently prayed, *Please, God, don't let him change his mind. Please.* She wondered whether God listened to naughty requests from good girls, and then told her inner Puritan to take a hike.

In the next instant, Tulane pulled off his golf shirt. Sarah had only a moment to marvel at the pale moonlight on his chest before the man shucked his loafers and unbuckled his belt. He was naked about thirty seconds after that and dived into the water no more than five seconds later. She hadn't had more than an instant to get a good look at him in the wan light. But what she had seen was enough to make a woman's insides go completely haywire. Maybe stock car racing *was* a bona fide sport, because Tulane was built like an athlete.

His head emerged from the water a minute later. "C'mon in, the water's great," he called in a low-pitched voice.

She pulled the banana clip out of her hair. Her tresses tumbled down past her shoulders, creating a veil where she could pretend to hide.

She started shucking the pieces of her black tropical-weight worsted, which had been required attire this time, since someone *had* died. Cool, humid air touched bare skin, and her arms and backside pebbled with gooseflesh. She moved fast, completely aware that he watched from the water. When she was as bare as Lady Godiva, she took three steps to the edge of the pier and dived into the dark river below.

Her entire system went into shock the minute she hit the water. Her feeble brain registered two facts: The Edisto River was about the temperature of the Arctic Ocean, and it had a swift current that the night had hidden from view.

She broke the surface almost paralyzed with cold, only to realize that if she didn't swim hard, the current would sweep her away into the darkness. She shrieked Tulane's name, suddenly both furious and terrified.

He was beside her in the next instant, treading water, his voice an island of calm. "Relax, just float. Let the current take you."

She tried to relax but suddenly the night seemed exceptionally black, and the water seemed potentially dangerous and probably infested with all kinds of creepy crawlies. Why had she wanted to break the rules? Someone should examine her head.

"See the big float over yonder?" he said. "Just float on down to it and grab hold of the chain."

The current sucked at them and propelled them forward. A wooden platform built over plastic drums floated in the middle of the channel. Chains connected it to a cable suspended across the river.

Tulane took off in the direction of the float, and she followed, allowing the current to propel her forward toward the looming object.

Tulane reached the float before her, grabbing the chain with his right hand and reaching out with his left arm to haul her close. He snaked his arm around her waist like a fisherman drawing in a purse seine net.

She came to rest against him, chest to chest, her hands suddenly finding an anchor around his neck. He held them both against the current, which sluiced around them and dragged at their feet, pulling them upward in its frenzy to sweep them away downriver.

Her breasts pressed against the surprising warmth of his chest while her legs bumped and slid against his as the current tugged at them. She was completely at his mercy. If he let her go, she would drown. She didn't know whether to trust him or to scream.

"Well now, this is an interesting development. It's a darn shame the water's so cold." Even in the darkness, humor glinted in his eyes. "On the other hand, maybe it's a good thing the water's cold," he continued. "I'm thinking cold water is precisely what we needed to clear our heads."

He had a point. Her mind was definitely distracted by the strength of his arms, the warmth of his chest, and the texture of his buzz-cut hair against the palm of her right hand. The water wasn't nearly as icy as it had been a moment ago.

They hung there for an instant, their eyes meeting, even in the darkness. Intimacy bloomed.

She moved her right hand upward along his skull, indulging her curiosity about his short-cropped hair.

He pressed into her touch, cocking his head.

She stretched up toward him.

He leaned down toward her.

And then he slanted his lips across hers in a kiss so hot that it should have made the cold waters of the Edisto boil.

Her brain took the brunt of the kiss's shock wave. Her brain cells pretty much stopped functioning after that, except to record the man's technique. Tulane didn't seem too interested in invading her mouth. He was too busy taking little nibbles at her lower lip, sucking it into the warmth of his mouth, running his tongue over the inside of it.

His kiss was an invitation, soft and sultry,

but also distressingly polite. She didn't want polite. She was tired of polite.

He opened his mouth a little, and she moved in on him. He met her tongue with his. Tulane didn't intend to lead this dance. He seemed a whole lot more interested in following where she wanted him to go. And she wanted to know every square millimeter of his mouth. And when she was finished with that, she wanted to explore the rasp of his beard and know the planes of his chest and touch him everywhere.

Her body exploded with sensations that shouldn't have been possible while floating in freezing water. She found herself fighting against the current, wanting to press herself against him, only to have the river suck him away as if it were trying to pull them apart before they even got together.

And then, just as she was about to suggest that they climb up on the float, she was blinded by a light so bright and piercing she thought for an instant that God had sent a lightning bolt down to strike her dead.

Tulane pulled his lips away just as a disembodied voice said from the shoreline, "Okay, y'all, why don't you take this to a no-tell motel. But don't you dare take it to the Peach Blossom Motor Court, you hear? There's a place over in Bamberg where Lillian Bray is unlikely to catch you."

"Shoot, Stony, why don't you just turn that damned flashlight off. I know you're angry at me, but trust me, it's not my fault. I can't help what Pete put in that letter," Tulane hollered at his older brother, just as something downshifted in his head.

The light disappeared, leaving a night that seemed darker than before. "Tulane, this has nothing to do with Pete's letter," Stone said from the shoreline. "Miz Bray is sure there's an orgy going on out here, and near as I can tell, that isn't too far from the truth. She made a call into the county, and I was dispatched to check things out. I guess the old biddy is spending the night at her river house tonight, instead of in town."

Oh, crap. If Lillian Bray figured out that he and Sarah were out here naked on the eve of Pete's funeral, Momma was likely to wear out his backside. Lillian would be disappointed about the whole Reverend Ellis–Sarah Murray matchup. Even worse, the church ladies would start getting all kinds of ideas about Sarah and him. And that would not be good.

Sarah took that moment to tuck her head under his chin, and the intimacy of it felt both wonderful and scary.

Whoa . . . wait one minute there, boy. Sarah

sure did have a nice little curvy body, and an even more twisted mind, but he wasn't interested in anything long-term. And Sarah was the kind of woman you did long-term with.

"What the hell is the matter with you, anyway?" Stone said, like he had come for the express purpose of pointing out the error of Tulane's ways, which wasn't far from the truth of it. "Uncle Pete is dead, and you're out here acting like an out-of-control teenager. When, exactly, are you planning to grow up?"

It was a rhetorical question, which was why Tulane didn't bother to answer it. Stone asked this question with distressing regularity, so he just forged ahead in true big-brother fashion.

"Get your clothes on, you hear? If you aren't out of here in ten minutes, I swear I'm going to cuff and stuff you, take you down to the county lockup, and charge you with trespassing and indecent exposure and anything else I can think up. I wonder what Pete would think about that, especially since you'd be missing his big send-off."

Stone paused for a long moment and then spoke again. "And Sarah, you, of all people, ought to know better."

Sarah made a little noise that didn't

exactly sound remorseful.

"Well?" Stony said. "Did you hear me or not?"

"You wouldn't put me in jail, Stony. I'm kin."

"Ha, just try me. It's about time someone kicked some sense into you. I've had reports from all over the county about you running *my* truck like it was some kind of dragster all up and down the back roads around here. You know, Tulane, it's the only truck I have. Did you think of that before you drove it like a maniac?"

"I could buy you a new truck, Stone."

"Just like you could buy Golfing for God. Tulane, there is more to life than money. It's not about the truck. Get your butt out of that river and try for once in your life to act your age."

Tulane's brain switched on. Sarah had pretty much succeeded in turning his brain off there for a little while. Wow, that woman could kiss.

"You hear me?" Stone said.

"Yeah, I hear you."

"Good."

Tulane heard the sound of Stone's footsteps along the bank, followed by the sound of his Crown Vic cruiser crunching down the gravel road. Stone would be waiting right outside the gates to ensure they actually left within the allotted time. And he would probably escort them back into town, too, which would be embarrassing.

Stone was always doing stuff like that, on account of the fact that he was a grown-up and had been a grown-up from the time he was seven. Tulane needed to listen to his brother. Shoot, he needed to *become* his brother.

That was a depressing thought.

"Well, honey, I reckon our night of raising hell has come to an ignominious end," Tulane said as he released the chain. They began to drift downriver.

He ducked under the water, shaking free of Sarah's death grip around his neck. He resurfaced a little ways downriver. "Over here, Sarah, follow me. There's a shallow spot where you can get out," he called quietly before the woman completely panicked.

Sarah followed him toward the shoreline and stood up, the water coming up to her collarbone, the moonlight shining on the droplets that clung like quicksilver to her shoulders and eyelashes. She resembled a sea goddess, and he wanted her in an entirely carnal way.

She waded toward him, the water coming

up just to the level of her nipples. He gazed down at her, and desire tugged at his body. But the minute his body stiffened, he looked up, training his gaze on her face. The moonlight glinted in her eyes, seductive and heavy with the promise of heat. She resembled a starry-eyed kid, drunk on the possibilities laid out before her. It would be so easy to take advantage of that. He was sad and angry enough at Pete to be fully capable of it.

But tonight was a terrible night to do something stupid like this with a woman like Sarah. He probably would have stopped things before they got too out of hand, anyway. But, of course, Stone got there first.

"So where exactly is the Peach Blossom Motor Court?" Sarah asked.

Tulane squeezed his eyes closed, shutting out her soft, unfocused gaze and the promise it offered.

"We aren't going to the Peach Blossom Motor Court, so you can put that right out of your mind. I know you want to break the rules, but we aren't going to break that one. You're spending the night alone at Miz Miriam's."

Something changed in her gaze, and he could almost see how his rejection had hurt her. "This was a big mistake," he said into the charged silence.

"But —"

"Look, Sarah, this is just me being depressed about Uncle Pete, okay? I wasn't thinking . . ." His voice faded out. That was the absolute truth. He'd been on autopilot most of the day, since the will reading.

But he *was* thinking now. Sarah and the Peach Blossom Motor Court were things that didn't go together.

She crossed her arms across her breasts, and he read the gesture for what it was. Her defenses were coming up, and he was halfway glad of it. She needed to defend herself. She needed to get angry at him. If she were angry, then he wouldn't have to feel like such an a-hole for pushing this thing way beyond the limits of reason.

"What did I do wrong?" she asked.

The question jolted him. That wasn't exactly what he expected her to say. "What did you do . . . ? Honey, you didn't do anything wrong. This is just not a good idea."

"But —"

"I shouldn't have kissed you. I should never have brought you here or suggested getting naked. That was pretty stupid on my part. And as Stone points out all the time, I usually act first and think about it later. It's my signature fault.

"From now on, I plan to do a lot more thinking before I act. NASCAR wants me to do that, Stony wants me to do that, Momma wants me to do that, and, to tell you the truth, Uncle Pete used to tell me that all the time. I've decided I'm going to listen to authority for once in my life."

"Oh please, do not give me this claptrap. Was it the way I kissed?"

Oh boy, he was such a fool. He should have expected this when he suggested skinny-dipping. He should have known that little, inexperienced Sarah wanted something that she thought she needed in order to be grown-up.

Well, he didn't want to be the one to teach her about how casual some men could be about sex. He could almost imagine the regret in her pretty face tomorrow morning. This stupid thing that he'd almost done would change everything between them. His throat closed up at the thought.

"Sarah, please —"

"Please what? Stand here while yet another man kisses me and then invents all kinds of reasons why he won't do it again? Why am I so pathetic that I can't even interest a red-blooded male in taking me to the Peach Blossom Motor Court?"

Was she nuts? He sincerely wanted to take her there, but he wasn't going to do that. She was the kind of woman a man took to the Ritz and made love to.

"You aren't the kind of woman who ought to see the insides of the Peach Blossom Motor Court. And you sure as hell shouldn't see it with a guy like me. You're a nice girl, and I'm not taking you there, okay? We've ended our hell-raising session for the evening."

"Here is a news flash for you," she rejoined in a flat voice that telegraphed her ire. "I'm here trying to have a bad-boy experience. The entire point is for me to see the insides of a place like the Peach Blossom Motor Court with somebody like you."

Of course she wanted a fling with a bad boy, every woman did. But he was tired of being the designated bad boy. These relationships were great until the inevitable moment when the good girls realized that he was not good at things like lifelong commitment. There were always tears and recriminations when that happened.

And just imagining Sarah in tears twisted up his gut. He didn't want to hurt her. He liked her way too much for that.

"Well, I'm not the bad boy who's going to screw you tonight," he said, purposefully using that word to wake her up and make her realize the danger that she faced.

She was startled for a moment, clearly disturbed by the profanity. And that little hesitation told him all he needed to know. It confirmed that he was doing the right thing, even if it was one of the most difficult things he'd ever done in his life.

"Why is it that guys like you think you can egg on a girl like me, just so long as you stop before the action gets hot? If a girl did that to you, you would call her a tease," she said.

Tears gathered in her eyes. He'd just hurt her. But she would get over it.

"Look," he said on a long, frustrated sigh. "you stay here. I'll go get our clothes."

CHAPTER 11

Steve Phelps sat down at the computer, the lights of the New York skyline glowing dully in the darkened office. He glanced at the silver clock on Deidre's desk. Eleven o'clock on Saturday evening. National Brands was quiet as a tomb.

He waited for Deidre's workstation to boot up. When the log-in screen came on, he pulled a yellow sticky note from his breast pocket and carefully keyed in the user name and password.

"Yes," he hissed when Deidre's desktop appeared. He was in. Tracy down in IT had come through for him. She had actually given him the log-in information with few questions asked. He'd simply told her that Deidre was traveling in the wilds of South Carolina and had no Wi-Fi connection and needed someone to check an incoming e-mail.

Tracy, a born-and-bred New Yorker who

had never been farther south than Newark, actually believed that most of South Carolina was devoid of cell phone connectivity. Steve wasn't a complete dunce when it came to selling people the big lie. He knew that to do that, you just had to appeal to a person's inner prejudices.

Breaking into Deidre's computer was a long shot, but Steve was desperate. He couldn't let Deidre mess up a good thing, could he?

Cottontail Diaper sales had never been better, and he was reaping all the glory for that. But if Deidre moved forward with her car seat safety program, any future accolades wouldn't fall to him.

Besides, with Deidre protecting Sarah, Steve was in a precarious situation. What if Deidre found out that he hadn't written the Cottontail Diaper marketing memo? What if Deidre found out that he'd ripped off Sarah's ideas for the Cuppa Java campaign?

He needed to figure out something quick before Deidre took the NASCAR program back or Sarah outed him.

The easiest solution to his problem would have been to come up with some brilliant marketing strategy for Rice Doodles, the new snack-food product that had landed on his desk.

Unfortunately, Rice Doodles were tasteless and odorless. The fact that they were diet food was completely irrelevant. No one would eat that crap after tasting it once, no matter how desperate they were to lose weight. This probably explained why Deidre had given his team the task of coming up with the marketing program. In Steve's opinion, Rice Doodles were unmarketable.

Steve was up against a wall. If he didn't figure out something quick, he might have to join the swelling ranks of the unemployed. And that was not a good option for him. He had very expensive tastes.

Removing Deidre from his career path seemed to be the best option open to him at the moment. And for that, a little inside corporate espionage seemed reasonable.

He opened Deidre's e-mail program and began reading her messages. It didn't take long for him to find Sarah's memo on car seat safety.

So, Deidre was stealing Sarah's ideas, too.

Either that or the two of them had teamed up.

Deidre stealing Sarah's ideas didn't surprise him. But Deidre teaming up with Sarah scared the crap out of him.

Steve finished perusing Deidre's e-mails. There were a lot of messages between her and a couple of executives at Penny Farthing Productions, the owners of the Racer Rabbit cartoon character.

Holy crap, Deidre was far along in negotiating a deal that would permanently change the Cottontail Disposable Diaper bunny. Wow. Using Racer Rabbit was going to cost the company a fortune in licensing fees.

When he'd finished with the e-mails, he started opening Deidre's personal files. There wasn't much there, until he found a file named "Kelly."

He opened that one.

Oh, yeah. Pay dirt.

Haley carefully folded the pretty green-and-yellow prayer blanket the way Miz Miriam Randall had shown her. There was a big pile of blankets that she and her big sister, Lizzy, were folding.

They were helping Miz Miriam and some of the other old church ladies like they always did this time of year. Granny said that helping to make prayer blankets was probably the bestest thing that a girl could do for folks who were sick.

Granny said that the prayer blankets were kind of magic. They had so many prayers inside them that a sick person would just naturally get better because of it.

Haley kind of wished her momma had had a prayer blanket like this when they'd been in that car wreck. Then maybe Haley would have a mother instead of a Sorrowful Angel. All in all, Haley reckoned a momma was way better than a dumb old angel who didn't really know how to get back to Heaven.

She folded blankets and wondered if maybe the little old ladies at church could pray the angel back to Heaven. The little old ladies sure knew how to pray.

Haley had just finished folding the last of the blankets when the door to the fellowship hall opened, and Miz Hettie Marshall came into the room. The old ladies stopped talking and looked up.

Miz Hettie was old, but not nearly old enough to be making blankets, which probably explained why Miz Hettie took one look at all of them and got a strange look on her face and said, "Oh."

"What can we do for you, Hettie?" Miz Miriam asked. Miz Miriam was tying big ribbons around each folded blanket. She was doing this on account of the fact that her arthritis was too bad for her to do any sewing. Even so, Lizzy was helping a lot with the bow tying.

"I was looking for Bill," Miz Hettie said.

As usual, Miz Hettie was dressed real pretty. Granny said Miz Hettie had the best fashion sense in all of Allenberg County.

"Oh, I reckon he'll be here in a minute. Vivian just went up to get him. We're about to do some praying. Why don't you join us?"

Miz Hettie looked like she didn't really want to do any praying, and that made Haley feel kind of sad. So she spoke up. "Miz Hettie, of course you want to help."

"Well, I —"

"It's really great," Haley said. She climbed down from the chair she'd been standing on and went over to take Miz Hettie's hand. Miz Hettie had cold bony hands, but she was still real pretty. "We all get to pray for the sick people, and that makes the magic."

Miz Hettie didn't budge, so Haley dropped her hand. The lady looked down at Haley for a long minute. She wasn't mad. She seemed kind of confused, for a grown-up. "Magic?"

Haley shrugged. "Yeah, kind of. You know, like the magic of prayers."

"But —"

The preacher walked into the room right then, with Miz Vivian right behind him. "Don't try to talk her out of it, Hettie," he said with a big smile.

Haley liked this preacher, even though

there were times when he could be a little scary. But he was way younger than old Reverend Reed, and he was always nice to the kids in Sunday school. He could tell stories from out of the Bible using all kinds of funny voices.

It was cool.

Miz Hettie turned and looked at the preacher. The preacher looked back. They kind of got stuck looking at each other for a long time. That's when Miz Miriam coughed that kind of cough grown-ups do when they want to get someone's attention.

The preacher looked at Miz Miriam. "So, you ladies ready?"

"We are," Miz Miriam said.

The preacher took Haley by the hand. His hands were big and warm. And then he took Miz Hettie by the hand, too. "Come on, then, let's all gather around these beautiful prayer blankets ya'll have made today."

The old ladies gathered around the table where Miz Miriam finished tying the last bow on the last blanket. And then everyone laid their hands on the blankets, even the Sorrowful Angel, who had been hovering nearby all day. And then the preacher said a prayer.

But the praying went on for a long time after he finished speaking. And in that time, it seemed like the Sorrowful Angel's halo started to glow. For a moment, Haley thought maybe the old ladies would get the angel back to Heaven.

But that didn't happen. Instead, when the praying was over, Miz Hettie was crying almost as hard as the Sorrowful Angel.

"Hettie, what's the matter?" the preacher asked.

She shook her head and pulled a tissue from the pocket in her skirt. "I don't know, Bill. Do you believe in an ark big enough to hold all the species in the world?"

He smiled and looked down at Haley and then back at Miz Hettie. But he didn't say anything one way or another.

Miz Hettie sniffed, dabbed her eyes, and then looked the preacher in the eye once again. "I know. It's a silly question, and I'm not asking if you're a literal reader of the Bible. I'm asking about something deeper than that."

The preacher nodded. "Ah, I see. You're asking me if I believe in what Haley just called the magic of prayer?"

And durned if Miz Hettie didn't nod her head. "Yes, that's what I'm asking. You know, like the way you used to feel when you were Haley's age."

"Well, if that's your question, then yes,

Hettie, I believe very strongly in the magic of prayer. And I believe the Lord can make miracles."

"Bill, I really need to talk with you."

And with that, the preacher excused himself, and he and Miz Hettie went off to the church office. The old ladies immediately started talking about how Miz Hettie had started crying, but Miz Miriam only said it was about time for that dam to break.

Haley wasn't sure what Miz Miriam meant by what she'd said. She sure hoped Miz Miriam hadn't said a bad word.

A week after Pete's funeral, early on a Monday morning, Sarah's ringing cell phone destroyed her plan to sleep in on her day off. She groped around the nightstand for her cell and flipped it open. "Yeah," she said.

"Sarah, it's Ruby Rhodes."

"Is Tulane all right?" Adrenaline jolted her system. She and Tulane might not be speaking to each other, but that didn't mean Sarah didn't care.

"Well, I'm not sure, sugar. I'm not calling about him."

Sarah sat up and fluffed the pillows behind her. "Uh, you aren't? But —"

"Look, Sarah, first of all, I wanted to

thank you for all you did for us during Pete's funeral. We are all mighty grateful for your help."

Sarah squinted at her bedside clock. It was not even eight in the morning. "Oh, well, it was nothing, really."

"But that's not why I'm calling."

"No?"

"No, sugar. See, I heard all about what you told Hettie the other day about Golfing for God. And, well, you really lit a fire under her. She's usually so shy and soft-spoken and almost standoffish, but, well, I reckon you just helped her see what my husband's golf course is really about, and now she wants to form a committee."

Sarah flashed on a mental image of the blonde woman in Armani and Hermes.

"Hettie Marshall wants to form a committee?"

"Oh, yes. Reverend Ellis was so enthusiastic about the idea of resurrecting the golf course, especially after Hettie told him about how you have to just believe like you were a six-year-old. Sarah, that's so insightful. Really."

"Uh, well, that's real nice, Ruby, but —"

"To be honest, it was actually Bill who suggested that Hettie form a committee. But, you see, having Hettie be supportive of something like this changes everything. So, I know it's a really long drive, but I was wondering if you could come down here for the first organizational meeting."

"The first organizational meeting?"

"Yes, of the Committee to Resurrect Golfing for God. We're going to meet at the beauty shop this morning. And Hettie is quite adamant that we need some professional help with fundraising and marketing and just plain getting organized. And well, see, I've heard about all the work you've been doing on that car seat program. And, well, I thought maybe . . ."

"Uh, Ruby, Tulane won't be happy about this."

"Of course he won't be happy. That's why I'm asking."

Sarah leaned back on her pillows and let the silence on the line speak volumes.

"What exactly are you up to, Ruby?" Sarah finally asked.

"Well, officially, I'm just asking you to come and help us make a start with this committee. Unofficially . . . I have been known to be a real pain in the backsides of my offspring from time to time. And now that they've gotten too big to spank, I have to find other ways to make my point."

Sarah sat there for a long moment. She

should say no. But she was a scorned woman, and her fury knew no bounds. It would serve Tulane right if she joined up with the church ladies, especially after the way he'd treated her last Friday at the river. If he wanted her to be a church lady, maybe she should just join up with them and make his life miserable.

The irony of teaming up with church ladies because Tulane refused to take her to a cheap motel was not entirely lost on Sarah. But, by the same token, helping the church ladies rescue Golfing for God seemed like a worthy pursuit, especially because it was Sarah's own idea. With this request, the ladies were acknowledging her contribution. They wanted her professional help, which was like a victory all by itself.

And besides, it was Pete's last request.

The fact that it would drive Tulane insane was merely icing on the cake.

"Um, okay," Sarah found herself saying.

"Really? You'll help?" Ruby sounded surprised.

"Yes, but it takes two hours to drive there. What time is this meeting?"

"You've got plenty of time. It starts at lunch. Thelma is bringing a casserole and Millie promised some red-velvet cake for dessert."

■ ■ ■ ■

Sarah collected her notes and began stuffing them into her briefcase. The organizational meeting of the Committee to Resurrect Golfing for God had been a surprising success. Miriam Randall, Thelma Hanks, Millie Polk, Jane and Ruby Rhodes, and Hettie Marshall had all attended. Of course, Lillian Bray had not deigned to attend because she remained firm in her convictions that Golfing for God was a blasphemous eyesore.

So the initial attendees had all taken positions on an executive committee, and Sarah had outlined the steps they needed to take to get the group incorporated, obtain non-profit status, and begin to market their cause.

The ladies were going to consult a lawyer about the legal requirements but were already planning a group cookbook and a press release.

"Well," Ruby said as she closed the door behind the last of the committee members, "that went well, don't you think?" The hairdresser turned and gave Sarah a big smile. "Thank you so much for coming. Now, in return, I'd like to do something for you."

Ruby advanced, a surprisingly wicked gleam in her green eyes.

"Oh, it's not —"

"Oh, yes, it is, sugar. It's completely necessary. Now you just relax, you hear, and let me take care of it."

"Take care of what?"

"That awful hairdo."

"But —"

Her protest was cut short when Ruby seized her by the upper arm and gently guided her toward the hair-washing station at the back of the Cut 'n Curl.

"You are a beautiful woman, Sarah, but sometimes I get the feeling you're trying to hide all that beauty under a bushel basket." Ruby gently pressed Sarah into the seat and then pried the banana clip loose from her hair.

"You know, these things can be handy, but they shouldn't ever be a crutch." Ruby tossed the offending item into a trash basket. "And besides, pulling all that glorious red hair back like that makes you look like a librarian."

"It does?"

"Yes, sugar, it surely does. And if you want my advice, you aren't going to catch any interesting men wearing your hair that way.

Now just lie back and let me fix it."

Sarah decided not to fight it. Her hair did need fixing. And so did her wardrobe. Two hours later, Sarah emerged from Ruby's care buffed, waxed, made up, trimmed, painted, and detailed. Surely this was what the boys down in the shop meant when they talked about a full body-off frame-up restoration.

She looked fabulous, but she was still worried. After all, even a full body-off restoration didn't change the underlying automobile. Sarah doubted that anyone could fix what was really wrong with her.

And that was simple. She exuded some kind of reverse pheromone. Men took one look at her and ran for cover every time.

"I still look like the girl next door," Sarah said as she stared at Ruby's handiwork in the mirror.

"Of course you do. That's your charm."

"But I don't want to be the girl next door."

Ruby laughed aloud. "What are you talking about? Every man on the face of the planet wants the girl next door. You can trust me on this."

"But —"

Ruby held up her hand. "They do. But here's the secret. They want you to *be* the

271

girl next door, just not necessarily look the part."

"But that's the point. I look like the girl next door. I can't do a thing about it either. Even with a new haircut and makeup and everything. I still look like the redheaded, freckle-faced girl next door."

"There isn't anything wrong with your freckles or red hair. That just makes you adorable. I declare, Sarah, you have a cute curvy body. You need to quit hiding it in baggy chinos and man-tailored suits. All you need are a couple of pairs of tight blue jeans, and a few tank tops that show off your assets."

Ruby cocked her head and studied Sarah in the mirror for a long moment. Then she pulled her cell phone out of her smock and speed-dialed a number.

"Elbert, honey," Ruby said into the phone, "I'm not going to be home for supper."

She paused and listened. "No, it's not a dire emergency, but something extremely important has come up, and I have to go shopping."

She listened again. "Uh-huh, it's a beauty disaster. So you tell Stone to take the girls out for dinner tonight. And you can eat the leftover ham and butter beans. Clay and Jane are up in Columbia tonight with the band. I'll be home no later than ten."

She folded the phone closed.

"All right, sugar, you and I are going shopping together over to Florence. I'm just itching to dress you up in some green. And pink, of course." She laughed at that.

"No doubt because pink is such a power color." Sarah rolled her eyes. "I don't want to wear pink any more than Tulane does."

"Sarah, you would look good enough to eat in pink. You just need the right form-fitting tank top. And a pair of bad-girl high-heel boots, of course."

"Bad-girl high-heel boots?" she asked. The idea titillated her, even though it was suggested by Tulane's mother.

A grin touched Ruby's lips. "I'd recommend strappy little sandals, sugar, it being the summertime, but they have rules about open-toed footwear in the garages. But boots are allowed. And I'm thinking really naughty boots."

"Wow. I've never owned shoes like that. I've always been so practical in my footwear choices."

"Yes, I've figured that out about you. And I surely do appreciate your practicality. It will come in handy in the future. But for now, we need to play up the bad girl. If you want to look naughty, you have to kiss

273

'practical' good-bye. Now, mind, wearing boots like that will kill your feet, but I guarantee you they will get noticed down on pit row."

"You think?"

"I know."

"Well, okay, then," Sarah said with a nod. "Bring on the high-heel boots."

CHAPTER 12

Tulane lengthened his stride, pushing himself into a full-out run as he started another lap around the dirt harness track at Dover Downs. The horse track sat right inside Dover International Speedway. In a few hours, the Monster Mile would come alive with almost four dozen screaming machines, all trying to qualify for the next NASCAR Sprint Cup race. But for now, it was just a peaceful, slightly hazy Friday morning.

He concentrated on the *slap* of his running shoes against the earth, the burn in his thighs, and the pounding of his pulse. He wanted to find the zone where the endorphins kicked in. The zone where he could leave his head and live in his body.

He'd made several laps already — almost his five-mile quota — and he still hadn't managed to empty his mind of anything. He counted all the things that were distracting him from his job.

Sarah came first. Ever since Pete's funeral, the woman had been the last thing he thought about when his head hit the pillow and the first thing he thought about when he awoke. He wanted that woman, but having her would be a big honking mistake. If he wanted to be responsible and mature, he had to treat her professionally. Somehow, being responsible and mature wasn't all that much fun.

Then there was the whole what-to-do-about-Pete's-letter thing. The entire family was squabbling over this issue, and he just wanted to run away. Why had Pete made him responsible for this? It wasn't fair.

He also couldn't ignore the pile of business issues and offers that had suddenly materialized because of his interviews on nonsports television. Apparently a guy in a pink bunny suit was news. Ford Motor Company needed him to think about doing a bunch of television commercials. Half a dozen minor sponsors wanted him to think about die-cast cars and branded apparel.

It was totally insane. Why did anyone give a durn about a driver whose best finish was twenty-ninth out of a field of forty-three? He didn't want fame. He wanted to drive fast and win races and make Pete proud of him.

Shoot. All this thinking was driving him crazy. Especially the part of his brain that only wanted to think about Sarah.

Sarah had e-mailed him a few times since his boneheaded decision back at the river. Her e-mails were professional and kept to topics like the upcoming schedule, which involved a VIP dinner with the governor tomorrow night. Sarah seemed to have everything under control. The whole skinny-dipping-in-the-Edisto thing didn't seem to be bothering her at all.

A sign of true maturity on her part.

Tulane finished the lap, sweat pouring off him and his lungs working overtime. He continued to walk briskly toward the infield motor-home lot that was his temporary home away from home. The next complication to his life greeted him the minute he got back.

Lacy DuBois, an assistant to an assistant NASCAR assistant, sat draped over a folding lawn-chair like so much tarnished Christmas tinsel. Despite her job title, her appearance at this hour of the morning was strictly unofficial.

"Hey, good-looking," Lacy said in a lazy Louisiana drawl. "Have a nice run?" She unfolded all 5 feet 10 inches of her body from the lawn chair and tossed her Farrah

Fawcett do for effect. The woman was built straight up and down, like a boy, except for her artificially enhanced breasts. She resembled Trailer Trash Barbie in her tight lime-green jeans and the cropped Daisy Duke top that showed both her belly-button ring and a prodigious amount of silicone cleavage.

The boys down in the garages thought Lacy was about as hot as a Shelby Ford Mustang. Tulane found her singularly unappealing.

Lacy was a fabled pit lizard with an agenda as long as there were drivers and owners. It was a lead-pipe cinch that her appearance today meant Tulane had moved up from last to first on her to-do list.

Lacy sashayed across the infield grass and stopped just inches from him. "My, my, but aren't you impressive, all sweaty and hot," she said, reaching out and running a red-nailed finger down his cheek before he could flinch away. She made a great show of popping the sweat-dampened finger into her mouth.

"Yummy," she said in a husky voice. "I do like the taste of salty man."

He leaned in. "Lacy," he said softly.

She gazed at him out of a pair of brown eyes fringed in fake lashes and about three pounds of mascara. "What, honey?"

"Get lost."

She startled but didn't retreat. "Now, is that any way to treat a lady who is willing to make you a very good offer?"

She had to be kidding. Did she use that line with everyone? Good grief, that didn't say much about the boys of professional stock car racing, did it? He leaned in a little closer and was on the point of whispering into her ear that she was no lady and that her offer was pretty tawdry. Only he never got the words out, because Sarah Murray pulled up in a golf cart.

At the sound of approaching tires, he stepped away from Lacy and turned, hoping that whoever had just arrived wouldn't get the wrong idea. But Sarah *had* gotten the wrong idea.

His day took a simultaneous turn for the better and the worse. Sarah had let her hair down, and she wore a pair of jeans and pink T-shirt that hugged her hips and her waist and her curvy boobs, where a little golden crucifix nestled.

The sight of that little religious symbol should have cooled his ardor, but instead he reacted just like a horny teenager. She was the spitting image of the proverbial nice girl, right down to her adorable freckles.

Sarah was like some unearthly combination of virgin and harlot. Tulane wanted her deeply, and now. He didn't actually have to think about this reaction. This reaction had nothing to do with his brain.

Boy, he had really missed her these last few days. He wanted to walk over there and say something outrageous and kind of immature — something that would make her blush a deep red.

But the expression on her face — lips pursed, hazel eyes fiery — told him he was never going to get another chance with her, which was probably the right thing all the way around.

"Sarah," he said, trying to find some way to keep his voice even, "meet Lacy DuBois. She's an assistant to an assistant to a not-very-important NASCAR flack. She's here to make my day."

He turned toward Lacy, who was looking at him suspiciously. No doubt she was trying to figure out if he had just insulted her. Since Lacy didn't have much in the brains department, it took a while for her to process the thought. "Lacy, Sarah is the National Brands liaison to Ferguson Racing," Tulane said.

"Oh." Lacy managed a weak smile. "Nice to meet you."

Sarah said nothing to Lacy. The silence said enough, since everyone knew the best insult is simply to ignore the competition. Sarah did a real fine job of pretending that Lacy wasn't even standing there.

She hopped down from the golf cart onto a pair of pointy-toed, do-me boots. She tottered on them as she tried to walk over the grass. She reminded Tulane of a little girl who had just dressed up in her momma's clothes. Only in this case, Momma would be a streetwalker. The effect was adorable and deeply disturbing.

What the heck had happened to her? Where was his little librarian? Obviously escaped from the library and on a wild tear to raise some more hell. The fact that she was off doing this without his help made him ornery. He was going to miss out on some major-league fun.

She held out a FedEx overnight envelope for him. "I'm sorry to disturb you," she said in a polite voice. "But Deidre insisted that I deliver this to you right away. It came yesterday to the office. She thought you might be interested."

"What is it?" he asked, taking the cardboard folder.

"Artist's renderings for new paint schemes. National Brands is starting negotiations with the owners of the rights to the Racer Rabbit cartoon character. The artist is trying to make the car look like the one Racer Rabbit drives. It's painted green."

"Green?" *Hallelujah.*

"Pale *lime* green," she said soberly. "About the shade of Lacy's pants. With fuchsia trim."

He flicked his gaze to Lacy's green outfit and stifled a groan. This was not what he had in mind.

"And, just for the record," Sarah said, tossing her hair, "I wrote a totally bogus memo to Deidre about what happened at the funeral. I've kept all your secrets, but I'm telling you, Tulane, I'm really tired of lying for you. I'm starting to regret the promises I made."

She finished her piece and turned unsteadily on one spike heel. She headed back to the cart, fired up the electric motor on that baby, and zoomed off at an unsafe speed.

Tulane watched her leave. The folks in Last Chance were going to laugh their heads off when they saw him in a lime green and fuchsia car. And wasn't fuchsia a shade of pink? Thank goodness Pete wouldn't ever have to see that.

"Sugar, what did you do to that girl to get

her so riled up at you?" Lacy asked, pulling him away from his sour thoughts.

He leaned toward the long-legged blonde, feeling ornery as a snake with the hives. "Same as I'm going to do to you."

"What's that?"

"I turned her down."

With that, he turned and climbed the stairs to his mobile home, slamming the door right in Lacy DuBois' face.

"Tulane," she bellowed behind him, and he tried not to listen. "What the hell is the matter with you? Are you gay or something?"

Eight hours later, Tulane's mood had improved marginally. In an attempt to build more team spirit, Doc Jackson, Tulane's crew chief, had organized an impromptu cookout at Tulane's motor home.

Dwayne, the gasman, brought several cases of Budweiser. Kyle, the jack man and team driver, brought hamburgers and hot dogs and all the trimmings. Lori Sterling, the team's logistics coordinator and wife of Sam Sterling, the team manager, brought all the makings for her rum punch — a powerful concoction of Bacardi and orange, apple, and pineapple juices that Tulane never touched.

All Tulane had to do was sit back, sip his beer, and revel in the fact that, for once, they seemed to have gotten it right this afternoon. The No. 57 Ford had been the fastest car during today's two-hour practice.

Tulane's bliss lasted about two minutes, until Ken Lewicki showed up. True to form, the jerk hadn't brought anything to eat or drink. But he had the balls to show up with Sarah.

Her appearance at this impromptu gathering shouldn't have surprised Tulane. After all, she was detailed to the team as if she were actually a member of it. It was their showing up together that annoyed him.

What was she up to?

She gave him only the barest of greetings — a little nod of the head and that was it. Then she and Kenny snagged a couple of lawn chairs about fifteen feet from where Tulane was sitting. They sat there like a couple of kids with their heads together. Kenny the motormouth was doing his thing, and Sarah appeared to be hanging on every one of the man's three-syllable words.

He wanted to walk over there and smash Kenny flat. Only he couldn't do that. Kenny was exactly the right kind of man for Sarah. Just because he was an opinionated snob didn't mean that he and Sarah weren't made for each other.

Tulane sat there watching for the better part of an hour while Sarah and Kenny each downed a large cup of Lori's punch, as if that stuff were only fruit juice and not laced with both dark and light rum. When Lori headed out with another round, he decided Sarah had had enough.

He pushed up from his chair and grabbed Lori before she could deliver the drinks. He took the plastic cup of punch from her hand. "I'm cutting Sarah off," he said quietly.

"Hey, gimme that back. Since when are you her keeper?"

"Since right now. And while I'm at it, you've had enough, too."

"Gimme back that cup, Tulane." She attempted a lunge at the cup, and he backed away.

"Look, Lori, the thing is, Sarah doesn't drink all that often, and those rum drinks are really strong. You don't want to get her into trouble now, do you?" Tulane asked.

Lori tossed her mane of dark hair and rolled her eyes in disgust. "You know, Tulane, just because Sarah's not a pit lizard doesn't mean she isn't capable of letting her hair down and having some fun. Now gimme that back." Lori lunged again and managed to pull the drink right out of his hand without spilling too much of it. She turned around with a little sniff and marched on toward Sarah and Ken as if she were on a crusade.

"Leave Lori alone, Tulane," Sam said. "We're supposed to be having fun tonight. I'm sure Sarah can handle it."

Tulane wanted to argue the point, but he clamped his mouth shut. Arguing with Sam would be stupid, because Sam was the team manager, and Lori was Sam's wife.

So Tulane sucked it up and walked away.

Like a man.

Pete would be so proud.

"Hey," Doc shouted to his back. "Where you going?"

"Taking a walk," Tulane said, and didn't look back.

He walked for a good hour, around the mile-long asphalt track a few times, still searching for the no-head zone. It continued to elude him, so he focused on the problem of how to excise Sarah from his head.

Unfortunately, though, he had a deep-down hankering for Sarah. So that was a problem.

When the evening faded to twilight, the weekend concert got under way at the bandstand. Tulane figured the party had moved on, so he headed back toward his motor home. But when he came around the corner of the Prevost Coach, his little piece of the infield was still occupied.

Kenny had Sarah pinned against the motor home's exterior. The engineer was making a thorough and deep-throated inspection of the little librarian's tonsils.

Ugly and dangerous emotions welled up inside Tulane and made his hands ball up into fists. He ought to turn around and walk away, but his anger held him captive. He stood rooted to the ground while his pulse and respiration climbed into the red zone.

His anger turned into rage a moment later when Sarah's fisted hand pressed up against Kenny's shoulder in an unmistakable gesture that said she had had enough. Instead of letting go, Kenny grabbed her upper arm and slapped her tiny hand up against the motor coach, where he pinned it by the wrist. Then he spread his legs and used his much larger body in an attempt to smother her efforts to get away from him. She bucked against him and tried to twist away, but Kenny was larger and more powerful.

Tulane's raging emotions propelled him forward. Three long strides carried him close enough to grab Kenny by the shoulders of his golf shirt. He yanked the man back, whirled him around, and gave him a hard shove backward that sent him sprawling into a lawn chair, which promptly collapsed underneath him. The engineer and the chair tangled up and ended down on the ground.

Tulane took two steps forward and stared down at his adversary. "Get the hell out of here before I break your face."

Kenny untangled himself, scrambled to his feet, and stood there a little unsteadily. "What's the matter, Tulane? Jealous?"

"I said get going. I don't want to pick a fight. And I don't want to hurt you. But it's clear to me Sarah isn't interested in where you want to go. You're drunk. So just get out of here."

Kenny's gaze shifted a little. "C'mon, Sarah, let's take this somewhere else. The big, important race car driver has a problem with us being here."

"Sarah's staying here."

"The hell she is," Kenny bellowed, coming forward a couple of steps and taking a wild-ass swing.

Tulane ducked and instinct took over. He turned and came back at Kenny with a hard right cross that caught the engineer square in the nose. Tulane felt the cartilage in Kenny's nose crunch. Blood exploded out of the man's nostrils, and he staggered back a few steps, wailing in pain.

"Shit, Tulane, goddamn you, you sonofabitch." Kenny brought both of his hands up to his face, the blood splattering his shirt and his hands. "What the hell is wrong with you, anyway? You're such a loser."

The epithet knifed through Tulane. How many times had people called him that? "I didn't want to hurt you. I told you to leave."

Kenny just stood there swaying a little.

Dammit. He had worked so hard to avoid a fight. He didn't want to fight. He'd been trying to get on Kenny's good side for weeks and weeks.

But what was a man supposed to do in a situation like this? Stand there watching Sarah get manhandled?

No frigging way.

"I think it's broken," Kenny whined.

"I'm sure it's broken. You ought to find some ice for it before it swells up on you. I'm sorry I had to do that," Tulane said in a shaky voice.

He turned his back on Kenny, giving him a chance to take a little revenge if he wanted. But Kenny was a college boy who knew better than to get into fights. Kenny was well-educated and mature. And Tulane was just a hick from the sticks.

Tulane heard him moving away, muttering curses and insults.

Tulane turned back toward Sarah. She sagged against the motor home, eyes closed, her face as pale as his momma's bone china. Her cotton T-shirt had been ripped apart at the shoulder, exposing the pale lace of her bra. Three dark bruises in the shape of fingerprints had begun to darken her upper left arm. She cradled her left hand against her chest, a little smudge of blood welling out of a scrape along the knuckles.

His insides went haywire. Every instinct propelled him forward with the single-minded knowledge that his honor and his manhood depended on keeping this woman safe.

"Honey?" His voice came out as ragged and hoarse as his out-of-control emotions.

She opened a pair of unfocused eyes. The rum punch had taken a serious toll on her. "It's okay, Sarah, I'm here," Tulane said. He wanted to catch her up in his arms and hold her tight and tell her the bullies were never going to hurt her again. But he held back. The last thing she needed was some jerk making a sudden move on her.

"I'm so dizzy," she whispered. "I think I'm going to be —"

She never finished the sentence. She bent

over, clutching her stomach, and upchucked her dinner all over the toes of her silly high-heel boots and the hems of her tight blue jeans.

Tulane finally found the no-head zone he'd been searching for all day. He simply stopped thinking about everything *except* Sarah Murray.

CHAPTER 13

"Hey, honey, wake up."

Sarah fought against consciousness. Waking up this morning was going to be an unpleasant experience. So she curled in on herself, pulled the soft comforter closer around her neck, and burrowed deeper into the pillow. A hand with warm, rough fingers and a gentle touch caressed her temple.

"C'mon, it's almost eight, and I know you have business to take care of," a low-pitched voice whispered near her ear. Warm breath heated her skin. The voice spoke in a lovely accent full of dropped syllables, and soft consonants, and blurred vowels. The voice was as gentle and safe as the hand stroking her temple. She could listen to this voice for all of eternity.

But the voice kept talking about stuff that she didn't want to think about right now. Like a dinner tonight with the governor of Delaware.

The governor of Delaware!

Reality came crashing down on her like a ton of bricks.

Sarah opened her eyes and immediately regretted it. Wicked pain prickled through her frontal lobes, her stomach gave a queasy roll, and a raft of humiliating memories filled her head.

She shut her eyes and groaned.

This elicited a little chuckle from Tulane. He sat on the edge of the bed, stroking her temple as if he were some kind of gender-confused Florence Nightingale. "C'mon, now, I've got a couple of aspirin and about a gallon of water for you."

She tried to sink deeper into the bed. "No more, please," she croaked as she remembered Tulane feeding her copious quantities of water last night. She had become intimately acquainted with the toilet in the motor home's surprisingly sumptuous bathroom.

"C'mon, you've got to get up. You can't hide out all day."

She opened her eyes and squinted up at him in the semidarkness. Bless the man for having drawn the mini-blinds in his richly appointed bedroom on wheels. "Why would *you* be hiding out?" she asked in a rusty voice. "*I'm* the one who embarrassed my-self."

She was also the one who had decided to try kissing Kenny. *Why had she done that?*

"C'mon, get yourself up," Tulane said as he dragged her up to a sitting position. She looked down at herself. Her top had been replaced by Tulane's favorite Alabama T-shirt. The soft cotton hung off her body like a nightgown, and it smelled of him.

She wasn't wearing anything underneath.

Then she remembered that she had barfed all over herself, which was why Tulane had helped her into his T-shirt.

"C'mon. You need these," Tulane said, his voice serious in the dim light. Sarah gazed up at his outstretched palm where a couple of aspirin tablets rested. She snagged them and popped them into her mouth and then accepted a glass of water from him.

"Drink it all."

She obeyed. There was something in the timbre of his voice that said she would find even more trouble if she didn't.

She handed the empty glass back to him. Tulane was clean-shaven, clear-eyed, sober, and dressed in a pair of khakis and a golf shirt bearing the logos of Ferguson Racing and Cottontail Disposable Diapers. The logo shirt was white today, instead of pink

— a little change that she and Deidre had both managed to agree upon. This was his uniform at the track when he wasn't wearing his pink flame-resistant driver's suit.

"Is it really eight?" she asked.

"Yes, ma'am. And I have to get myself down to the garage. Qualifying starts early. And according to my sources, you have an early meeting with the catering department up at the Dover Downs Hotel to go over tonight's shindig."

She drew her knees up and rested her head on them. "I'm going to be late, aren't I? My clothes are —"

"I had Kyle bring your suitcase over from the hotel this morning, along with your purse and laptop and BlackBerry. I turned the BlackBerry off, but I'm thinking you probably better turn it back on and check your messages."

Sarah groaned and squeezed her eyes shut. She wanted to disappear. Everyone on the team must know what had happened last night. She could count on the good ol' boys down in the pits laughing their redneck heads off about it.

"Sweetheart," Tulane said softly. His hand found her back and began massaging it gently. His touch felt too good. "Pull yourself together now, and listen to me, okay?"

She nodded but kept her eyes closed.

"Lori should have known better than to give you that punch," he said. "That stuff is deadly."

"I didn't know it was spiked until I stood up and the universe tilted."

"Lori didn't tell you there was rum in the drink?"

"No, she didn't."

"Well, let that be a lesson. The next time someone hands you a fruit drink, you should ask."

"I'll keep that in mind."

"Good, you do that, because *I'm* the one who's going to pay the price for what happened last night."

This sent a wave of concern washing through her. "Why would *you* take the blame for anything? You didn't make a fool of yourself."

"You don't remember everything that happened, do you?"

She squeezed her eyes shut as she let every embarrassing memory flood through her. "Uh, yeah, I think I remember most of the important parts. Like where I got drunk and threw up on myself and you stayed with me all the way through the dry heaves. Uh, thanks for that, by the way."

"Aw, shucks, honey, wasn't nothing, just

your average Prince Charming stuff."

At the humor in his voice, she opened her eyes. But Tulane wasn't smiling.

"Actually, that's not the part of last night I was talking about," he said. "I'm talking about the stuff that happened before you threw up."

"You rescued me from Kenny?"

"What I did was to break Kenny's pretty little nose. His face isn't ever going to be the same. Kyle told me this morning the doctors down at the emergency room said he would probably need surgery to fix it so he can breathe right."

Sarah pressed her forehead down onto her updrawn knees. "I don't remember that part. But I remember being so relieved that you came and rescued me."

"Well, thanks, but I'm pretty sure I'm about to get sent off to the principal's office one more time. Jim Ferguson is going to rip me a new one. There just isn't any way a driver pops his engineer in the face without there being repercussions. The racing association is going to hear about this, and they'll investigate. They could put me on probation. And I hate to think what your boss lady would think about this, since she wants you to spy on me. They could ruin my career over this."

Sarah heard the misery in his voice. He was trying to behave himself, and she had ruined it for him. He wasn't a bad boy at all. He was a guy trying to get ahead in his career, just like she was trying to get ahead in her career. All of this was her fault — right down to his pink driving suit and car.

She looked up again, and their gazes caught and held. Sarah's body quickened like it always did whenever Tulane looked her square in the eye. Boy, she was hopeless.

Tulane's gaze shifted just a little, downward toward her left shoulder and then farther to her left hand, which was wrapped around her knees. He swallowed, his Adam's apple recoiling, while a muscle ticked in his lean cheek. Sarah could have sworn that Tulane was angry at her. She probably deserved it, too. But she was not going to admit that.

"I'm sorry," she said instead. Mother always said that an apology was the best policy when one had made a big mistake.

"Look," he said in a hard voice. "Breaking the rules is not a good way to get ahead in life. The racing association can get you for it. Deidre can get you. The press can run your name into the mud. I want you to stop trying to be something you aren't. It isn't safe. I would feel terrible if anything had happened to you. Is that clear?"

Apparently apologies didn't work for Tulane. He seemed even angrier. But there wasn't anything she could do about that.

"I need to get going," Sarah said, ignoring his question. She inched to the side of the bed and stood up gingerly, feeling a draft on her backside. She headed toward the bathroom in search of a toothbrush.

"Sarah," he said to her retreating back. She didn't respond. She reached the bathroom, picked up Tulane's toothbrush, and applied toothpaste to it. She popped it in her mouth just as he arrived at the door.

"Sarah, tell me you understand what I'm talking about here. Kenny could have hurt you. You *do* understand this, *don't you?* You're kind of naïve when it comes to some things, you know?"

She ignored him, although she was oddly aware of the intimacy of this scene — especially the fact that she had his toothbrush in her mouth, and he didn't even seem to care.

He leaned his body against the doorway and folded his arms across his chest. She spit out the toothpaste and rinsed.

"Where's my suitcase?" she asked.

"In the living room."

She pushed past him and made her way down a little hallway and through the galley. He followed her.

"Sarah, I'm trying to talk to you." His voice held an edge to it.

"Yeah, well, I hear you." She reached the living area. Her suitcase sat on one of the long leather couches that lined the bulkhead. She pulled it down onto the deep carpet and started rolling it back in the direction of the bathroom.

She got as far as the galley before Tulane leaned one hand across the archway, blocking her path.

"And?" he said.

She inched her chin up, trying to block out the headache and that familiar tingly feeling that vibrated through her whenever Tulane got this close.

"And what?" she asked.

"Do you understand that we're in trouble, and it's time for us both to grow up and be mature?" He said this slowly, like he was talking to a child.

"Okay, that's fair. I guess I was naïve and stupid about the spiked fruit juice."

"You were stupid about more than the punch."

"Like what?"

"Like wearing those boots and tight jeans."

"Wait one minute. What was stupid about that? And where is the rule that says I can't wear high-heel boots?"

"Those boots are not you, babe."

"Don't call me that. I tolerate 'honey,' but I am not a 'babe.' "

"You're right on that score."

Fury, white and hot, slammed through her, and she reacted without thought. She lashed out, slapping him across the cheek with all her might. The sheer force of the attack stunned her. She had never hit anyone in her life, let alone a man who had just spent the better part of the last night being kind to her.

Sarah stared up at him, trying not to be shocked at herself as she watched a little red stain color his left cheek. Remorse immediately flooded her system, tempered by fear.

She braced herself for his fury, only it didn't come. Instead, his lips twitched. She hadn't hurt him. She had amused him.

All remorse evaporated.

"You have to stop now," he whispered, leaning in closer to her, invading her space without even touching her. "You need to lose the high heels and the tawdry makeup and quit trying so hard. It's no wonder Kenny got the wrong idea. You shouldn't be messing around with jerks like Kenny."

"What do you mean? Kenny is okay. He even has a mother in Ypsilanti that he's devoted to."

"Yeah, and he put bruises on you. Stay away from him, you hear?"

"I'm sorry to tell you this, Tulane, but it's not your business. And besides, I'll bet Kenny didn't know the juice was spiked either. Kenny is usually a sober and serious sort of person. How was I supposed to know that a little alcohol would turn him into an asshole?"

"Asshole?" Tulane said, his eyes lighting up with amusement. "When did you learn to say that word? I'm pretty sure I didn't teach you that one."

Sarah raised her hand to slap him again only he was faster this time, catching her wrist in a grip that was as overpowering as it was gentle. Unlike Kenny's touch, Tulane's wouldn't leave a mark.

"Play nice," he whispered. Then he did the unexpected, pulling her hand forward instead of pushing her back.

In the next instant, he pulled her right in to his chest, placing her hand on his shoulder, letting it go, and then cupping the back of her head as he pulled her up into the most erotic kiss she had ever experienced in her life.

Not that she had that much experience in the kissing department, but she was pretty certain Tulane Rhodes wrote the book on deep, sexy kisses.

His lips, so unbelievably warm and soft, closed over her mouth. His tongue glided over her sensitive flesh in little tight circles as he explored every nook and cranny of her mouth. He kissed like a virtuoso. He knew every move and just the right rhythm; he found places she didn't even know existed, and he brought them completely to life.

The kiss tasted like Heaven itself, with hints of toothpaste and overtones of coffee, all overlaid with the taste of him. He tasted dark, and mysterious, and complex.

She pressed up on tiptoes, everything they had argued about forgotten in her surprise that he was even interested in doing something naughty like this. She slid her hand up into his short hair, the texture spiky against her palm as she rubbed it against its pattern of growth.

Tulane made a funny noise deep in his throat. He pressed himself against her hand at the same time that his own traveled all the way down her spine coming to rest on her bare, naked backside.

Liquid heat flooded her system.

He squeezed her butt cheeks, then cupped her bottom and pulled her right off the floor, forcing her to spread her legs and wrap them high around his hips. He fell back against the galley's countertop and rocked his pelvis against her.

Reaction bubbled up her windpipe and exploded into a noise that was completely inarticulate and utterly necessary.

The man had rhythm in every part of his body — especially his tongue and his hips. She felt like a play toy, and Tulane had her key, winding up the mainspring inside her until it felt like it would surely burst.

Just as this thought crossed her mind, Tulane twisted his mouth away from hers and said one of the FCC's seven forbidden words.

He loosened his grip on her backside and leaned forward, pressing her against the refrigerator and letting her front slide down his body until she was back on her feet. He placed a little chaste kiss on her temple, brushed the hair out of her face, and then tucked her head under his chin.

"I'm sorry about what just happened," he murmured.

Of all the things he could have said, that had to be the most humiliating. She pushed against his chest, and he let her go, just like a gentleman should. She really needed to go now. Embarrassment flooded her.

"I've got to get dressed." She tried to turn away from him toward the hallway, but he continued to block her passage.

"Sarah, look at me. I'm sorry about what just happened. I . . ." He strangled on the words.

She finally looked up at him. His dilated pupils made his eyes appear black. Two splotches of color stained his cheeks, while his ears had turned a flaming red. His heart was beating so hard that she could see the pulse pounding at the base of his neck.

Was he aroused? Or was he angry? She couldn't tell.

They stood there for a moment, staring at each other, and the longer she stared at him, the more aware she became of that low vibration jangling at her nerves.

"Uh," she said, after a long moment, "I'm not upset about what you just did. But I'm mad as hell that you stopped."

His mouth gave an ambiguous twitch. "I, uh . . ." He squeezed his eyes shut. "Sarah, don't you realize that you're driving me crazy?"

"I am?" Hope blossomed inside her.

He opened his eyes. "You have no idea."

"Then why did you stop? Did I do something wrong? Tell me, please, and be honest. I'm so tired of getting this wrong all the time."

"You haven't done anything wrong. Not in that department, anyway. I just got . . . I just got carried away, is all. You and me, well, it's just not a good idea, you know?"

Hope crashed and burned, right in the middle of her chest. "Yeah, I know. I've heard that line before, Tulane. That line explains why I've only had like three and a half bona fide sexual experiences. I know that's pathetic for a woman my age, but there you have it. I have this talent for turning guys off. Guys are always telling me that getting involved would be a bad idea because I'm a nice girl who should be with some guy who wants a little house and a picket fence. You're just the latest in a long line who've told me this."

"Three and a *half?* Honey, sex is not like horseshoes; either you score or you don't."

"Okay, then I must not have any talent for it. I'm not good at pool or poker or drinking rum punch either."

"It takes practice to be good at pool and poker."

"And what about the other? Doesn't it take practice for that, too?"

"No. What are you talking about?"

"I tried to tell you about this problem that night at the river. I seem to have this impact on guys. Either I'm not fast enough for them, or I'm too fast for them, or I'm . . . I don't know — a disaster is what I am. I clearly don't know what I'm doing. And that's the point. You can practice something all you want, but if you're practicing the wrong thing, you never get any better at it. What I need is a coach."

"A coach?" His voice sounded pinched.

She nodded. "A teacher. You know, someone I could trust, who wouldn't laugh at me and who could show me what it is that I'm doing wrong. That's why I suggested we spend the night at the Peach Blossom Hotel, or whatever. But you made it clear you weren't interested."

"You wanted me to be your sex coach? Honey, that's just crazy. Sex is something that more or less comes natural, no pun intended. And, trust me on this, sex between you and me would be a huge mistake."

"You're probably right about you and me. But you're wrong about the other. I hate to sound like a librarian, but it's a medical fact that sexual response in human females is

307

largely a learned behavior. Maybe for guys it's different, but —"

She didn't finish the sentence because Tulane backed her up against the refrigerator and kissed her right into silence. Goodness, the man knew how to kiss.

But the kiss seemed oddly restrained compared to what had happened a moment ago. It didn't last long, but when he disengaged, it was accomplished with several little nibbles at her lower lip that made her want to cry out loud because they were so sweet.

"Honey, there isn't one thing I can teach you about kissing." His voice was husky.

She wanted to dispute that, because in her judgment he was the only man who had ever actually given her a chance to kiss back. "Tulane, I —"

He pressed his fingers against her lips. "It's getting real late, and we both have jobs to do."

"You're turning me down again, aren't you?"

"Honey, I am not going to be your sex coach. So you can put that right out of your mind. You are too good for that, you understand? And besides, I need to focus on my career, which isn't going too well at the moment." He leaned back, clearing the path to the bathroom.

That was it. Tulane and Kenny had combined to make her feel about as small as an ant. Her humiliation was utterly complete.

CHAPTER 14

Jim Ferguson had a reputation for having the patience of Job. But even Job reached his breaking point.

"I ought to send all three of you right to the unemployment line," Jim said to Tulane, Sam Sterling, and Doc Jackson. The four of them sat in the team's hauler, directly after qualifying, where the No. 57 Ford had managed to come in thirty-ninth out of a field of forty-three.

Sam and Doc started talking simultaneously. Tulane sat there studying the vinyl flooring, trying to figure out what, if anything, he should say.

He kept wondering what Pete might do in a situation like this, and there were a couple of things that seemed clear. Pete would protect Sarah, no matter what. His uncle wouldn't make any excuses either. He'd man up and admit that he was wrong.

So Tulane winged a little prayer to the

Almighty. He was going to try to behave like the grown-up that Pete and Stone always wanted him to be.

"Okay, who's going to go first? Doc?" Jim's voice sounded brittle with suppressed fury.

"We were just having a little fun, is all," Doc said. Tulane looked up at his crew chief, suddenly aware that this was not the right way to start out this conversation.

"Uh, Jim —"

"Be quiet, Tulane. Let Doc tell it. You'll get your turn." Jim turned toward Doc. "You were just having some fun? You call sending Kenny to the hospital 'fun'?" Jim's face had gone red. The boss was not very happy, and Tulane didn't blame him, right at the moment. The fight with Kenny had not been about having fun.

Doc leaned back in his chair. The man weighed in excess of 250 pounds, and every ounce was Georgia good ol' boy. He crossed his hamlike arms over his chest, and his beer belly almost showed from beneath the hem of his pink shirt.

"Yeah, as a matter of fact. To be honest, Jim, I've wanted to break Kenny's nose myself on occasion," Doc replied.

Tulane had to stifle a groan. Someone needed to stop Doc before he got them all hanged. "Uh, Jim, can I —"

Jim turned on Tulane, his eyes hard. "You, be quiet. We'll get to you in a minute."

Tulane straightened in his chair and wondered when the world would ever give him a chance to be mature and grown-up.

Jim turned back toward Doc. "Are you telling me you have a problem with Ken?"

"Yeah, I do. He doesn't know his butt from a hole in the ground." Doc gave Tulane a glance of solidarity. Tulane was glad to have Doc taking his side, but, on the other hand, Doc was making a total hash out of things.

"Ken has a degree from University of —" Jim began.

"Don't mean he knows squat about race car setups," Doc said. "He doesn't listen to what Tulane says. And if you want to know why we're having trouble as a team, that's pretty much the reason. Kenny has never respected Tulane's experience, and Tulane deserves some respect. He's been driving for a long time. He knows cars."

Wow. Tulane had no idea Doc Jackson — one of the legendary crew chiefs in professional stock car racing — thought those things about him. For weeks now, Doc had been telling Tulane that he just needed to find some way to work with the engineer. It was the sort of thing Pete would have told him. And Tulane had been trying his best, letting Kenny win at pool week after week, and not arguing with the guy when he made some stupid adjustment to the car. The whole Kenny thing had been very frustrating.

But that's not why he popped the guy in the face. And Doc needed to shut up *now.*

"Um, Jim, can I speak, please?"

Jim turned on Tulane again. "No. I'm not all that interested in your excuses. Picking fights is not a good way to solve problems on a race team. You would think with your experience and age, you'd know that by now." Jim said the words real slow, like he was speaking to one of his many children.

"But —"

"Shut up and listen. I had to take a call this morning from National Brands. Deidre Montgomery wants me to fire you. She doesn't think you're a good spokesman for their brand image. And right now, I have to say, she's got a good point."

Tulane clamped down on the angry retort that rested on the tip of his tongue. He was not going to yell. He was going to be mature.

"Well?" Jim asked. "You wanted to say something?"

"Yes, I do."

"Okay then, go ahead."

"I hit Kenny all right. But not because of the stuff Doc said. I only hit him because he came after me. But see, he was drunk. He'd been drinking rum punch. And I was sober. So, all in all, I probably could have handled it better."

Good, his voice came out real natural, without any emotions, but he'd confessed like a man. Pete would have been proud of him for simply taking the blame. He stared up at Jim directly, man to man, and waited to be told that Jim was letting him go. A huge knot formed in his throat, but he controlled his emotions.

Sam cleared his throat, but the team manager didn't say anything out loud about how the rum punch had been made by his wife. Sam was going to protect his wife and Sarah, too. Both Doc and Sam were. Tulane understood and approved.

Jim turned to stare at Sam. "What?" the boss asked.

"Nothing." Sam crossed his arms across his chest, too, and met Jim's stare head-on.

"All right, what's going on here?" Jim asked.

"Not a thing, Jim," Sam said. "Kenny is an idiot, and Tulane didn't start the fight, he just finished it. Simple as that."

Jim turned and stared down at Tulane for a long, long moment. "You are an idiot, you know that? You've got a good thing going here, and you're about to screw it up, son. You need to grow up."

Tulane nodded. "Yes, sir, I understand. I'm trying real hard on that score."

Jim shook his head and stared up at the ceiling for a moment. "Well, try harder. As of this moment, you are on probation, young man." Jim turned and glared at the rest of them. "All ya'll better grow up, too. Now get the hell out of my sight."

The men piled out of the team hauler, and Sam clapped Tulane across the shoulders. "Don't worry, kid. It'll blow over. And thanks a bunch for protecting Lori; I've got your back."

"Yeah," Doc said. "And we'll keep quiet about Sarah. You can count on it."

Tulane nodded. The knot in his throat was so thick he couldn't speak. Maybe Doc and Sam understood why he couldn't simply stand there and let Kenny manhandle Sarah. Just thinking about the bruises that Kenny had put on her tore him up inside.

"Sure, great," Tulane said, clamping down on his feelings and managing a phony smile for his bosses. He turned and walked with them back to the garages, determined to put Sarah and Kenny out of his head.

He just needed to win a race. If he could just win, everything would work itself out.

It didn't take long for the bad news to make the rounds. Sarah was working with the caterer at the Dover Downs Hotel when one of the marketing people at headquarters texted her.

Kenny had given a self-serving statement to someone at Speed Channel, and as usual the press had jumped to all the wrong conclusions about Tulane Rhodes, bad-boy stock car driver.

The rumors were running wild that Jim Ferguson was about to fire Tulane because he'd gotten into a brawl with his team engineer. The various sports news feeds also said NASCAR was going to put Tulane on suspension. The general view seemed to be that Tulane was an immature hothead who had no business driving a Cup car. Maybe if he'd been winning races the critics might have been less hard on him. But, so far, Tulane's record in the Sprint Cup series had been less than stellar.

Sarah read the news on her BlackBerry while a slow burn consumed her middle. Why hadn't Tulane told Jim the truth?

Short answer: Tulane had protected her reputation.

At the expense of his own.

Tulane Rhodes was proving to be maddeningly chivalrous. Where the heck was the bad boy he was supposed to be?

Tulane was loyal to a fault, protected his family at all costs, took care of his friends when they made stupid mistakes, and was manly enough to cry when someone he loved died.

Well, if he could be mature about this, then she could be mature, too.

She wasn't about to let Tulane take the fall for her mistake. She'd been letting him do that for a long time. She needed to rescue him.

She found a quiet corner of the hotel, took a deep, calming breath, and placed a phone call to Deidre.

"I was just about to call you, Sarah," Deidre said without preamble. "What the hell is going on? Did Rhodes really break his engineer's nose? Please don't tell me he was drunk."

"Tulane was sober as a judge when it happened. Kenny, not so much," Sarah replied.

"Tulane attacked a drunken man? Oh boy."

"Deidre, there are a few things you need

to know about Tulane and what happened last night. Things I haven't told you, and which he obviously didn't tell Jim Ferguson."

Silence beat on the phone for a moment. "You've been lying for him, haven't you?"

"No," she lied, hoping Deidre couldn't see through her. She was not about to tell Deidre the secrets she had sworn never to reveal, even though telling Deidre the truth would have made everything easier. A promise was a promise.

"No?" Deidre sounded surprised.

"Uh, no, it's actually the other way around. See, Tulane rescued me last night, and then he lied about it."

She told Deidre the truth about Kenny Lewicki, and had to sit there for a solid ten minutes while her boss gave her an ear-blistering lecture about the stupidity of drinking on the job and getting involved with work colleagues.

Sarah fully expected the Dragon Lady to fire her on the spot, but for some reason Deidre decided to merely put her on probation, with the warning that any future slipups would end in her termination.

The next day, feeling suitably chastened, Sarah found herself in one of the luxury suites at Dover Downs, along with fifty handpicked executives from Value Mart and National Brands. A handful of Delaware's political elite, including the governor, made this hospitality event the must-attend gathering at the races this weekend.

She was utterly exhausted. Last night's swanky dinner at the hotel had gone off without a hitch. Tulane had shown up, wearing a tuxedo. He'd charmed the executives and the politicos. He'd made everyone laugh, cracking a couple of great jokes at his own expense.

He had also given her about as wide a berth as a man could give a person who was supposed to be handling his personal appearances. He was officially on probation with NASCAR and Ferguson Racing.

Now, eighteen hours later, Sarah watched the race through the big picture windows that provided an eagle's-eye view of the front straightaway and pit row. Tulane was running a very good race today.

She stood near one of the windows, and despite the soundproofing, the combined rumble of the race cars compressed her chest every time they came around the track.

Tulane was in the middle of a pack of three side-by-side cars, going unbelievably fast, only inches apart. The cars screamed past, the pitch of their engines dropping from the Doppler shift, their bright colors blurring by as they headed toward turn one. For the last thirty laps, Tulane and Augie Tallon had been doing a dance with each other.

But the race was down to just a few laps left, and everyone was getting tense, including Sarah. If Tulane could keep his cool, he might finish in the top five. Heck, he might win. He and Augie had been trading the lead all day.

She kept her eye trained on Tulane's pink car as he and Augie raced for the lead with just eight laps to go.

And then, as they headed into the turn, the very worst happened. Augie's car came up on Tulane's bumper, and bedlam broke out in the very next instant.

The back end of Tulane's car bobbled and turned sideways. The car slipped up the track and slammed into the turn-four wall. Sarah could hear the sound of metal bending with sickening force. A plume of smoke bellowed from the back wheels, and everyone in the VIP suite gasped.

The Ford caromed off the wall, spinning 180 degrees and sliding backward down the track. Sarah lost sight of it in the smoke, but she heard the second impact as someone collided with it, shooting it forward into the grassy infield. The car kept coming like gangbusters. A wheel popped off, spinning high into the air. Behind it, a nutty demolition derby played out, but Sarah kept her horrified gaze fixed on the battered pink machine as its nose dug into the grass.

The speed propelling the car pushed it airborne, back end over front. It flipped three times, churning up the sod. Finally it skidded to a stop upside down, not far from the pit road entrance, fire flickering from what had been the right-rear wheel well.

The accident took about ten seconds to play out — too short a time for anyone to completely grasp the fact that a fragile human had just been slammed against a wall at almost 200 miles an hour and then flipped several times like a pancake.

But now the horror of it hit.

Sarah's throat closed up. Her heart dropped to her stomach. She cared about the man in that car. He was funny, and charming, and sweet. He had taught her about two-stepping, and poker, and pool. He had stayed with her Friday night when she was drunk and sick. He had rescued her from her own worst intensions.

He had behaved responsibly, even when

she'd been out of control.

What if . . . ?

She couldn't complete that thought. She said a truly filthy cuss word right out loud.

It occurred to her at that moment that Tulane was an honorable man who valued the most important things in life, like his family and his good name and doing his job the best way he knew how. He had protected her honor this weekend at his own expense.

She shut her eyes and sent a prayer winging heavenward. She was not one to pray for much, but this time, she prayed very hard for Tulane, and she asked the angels to please, please protect him.

No movement came from the car. A crash van and ambulance pulled up, and a team of men dressed in red spilled out carrying fire extinguishers. Three of them made short work of the fire in the car's back end, while a fourth got down on his belly and used a knife to hack through the netting on the driver's-side window.

Officials waved a red flag and stopped the race. The safety crew reached into the cockpit and finally pulled Tulane from the wreckage.

His pink driver suit looked pretty darn bright against the muddy infield, the cottontail bunny on its back oddly incongruous. The suit was relatively clean and not blood-spattered.

In fact, the suit appeared unscathed, and so did the man in it. He stood up on his own two feet and didn't even appear to be wobbly as he waved to the crowd and walked calmly to the ambulance.

Sarah turned away from the sight, swallowing down bile. She took off toward the bathroom at a dead run. When she reached the stall, she heaved up the contents of her stomach. Then she sat there for a good ten minutes, weeping silently.

It had been an awful weekend for everyone, and it had almost ended in disaster. What if he'd been worrying about all those stupid things she was responsible for unleashing instead of keeping his eye on the road?

What would she do if anything happened to Tulane?

She sniffled back her tears. She had just discovered that she had more than a crush on him.

God help her, she was falling in love with the guy.

CHAPTER 15

Tulane eased himself into a window seat near the back of the Boeing 737 charter. He was the first one on the plane, because he'd gotten a helicopter ride from the track, and the rest of the Ferguson crew had to fight the post-race traffic in an Econovan.

He buckled his seatbelt loosely around his bruised hips, reclined the seat, and tried to get his battered body into a position that didn't hurt too much.

Well, at least he had made Jim Ferguson happy today, even if he hadn't won the race. Instead of punching Augie in the nose for bumping him and causing a multi-car wreck, Tulane had simply shaken the man's hand and accepted his apology. On camera, no less.

Tulane sank back in the seat and closed his eyes and tried to focus on staying calm. Fear of flying wasn't the only reason that he was back here in the safest part of the airplane. He needed to keep his distance from Sarah.

That woman made him feel like he was driving 300 miles an hour in a car without brakes. Maybe if he kept a low profile back here, she wouldn't find him and make his day.

He wasn't that lucky.

"Hi," Sarah said in that straitlaced New England voice of hers.

He opened his eyes. There she was, his irresistible little librarian, leaning over the seat in front of him, concern all over her pretty freckled face and in her warm hazel eyes.

"Are you okay?" she asked in a near whisper.

He managed a little smile. "I'm okay."

She smiled back. His heart took flight. "I saw you shake Augie's hand after the race. That was very mature of you."

"Thanks. I'm trying my best. Why don't you sit down?" He said the words without thinking. He almost regretted them.

"No, I don't think that's a good . . ." She stopped for a moment and took a deep breath. "I'm so sorry for everything that happened this weekend. I was a huge distraction, and I hope that Deidre has straightened things out with Jim. If you need me to talk to Jim, then I'm more than —"

"Sit down, Sarah."

"No, I think maybe I should go . . ."

"Please?"

Her eyes darkened a little, and he had the urge to stand up and drag her into the seat. "I think we are both capable of being adult about this if we try hard," he said. He didn't actually believe it, but he said the words anyway.

Her eyes seemed oddly bright as she nodded. "Even though I behaved like an immature teenager most of the weekend?"

He chuckled. "Yeah. I think you have the capacity to behave."

A little smile touched her lips. To his delight, she sat herself down in the seat beside him. "I wanted to thank you and the rest of the guys on the team for keeping my name out of the press. Really, I should have known better, all the way around."

"It's okay. I forgive you for Friday night, and I thank you for being honest on Saturday." Holy crap! Saying what was really on his mind felt good.

Sarah turned her head away. She had the most amazing skin on her cheeks. Pale, translucent, dusted with freckles. She didn't wear a lot of makeup, and he liked that about her. But her face was oddly pale tonight.

"It was terrifying watching your car cartwheel like that. I was so worried that you had lost your concentration because of . . . well, you know." She turned back, and her lips, the palest pink, parted slightly. She was shaken up by what had happened today. He needed to put her mind at rest.

"I'm not hurt."

Her gaze did a little nervous circuit of his body and his face. Her inspection made his heart rate kick up a little bit.

"That's a lie. You're sitting there like everything hurts."

Just then, the jet lurched back from the gate. "Sarah," he said, trying to ignore the icy clutch of fear in his belly, "the cars are incredibly safe. Accidents happen all the time. It's part of what I do. You know that. You've seen me hit the wall before. And in this case, the whole thing was Augie's fault, not yours. You had nothing to do with it. In fact, in a way you did me a favor. I needed to get rid of Kenny, one way or another. And the truth is, this weekend, for the first time, Doc and I were really communicating. We didn't have Kenny getting in the way. Doc had that car dialed in, and if Augie hadn't bumped me, I might have won that race. So don't worry."

The jet's engines roared to life. He felt a little pain in his chest. God, he hated this. "Racing is what I'm good at. Everyone likes to do the thing they're good at. Like you're good at marketing, and numbers, and selling stuff to consumers." He paused a moment. "And you're not good at drinking hard liquor, or playing pool, or poker, or breaking traffic rules. Just remember that, okay?"

Her mouth pursed. And he could almost read her thoughts.

"Look, Sarah, I know what you're thinking. But trust me, one day you'll meet some guy, and he'll be just what Miriam Randall predicted, and it'll all work out. They say Miriam is never wrong."

She turned toward him. Her face was only inches from his, her hazel eyes locking with his. He felt a rush, like when they waved a green flag at him at the beginning of a race. He could lean in and kiss her. He surely did want to. But he wasn't going to. It would be dumb and unprofessional. He wanted to make Jim Ferguson proud of him.

"So we understand each other, right?"

She nodded. "Yes. It would be stupid for us to break any more rules or things like that. I've learned my lesson."

"Good. So have I."

He settled himself back into his seat. "Now that that's settled, I'm going to lie back here and concentrate on not moving anything painful. I'm going to do some deep breathing. Anyone comes around, you tell them I'm asleep, okay? You won't tell them I'm a sissy or anything, will you?"

"I've promised not to tell your secrets."

Tulane leaned back and closed his eyes and tried not to think about the panic that gripped him when the plane rolled down the runway. The minute he felt the wheels leave the ground, he clutched the armrest.

A second later, Sarah's cool fingers closed over his. She gave him a little squeeze, and he let go of his left hand and turned it palm up. She fit her hand in his. Her itty-bitty hand felt steady and strong and brave. He could get used to holding her hand like this.

But that was against the rules that Jim Ferguson had outlined for him. So he told himself he'd hold her hand for just a little bit, and then he'd let her go. Completely and forever.

All of Tulane's efforts to control his anger hit a major roadblock the next morning when his cell phone rang at 7:30 in the morning. It was Stone.

It took about thirty seconds of listening to his brother rant over the line before Tulane figured out that someone had written something unkind about the Rhodes family in a racing blog.

Tulane listened to Stony's invective while he got up and headed into his home office. He fired up his computer and found the website: OnlyLeftTurns.com, the quintessential NASCAR gossip blog penned daily by Arnold Simons.

The article this morning had the provocative title: "Is Tulane Rhodes NASCAR Material?" It began innocently enough, rehashing the events of the weekend. But then the article took a nasty right turn. Tulane started reading:

One has to wonder whether Rhodes has the emotional makeup necessary to find success in the big leagues of motorsports. It's not merely a question of his antics on and off the track, but a question of his background.

Although his official biography claims that his father, Elbert Rhodes of Last Chance, South Carolina, is a mechanic, the truth is far more colorful and disturbing. Tulane's father, a Vietnam veteran, has a history of mental illness.

"It's a fact," says Lillian Bray, chair of the Last Chance Garden Club, who has known Tulane Rhodes since he was a child. "Tulane's daddy is real different, bless his heart. He says he sees angels. And he's not the first one in his family to do so. Elbert's own daddy claimed that the angels told him to build the golf course outside of town."

The golf course in question is a putt-putt establishment, with 18 holes featuring Bible stories . . .

By the time Tulane had finished reading the article, he was ready to punch something. Simons had made the family look like a bunch of inbred hillbillies. The idiot had spared no one, not even Haley, who he suggested had "inherited the family's angel madness."

It was a hatchet job, pure and simple.

"So," Stone said, "what are you going to do about this? I'll bet those high-and-mighty people from New York are responsible for this. Folks up that way really don't understand the way we are in Last Chance."

Tulane stared at the words on his computer screen, feeling useless as udders on a bull. "You mean Deidre Montgomery?"

"Who?"

"She's Sarah's boss."

"Well, hell, I'm not so sure Sarah isn't responsible for this crap. After all, she isn't really one of us, no matter what Momma or the church ladies say."

Stone's accusation fried Tulane's nerve endings like the shock of a cattle prod. For an instant he entertained the thought, and then he dismissed it. The woman who had been worried about him and held his hand last night would never have had anything to do with an article like this. No doubt some reporter hit town and Lillian Bray told all.

"Stone, Sarah had nothing to do with this. I'd bet my life on it. And Deidre didn't have anything to do with it either. Deidre might have wanted to know all the nasty details of my life, but she would never have handed them to Arnold Simons. This is not good for diaper sales."

"Shoot, Tulane, you're starting to sound like them. I don't give a holy hell what they might have done. You need to fix this. Did you read what they said about Haley?"

"How am I supposed to fix this? There's nothing I *can* do."

"There has to be something. Thousands of people are going to wake up this morning and read that my daughter is crazy. She's not crazy."

"Well, she *is* seeing a therapist. Maybe if she wasn't I could sue for libel."

Stone started cussing, and he kept it up for a full minute before finally hanging up on Tulane.

Tulane propped his head in his hands. He could count on one hand the number of times his brother had been that angry. In fact, he could do the counting and still have ten fingers left.

Arnold Simons was a bully.

But he was a bully who was beyond Tulane's reach. Otherwise, the guy might be in danger of having his face broken. Tulane had to get up. He had to move. Sitting still was no longer possible.

He started pacing, both his body and his mind raging. A few minutes later his cell phone rang again. He stopped midpace and checked the caller ID.

He didn't recognize the number.

It was probably some reporter looking for a comment. He thought about answering the phone and screaming at the person on the other end of it.

But that wouldn't be mature. He was trying to control his anger, not unleash it on the world. And he knew one thing — cussing out a reporter was something Jim Ferguson would not be happy about.

So, before that happened, he needed to disappear. He needed to get his head straight before he figured out what to do about this awful thing. He needed to think things through.

He turned off his phone, threw on some clothes, and climbed into his Mustang fastback. He didn't have any particular destination in mind. He just drove. Taking his fury out on the pavement seemed like a reasonable thing to do, so long as he didn't exceed the speed limit by more than fifteen miles an hour.

An hour later, he looked up from the road.

Dammit all.

Like some old horse that always managed to find his home barn, Tulane had driven to Last Chance. It was an old habit when things started falling apart. But this time, Uncle Pete wasn't around for the usual man-to-man talk.

A hollow place opened in Tulane's chest as he cruised through town and continued heading south. Pretty soon Golfing for God came into view on the left side of the road. He slowed and pulled into the gravel lot.

He turned off his engine and sat in the car for a few minutes as the sun heated the interior. He contemplated the remains of the statue of Jesus that had once stood at the edge of the parking lot. Tulane's career and Jesus were pretty much in the same shape — wrecked beyond recognition.

Who wanted a driver with a reputation for being an immature hothead and who had insanity running through his gene pool? It was over. And he didn't know what to do about it.

The heat eventually drove him from his car. He headed down the path toward the ark. Weeds choked the main walk, and the place looked good and truly abandoned.

Kudzu vine was burying the place faster than anyone might have expected. In a couple of years, if nothing was done, the place would fade into obscurity.

He walked to the eighteenth hole and sat on the little bench by the 8-foot statue of the resurrected Christ. Jesus looked down on him with a half-smile on His fiberglass face and His hands outstretched. Stress fractures were forming along one hand.

What had Daddy been doing all these months since the lightning storm? The place was falling apart.

Tulane could almost hear Pete's voice in the back of his head, answering the question. Daddy didn't have anything to do anymore. And without Tulane's help, there wouldn't be any money to rebuild Golfing for God. Daddy could retire.

And do what?

All the times Tulane had wished for calamity to strike this place, he'd never stopped and really thought about how losing Golfing for God might affect his father.

A huge load of guilt slapped Tulane right upside the head. For one small instant he understood how Daddy might feel. What the hell would Tulane do if he couldn't drive a car around an oval racetrack? Driving a car was what he did, just like running a putt-putt was what Daddy did.

Daddy had always loved his job. He was good at it. And hadn't Tulane told Sarah last night that everyone wants to do the thing they are good at?

Tulane stood up and started toward the ark. Maybe he could find Daddy's power saw and cut down some of the burned pines that lined the main walk. That would certainly be a productive way to burn off his anger at Arnold Simons. And it might make Pete happy, too.

He had just taken a step toward the ark when Haley's little-girl voice called out, "Uncle Tulane, are you here? Me and Granddaddy saw your car."

Tulane turned, and Haley appeared an instant later, running down the walk and looking no worse for having been trashed on a blog read by thousands. Her shorts and T-shirt were a little dirty, her hair was a big mess, and she had a Band-Aid on her left knee. She pounded down the path on sneakers that flashed a pink light with every step. Then she jumped right into Tulane's arms.

Haley didn't seem angry at him, which was a huge relief. But of course, she was too little to understand what had happened to her reputation.

He gave her a big hug and buried his nose in her soft little-girl hair. Something in his chest eased. He wanted to hold her tight and keep her safe, but she wiggled out of his grasp.

"Are you gonna help us?" Her dark eyes danced with delight, and Tulane felt his mouth tip up. He adored this child.

"Hey," Daddy said.

Tulane looked up. His father stood by the Tree of Knowledge, wearing one of his signature black T-shirts and a pair of patched blue jeans. The message across Daddy's chest today: "America Needs a Faith Lift!"

"What you doing here?" Daddy said.

Tulane shrugged. "Thinking, I guess."

"You guess. Don't you know?"

337

"No, sir, I guess not."

"Hmmm. I know the feeling."

Haley tugged on Tulane's jeans. "So, you gonna help?"

He squatted down to be at eye level. "Help with what?"

"Well, see, Hettie Marshall has started this committee called the Resurrection of Golfing for God, and some people are coming today to do some cleaning and to figure out what needs fixing up." Haley had managed to lisp through her speech, and then she gave him the most beautiful gap-toothed smile. He wanted to hug her again and never let go.

"I'm so glad folks are going to fix this place up," Haley continued, " 'cause, honestly, I don't think the Sorrowful Angel wanted Golfing for God to go out of business because she had to smite the bad guys who came out here that time. But she's an angel, you know, and angels always smite the bad guys, like in the Bible."

Tulane swallowed hard. Maybe she would grow out of it. He could only hope. "I'm sure your angel didn't mean to break stuff," Tulane said aloud. He already knew there was no point in telling Haley that the damage to the golf course had been caused by a violent lightning storm.

"So you'll stay and help? I heard Granny say you were never, ever going to help with the golf course, even though Miss Sarah says the golf course is the bestest thing in Last Chance, and you and Miss Sarah are friends. So did Miss Sarah change your mind?"

"Uh, yeah, I guess," he managed, even though the hollow place in his chest opened up into a wide chasm. For the first time that morning, he thought about Sarah and what Arnold Simons's article was probably doing to her career.

Deidre was going to be furious when she read this stuff. All the more so because Tulane had asked Sarah to lie for him.

Maybe he should have listened to Sarah a few weeks ago. Maybe if they had told the truth, they could have minimized the damage.

What an idiot he'd been.

Just then, Hettie Marshall came striding down the walk with Bill Ellis by her side. Both of them were wearing jeans and T-shirts.

Hettie had graduated from Davis High a few years ahead of Tulane, but even back then, Hettie never wore T-shirts. And as for Bill, well, seeing a minister at Golfing for God was a whole new experience. The pastors of the past had never been big fans of putt-putt.

What was going on?

"Where do you need us, Elbert?" Bill said.

Elbert dug in his pocket and pulled out a key chain. He tossed the keys to the minister. "Why don't ya'll go unlock the ark and get out the wheelbarrow and the garden tools? I'll be with you directly. I need to talk with Tulane for a minute."

"I'm so glad you changed your mind, Uncle Tulane," Haley said. Then she turned and scampered toward the ark. "I can show you where everything is," she said to the preacher. Hettie and Bill let the little girl lead the way.

Tulane jammed his hands into his pockets. "So I guess you heard about the article on OnlyLeftTurns.com?"

Daddy strolled over to the eighteenth hole, took a seat, leaned back, and rested his arms along the back of the bench. "Afraid so. Stone woke us all up this morning at some ungodly hour." He chuckled.

"You think it's funny?"

"No, but haven't you wondered exactly how Stone found out about that article? I have a theory that your big brother has been following your career with more interest than he lets on. He's proud of you."

"Stone? Proud of me? I don't think so."

"Well, you can think what you want. You usually do."

"C'mon, Daddy, we all know the truth. I'm famous because I wear a stupid pink bunny suit and drive a stupid pink car. I'm not admired because of what I do behind the wheel. And the bullies just want to use the bunny on my back for target practice. Most folks don't give a rat's ass about what all this meaningless publicity is doing to my family. I'm sorry about what happened. I tried real hard to keep this stuff about Haley and you out of the press."

"Uh-huh. I reckon that's what you call lying in your biography and picking fights with anyone who looks at you crosswise."

"Daddy, don't start."

Elbert leaned forward where he sat. "Son, I'm only going to say this once. You don't have to defend me or lie about me. I'm comfortable with who I am. I am tired of you trying to make excuses for me. I don't want them."

"But —"

"Look, I know there are unkind people in this town and in the public who have made your life difficult. But the best way to handle them is to ignore them. Take a page from Haley's book."

"She's too little to —"

"Yeah, and see how it works for her?"

"Daddy, don't be ridiculous. You know good and well that walking away from bullies doesn't work."

"Ignoring a bully is not the same as walking away from a fight with one. See, son, if you don't care, they can't hurt you. I love you, and I love the way you have tried to protect and defend me and Haley. I'm glad to see you're angry about what was written. But I don't need your protection, and Haley has her angel. Sometimes I think you and your oldest brother were cast from the same mold."

"Ha, that's a laugh. I've never been like Stone."

"You're more like him than you know."

Tulane took his hands out of his pockets and braced them on his hips. "Uh, Daddy, I don't think so. Stone is strong, silent, mature. And I'm, well . . ." He shrugged.

"Why do you do that?"

"What?"

"Sell yourself short all the time. You let what everyone says about you get inside your head. And I can see how it shakes your self-confidence."

"Pete used to say that all the time. He used to say I needed to man up."

"Yeah, I know. I don't happen to agree with that advice. In my book, manning up does not mean picking a fight every time the opportunity presents itself. It means cleaning out the garbage between your ears."

"Garbage?"

"Yeah. The stuff you've decided to believe about yourself because some stupid person said some hurtful thing a long time ago. You need to learn to ignore that crap. Tulane, you are a talented, smart, and caring man. I'm proud of you, too. When are you going to learn how to be proud of yourself?"

"Hey, Elbert, where should we start?" Bill Ellis called from the ark.

Elbert looked over his shoulder. "I reckon the first thing we should do is pull down the kudzu that's overtaken the trees over by the Red Sea." He gestured toward the southern boundary of the course and the hole depicting Moses parting the waters.

Elbert stood up. "I can't help you figure out your life, Tulane. But I can tell you that I don't need or want you to fight my battles. And I sure as hell don't need your financial help with Golfing for God — especially not if it's just because Pete asked you to do it. I'd rather take my chances with Hettie Marshall. Hettie gets what Golfing for God is all about. I'm hoping one day you'll figure it out, too."

Tulane turned and watched as Hettie picked up a pair of loppers in her carefully manicured hands and headed toward Moses and the Red Sea. "How in the hell did you get Hettie Marshall and Bill Ellis involved in this thing?"

Elbert grinned. "A miracle. Or maybe just a force of nature from up north named Sarah Murray."

"Sarah? What are you talking about?" Tulane flashed on Sarah's little hand in his during the flight from Delaware. She *was* a force of nature. A force he needed to stay the hell away from.

"Well," Elbert said, "I don't rightly know what Sarah did exactly. But Hettie says Sarah helped her to see Golfing for God for what it is. And then Hettie talked to Bill, and I don't know what Hettie told him, but now Bill is a believer. I never expected an actual minister of the Word would get it. But he does.

"I don't know if Sarah can see angels, but she sure has managed to find me a couple of flesh-and-blood helpers who have gotten me out of my funk. To be honest, son, without Hettie's enthusiasm for rebuilding this place, I might have given up hope. Or faith. I might have listened to Jimmy Marshall and sold this land to a developer."

"Jimmy Marshall wants you to sell out, but his wife is trying to help you?"

Elbert chuckled. "Well, son, you know how complicated things can get in Last Chance. I'm not entirely sure that Hettie knows her husband has been after me to sell. But it doesn't matter, because thanks to Hettie, Bill, and Sarah, I've decided to stay."

Just then, voices came from down the walkway. Tulane turned just in time to see Millie Polk and Thelma Hanks and a handful of other members of the Last Chance Garden Club strolling down the ruined walk. And with them, looking like she belonged, walked Sarah Murray, descendant of Pilgrims.

Sarah was a whole lot younger than the rest of the church ladies and gardeners, with a better shape and brighter hair, but she still looked like one of them. And seeing her there made something ease down deep inside Tulane.

Then he noticed that Sarah's eyes were red, and her skin was splotchy, and she looked like she'd spent the morning crying her eyes out. After that, he was a goner.

■ ■ ■ ■

Sarah stopped in her tracks the moment she saw Tulane.

He looked like he'd tumbled right out of bed and thrown on the dirty laundry lying on his floor. His jeans had holes in the knees and he was wearing a faded Atlanta Braves T-shirt.

He needed a haircut and a shave, too.

He looked kind of like Sarah felt. Her morning had been pretty much the worst day of her life. There was nothing like being awakened by an angry Dragon Lady and being told that your career was over for all time to come.

If Sarah had been good at profanity, she would have picked up the phone this morning and cursed Arnold Simons to hell and back. But her skills at cursing were still rudimentary, and Simons deserved better than she could dish out on her worst day.

So she'd cried instead, until she remembered that she'd promised the Last Chance Garden Club she'd lend a hand with the cleanup of Golfing for God. She decided doing something like might be just what she needed before she tried to figure out what to do next.

During the drive from Florence, she'd convinced herself that coming here to clean up Elbert's putt-putt was like a nonviolent statement in opposition to the idiots like Arnold Simons. God would smile on the people who chose to clean up the place instead of ridicule it.

Of course, in all the thinking she'd done between Florence and Last Chance, it had never occurred to her that she'd find Tulane here.

She sucked up her complicated feelings and headed toward him. He watched her approach in a way that made her whole body vibrate. Darn it, why did he have to be so handsome and appealing? She needed to get over her crush.

"What are you doing here? I thought you hated Golfing for God," she asked as she stopped in front of him.

"It's not my most favorite place, but given that I'm a native and you're not, I'm the one who ought to be surprised. What are *you* doing here?" He glanced away for an instant, watching the members of the Last Chance Garden Club as they fanned out like an army and began attacking the weeds.

She squared her shoulders. He wasn't going to be happy about her getting all involved with his family's business, so she braced herself for one of Tulane's outbursts. "It's my day off and I can do what I want. Since the ladies needed help for their cleanup day, I decided I would —"

"You've been crying," he interrupted in a surprisingly calm voice.

"No, I haven't," she lied.

He saw through the lie. "Were you crying about Arnold Simons's blog?"

"So you heard about that, huh?"

He nodded.

"For the record, Tulane, I didn't tell that idiot anything about your family."

He held up his hands. "I didn't accuse you of that. What, do you have a guilty conscience?"

She shook her head and looked away from him. "No, it's just that I know you can get angry about things and, well . . ."

"Well what?"

"Well, I've already been bawled out once today because of your secrets. I don't need to be yelled at again, okay?" She sidestepped and started heading toward the Red Sea, where Bill and Hettie seemed to be having way too much fun pulling down kudzu.

Tulane snagged her wrist before she could get away. "Bawled out? By whom?"

She turned. "Who do you think? I've been lying to Deidre for weeks now. She was not

348

amused when she read that blog. I was supposed to clue her in on all that stuff, remember? That's why she sent me here. I didn't do my job and she fired me because of it. So I guess you're on your own from now on." She tried to pull her wrist out of his grasp.

"She can't do that to you," Tulane said.

"Wanna bet? After what I did last weekend? Deidre can do anything she wants."

He held up his finger. "Be quiet," he commanded. "And don't run away." He let her go and pulled out his cell phone. "You saved my butt this weekend. It's my time to save yours."

He pressed a few buttons and a minute later he was speaking with the Dragon Lady herself. Sarah stood there, feeling things she didn't want to feel as she listened to his side of the argument.

He didn't yell. He didn't whine. He just approached the conversation like a grown-up. He took all the blame for the fact that Sarah had kept his secrets. Then he explained in exceptionally calm tones all the facts that Arnold Simons's blog had left out — like the fact that Haley had been in a serious car accident that had taken the life of her mother. And that Haley had also been traumatized last October in a hijacking that

had almost taken the life of her grandmother. He also explained that he was
frankly amazed that Sarah had kept his
confidences. He had not expected her to do
that at the expense of her own job.

He listened to Deidre for a few moments,
and then handed his phone to Sarah. "She
wants to speak with you."

Sarah swallowed hard and pressed the
phone to her ear. "Deidre?"

"Sarah, why didn't you tell me this? It
changes everything. I had no idea Tulane's
family had been touched by tragedy."

"Uh, well, I promised him that I would
keep this stuff to myself. I mean, it involves
a minor child, and I thought —"

"Is she photogenic?"

Sarah closed her eyes. "Very. But don't go
there."

"But we have to go there, don't you see?
Arnold Simons has made it a complete
necessity for us to set the record straight.
Our negotiations with Penny Farthing have
hit a very delicate phase. Things could go
either way. I'm sure you want to see Tulane
out of that pink car and into a car with
Racer Rabbit on the hood. Don't you?"

It was like Deidre knew all her hot buttons. Of course she wanted to see Tulane
out of that pink car. She felt so guilty that

she'd do almost anything to help him, especially now that she'd fallen in love with him.

"Yes, but —"

"Look, I'm sorry I bawled you out before. I was very angry. I'm calmer now. And I understand how you might have wanted to protect this little girl, but you made the wrong decision. I hope you see that now. Being blindsided by this thing is way worse than having come out with it in the first place. And now that I understand why Tulane cares about car seats, well, it changes things. You see that, don't you?"

"Yes, I understand, but he also wants —"

"So, I need you to set up a time and place where everyone can meet this kid, and maybe her father. How about next weekend? They're racing in Darlington, aren't they?"

"Who is 'everyone'?"

"The people from Penny Farthing, who own the license for Racer Rabbit, and myself. I think Penny Farthing Productions needs reassurances after this blog disaster. Hell, Sarah, *I need reassurance.* You understand, don't you? We have to make his family look less eccentric."

"Yes, but, Deidre —"

"Good, get them passes. I want to meet

this child who sees angels. If she's as photogenic as her uncle, I'm pretty sure we can use her in our campaign. Don't disappoint me this time, Sarah."

Deidre hung up. Sarah handed Tulane his phone.

"I'm in such trouble," she said, feeling more tears well up in her eyes.

Tulane frowned. "Trouble? Honey, I thought I had her eating out of my hand. What did she say?"

"She wants to *meet* Haley. No, actually it's worse than that: she wants everyone from Penny Farthing to meet Haley because she has this notion that telling the rest of Haley's story is the only way to undo the damage done by Arnold Simons. I have to get passes for your family for next Sunday's race, and if Haley isn't there for inspection, the Dragon Lady is going to completely char my career. As it is, my career is already toasted."

The tears she was holding back suddenly erupted. "I could have handled this so much better. Now what am I going to do? I can't let the Dragon Lady get her claws into Haley. Can I?"

Tulane's face softened. "Aw, honey, we'll think of something. But maybe to start out we could just pull down some kudzu and maybe saw down some of those burned trees."

She tried to smile through the tears, but the tears won.

The next thing she knew she was up against Tulane's very hard chest, getting snot all over his T-shirt.

"Now, honey, none of this was your fault. It was all pretty much my own pride that got in the way."

Sarah knew she ought to explain about the pink car memo and how all of this was actually her fault. But she was having way too much fun being wrapped up in his arms, and pressing her cheek against the sturdy muscles of his chest. He held her a long time — way longer than entirely necessary for a man to comfort a woman in distress.

And during that time, Sarah let herself lean on him. He was strong enough to hold her up, which was really nice, because she was tired of holding her own self up and she needed this rest.

When they parted they looked into each other's eyes for a long time.

And blushed.

Both of them.

Her cheeks heated and his ears turned an amazing shade of red.

That was *before* they realized the busybodies of Last Chance, South Carolina, were watching them and taking notes.

CHAPTER 16

"Well, would you look at that," Thelma Hanks said.

"What?" Millie Polk asked.

"Over there on the eighteenth hole. My goodness. We need to tell Miriam and Ruby right away. That looks like a serious problem to me."

"Well, I never," Millie said.

Hettie looked over her shoulder to see what the girls were talking about. Tulane Rhodes and Sarah Murray were in each other's arms, and they didn't look like they were about to let go of each other anytime soon.

Bill laughed. He was working beside Hettie, pulling down kudzu like a he-man. She turned toward him in time to see him trying to smother his grin. "I heard that," she said. "And what do you think is so funny?"

"Guess I'm off the hook," he said as he tugged on a stubborn vine. Laugh lines flashed for just a moment on his left cheek.

He was devastatingly handsome, all the more so dressed in worn secular garb that fit his body well. He was a little bit sweaty and didn't look at all like a preacher in that T-shirt. But then, Hettie was hardly dressed like a Queen Bee.

Something about the casual clothing made the moment feel naughty and forbidden.

She turned away and tried to collect her wits. She needed to put distance between herself and Bill Ellis. It was simply not right to find the pastor of Christ Church so attractive. She picked up the heavy lopping shears and cut the vine he was tugging.

He tossed the severed vine into the debris pile, then captured her attention with his 3,000-watt blue eyes. "Don't be so shocked, Hettie. I live in Last Chance, and you can't live in this town without knowing about Miriam Randall's various matrimonial projects." The corner of his mouth quivered as if he were struggling to keep a straight face.

"Well, it would appear she's gotten it wrong, for once." *Probably because Miriam had made the whole thing up.* But Hettie wasn't about to give away Miriam's secrets.

Bill looked over his shoulder at Sarah and Tulane. They had just stepped apart, but anyone with eyes could tell the two of them were burning up for one another.

He looked back. "Well, I don't think I'd want to get between those two, right at the moment, regardless of what Miriam might have to say. Besides, Sarah is not the woman for me. She's way too corporate."

Hettie pulled the brim of her big, floppy hat down so Bill couldn't see the relief that probably showed on her face. Feeling relief was not a good thing. She should be trying to find Bill a proper wife, like all the rest of the Ladies Auxiliary.

He turned back to the vines and started pulling down another one. "I guess I'll have to continue to deal with Lillian Bray's matchmaking," he said, as if he could read her mind. "Although, to be honest, Hettie, she's got very high standards for me. I'm afraid she's unhappy about my relationship with Jenny Carpenter. I gather Jenny being a Methodist puts her completely out of the running."

A wave of adrenaline hit Hettie's bloodstream. "Are you serious about Jenny?" The words jumped right out of her mouth.

He shook his head. "What, Hettie, have you got a problem with Methodists, too?"

"No, it's just that . . ." She clamped down on her thoughts and took a deep breath. "I guess I was just surprised."

"Well, the thing is, Jenny is a real good cook and she doesn't have anyone to cook for now that her momma is up at the nursing home. And I have a weakness for homemade apple pie. The truth is, Jenny is lonely. And I am, too, sometimes. So I let her cook for me. Jenny and I are just friends."

"Uh-huh. I've heard that one before."

"Well," Bill said, "I know how it sounds when I say that Jenny and I are *just* friends. But it's true. I go over there every couple of weeks and she cooks a dinner for me and we talk about books. I see you more often than I see Jenny. After all, you sit on the church board of directors, you've roped me into being an advisor to the Committee to Resurrect Golfing for God, and you come to the church on a daily basis. I enjoy your company. But we're *just* friends, too."

Hettie's heart leapt to her throat and she looked up, past the brim of her hat, into his serious blue eyes. His gaze was far more direct and eloquent than his words had been.

She took a deep breath, collected her scattered emotions, and asked, "Do you think I should cut back on my church activities, then?"

He dropped another vine onto the debris pile and then turned back toward her. His smile was kind and gentle, as it always was. He was a friend. A very good friend.

"I would never dream of telling anyone to cut back on activities at the church. You can come to church as often as you like or as you need. I know something is troubling you very deeply. But I'm not the answer. I'm just a priest who can guide you, but not much more. The answer you're seeking lies in your faith. Trust in the Lord and He'll show you the right way. I'm worried about you."

She turned and looked up at the giant statue of Goliath. "Sometimes I'm worried about me, too," she finally said.

"Do me a favor, then."

"What?"

"Pray about it. I've been praying a lot for you recently."

She turned back. "Have you?"

He smiled. "Every day. But please, dear friend, remember that this town is a gossip mill." One of his brows inclined just a fraction.

She met his stare straight on as something wonderful and awful blossomed in her mind. "And you're saying I'm not the only one who could get hurt."

He nodded. "Yes, that's exactly what I'm saying."

After they helped the garden club, Tulane took Sarah to the Red Hot Pig Place, where they discussed the Deidre problem over hush puppies and pulled pork. They came to absolutely no conclusions, except that getting passes for next week's race for Haley and the rest of Tulane's family wouldn't do any more damage than had already been done.

That would appease the Dragon Lady for a few more days while they tried to figure out a way to rehabilitate Tulane's reputation and save Sarah's career.

It wasn't his reputation that Tulane was thinking about, though, as they sat there in that seedy barbecue place off Charleston-Augusta Road. Nope, all thoughts about his reputation took a hike the minute Sarah took her first bite of hush puppy and let go of a groan of pleasure that was triple-X-rated.

It was hard to think about anything after she made that noise. He wanted to reach across the table, take that stupid clip from her hair, and pull her up into his arms.

He'd been having random thoughts along those lines for most of the day. He was about to explode from those random and utterly immature thoughts.

Although, in truth, he had to admit that the lust he was feeling for her was overlaid with something else entirely. Something really complicated.

The fact was, he liked her. He liked her even though she'd managed to wrap herself around his life and his family and his hometown. He liked her because she didn't laugh at his folks. He liked her because she loved Golfing for God. He liked her because she treated Daddy like he was a human being and not some joke.

He liked her. A lot.

They finished dinner and walked to their separate cars. It was time to say good night. She gave him a lame little smile and told him she'd see him around the office.

He smiled back, got into his car, and followed her onto the Charleston-Augusta Road heading east toward Bamberg and Route 78, and the two-hour drive back to Florence. But when he got to the exit off I-95, where he should have turned off to go home, he kept following her car's red taillights.

Was it immature to want Sarah Rhodes?

He didn't have an answer. But he sure knew what Pete would say. Pete would tell him that if he cared about Sarah, he needed to let her know. Up until this moment, Tulane had been dodging that bullet, mostly because he hadn't been sure.

But he was sure now. A day watching her with the Last Chance Garden Club had pretty much sealed the deal.

He followed her into her complex's parking lot and parked beside Sarah's nondescript rental car. He got out of the Mustang and intercepted her between their cars.

"I thought you were going home," she said. "I sure hope you didn't follow me because you thought I needed protection. Because I'm a big girl, you know."

He jammed his hands into his front pockets and screwed up his courage. "Yeah, I know. And that's why I was wondering . . ." His mouth lost steam. Man, this was as awkward as that time Old Man Nelson had aimed a shotgun at Tulane to protect his granddaughter's honor. Tulane had only wanted a little kiss that time. He wanted more than that tonight.

He looked around the suburban parking lot. No hillbillies seemed to be lurking in the shadows. The coast was clear.

He started again. "Uh, look, Sarah, about that thing you said this weekend."

"What thing?" She pretended ignorance,

but she knew exactly what he was talking about. A little fire ignited in her hazel eyes, and it didn't have anything to do with the complex's security lights.

He stepped a little closer. "You know. That thing you wanted me to do for you." His heart ricocheted off his rib cage. He was going about this all wrong, and he suddenly knew it.

He should start over and tell Sarah that something had changed during the flight last night when she'd held his hand. But he wasn't brave enough for that.

She looked up at him, wide-eyed, kind of innocent. And then she bit her lower lip and something clicked in his head.

He leaned in, bracing himself on the car. He caged her between his arms. She didn't try to get away, so he wasn't being like Kenny. He didn't ever want to hurt her like Kenny had.

She thought she was easy, but he knew better. She'd been playing that part, and he'd ignored her. But he had just changed his mind, because he knew he was never going to hurt her. And he was ready. Somehow he knew he was ready for this.

He pulled in a deep breath. "You know, Sarah, I'm thinking we need to do this. I know I'm trying not to break rules and be mature and all that, but —"

"We can still be mature and do this," she said.

"Really? You think so?"

"Absolutely. This is about you giving me an experience I need. We can set some clearly understood ground rules before we start."

His heart slowed a fraction. What was she talking about? "Ground rules?"

"Well, you know, we just need to understand that it's a onetime thing. And then we'll be over it and I'll have had my experience and no one will be any worse for the wear."

He stood there leaning into the car, her warm curvy body so close, her scent messing with his mind.

He wanted her on every level a man could want a woman.

And she wanted a one-night stand?

He almost turned away. But something kept him there, glued to the blacktop as he stared down into her pretty, freckled face.

She had no idea of her power over him, did she?

If he turned and walked away, or got angry, she would misread his intentions. And she'd think she had done something wrong.

If he cared about her, he had to get her beyond that kind of foolish thinking.

But standing here discussing it maturely was only going to confuse things. It would be simpler, all the way around, if he could just show her how he felt. And then tomorrow morning she would understand.

That seemed like a perfectly legitimate plan of action. So he put on his most earnest voice and said, "Okay, honey, I think ground rules are good." Of course, he never said that he was going to agree with *her* ground rules. He had his own set of rules. Sarah would discover them soon enough.

She straightened her prim little shoulders. "All right, I'm glad we understand each other clearly. Because, well, our bosses would kill us if they found out we were . . . you know . . ."

"No, I don't know. What?" He was having fun teasing her now. What was it about Sarah that made teasing her one of life's greatest pleasures?

She rolled her eyes and blushed. "You know . . ."

Boy, she was adorable. And she was in for the surprise of her life. "Okay. I think we're all clear with one another." *Not.*

She stood there, kind of frozen. She was scared. But he was going to take care of her.

He was looking forward to the moment her fears disappeared. Like that time in the river, before he decided to be mature and walk away.

What an idiot he'd been that night.

"So, can I come up? See your place?" he asked.

She let go of a deep sigh. "You mean you want to do this *now?*"

"Strike while the iron is hot, you know." He had trouble keeping the grin from his face. It was just so much fun to call Sarah's bluffs.

"Uh, yeah, okay." She looked like a deer staring down headlights.

He needed to break the ice, so he dipped down and gave her a little kiss on the mouth that soon became a middle-sized kiss and then escalated to something that was hotter than the hottest day in July. And, boy howdy, did she ever taste like barbecue and summer heat. His whole system went hay-wire.

They stood there for a good five minutes, just kissing and not much else. It was so much fun — like being a teenager all over again and learning how to make out.

After a while he finally drew back. "So, we going upstairs?"

■ ■ ■ ■

Sarah took off toward the entrance of her building, her heart beating so fast she could hardly get her breath. She didn't look back to see if Tulane was following her. She was going to get hurt if she let this happen, wasn't she? On the other hand, if she chickened out now, she would regret it for the rest of her life.

She opened her front door, turned on the lights, and let Tulane into her apartment.

Tulane sauntered into her living room and studied the place for a long moment as Sarah did battle with her inner Puritan.

Her living room was decorated in shades of burgundy with a neutral carpet, floral couch, and utilitarian blinds at the balcony doors. The place was sterile — a temporary home for someone who didn't plan on staying too long in Florence, South Carolina.

Somehow the temporary nature of her home underscored the temporary nature of what she was about to do. Well, things never lasted forever, did they? She could deal with the heartbreak of her decision, especially since she was going into this clearheaded and with the rules well established.

Tulane strolled to the stereo on the bookshelf and studied her small collection of CDs. "Ah, this will do," he said as he pulled one from the stack and popped it into the CD player.

A moment later, the soft sounds of Norah Jones's unique and sexy blend of jazz-soul-folk filled the air. "If you'd had Barry White, I would have put that on. But Norah is almost as good for making out."

Sarah stood by the couch while her stomach clutched. Suddenly, this scenario was looking like something that should be filed under the heading of "Be Careful What You Ask For."

"I . . . uh . . . maybe we should . . . um."

Her sudden confusion elicited the sweetest smile from Tulane. It curled up both corners of his mouth and folded laugh lines into his cheeks and around his eyes. He crossed the room to stand right in front of her. "So, you want me to stop?"

Her voice didn't seem to want to work, but Tulane seemed to understand about that. He ran the back of his finger across her cheek. The touch, even as gentle as it was, generated a contrail of fire across her skin. She closed her eyes.

"You like that, don't you?"

She didn't say anything as his finger traveled across her cheek, and over her jaw, and down her neck to her collarbone, where he played with the little crucifix she always wore. Obviously he didn't find the jewelry any obstacle to the seduction he was planning, because in the next instant he said, "Let's find out where your erogenous zones are."

Her eyes flashed open, and she found her voice. "Erogenous zones? Uh, aren't they kind of obvious?"

He shook his head. "No, ma'am."

"No?"

As if in answer, he stopped playing with her necklace and reached for her right hand. He cradled it in his much larger palm for a moment, sending little shocks of reaction running all along her arm wherever his rough skin abraded hers. And then, like a courtly gentleman, he brought her hand to his lips.

He brushed his mouth across her fingers, and his lips parted just enough for the tip of his tongue to lave the back of her knuckles right in the crease between her first and second fingers.

Sensation curled around her insides and bubbled right out of her in the form of a groan. His lips retreated. "Nice," he murmured.

Tulane placed her hand on his shoulder,

and then he pulled the clip from her hair. Her tresses spilled down to her shoulders, and he let go of a long, vocal sigh. "I love your hair down."

He brushed her hair away from her face at the same time as he pulled her closer, his fingers running across her neck and up into her hairline.

Tension coiled in her belly the minute his lips found the flesh of her neck. He nibbled at her skin, sending heat shooting through her like a supernova. But that sensation wasn't anything like what happened when his tongue found the lobe of her ear.

Once again, something unspeakably exciting bubbled right out of her in the form of a noise that should have embarrassed her, but didn't, because the minute she made that noise, she heard Tulane make a noise of his own.

And that noise did something wicked to her soul, and her body, and her mind. It occurred to her that he might have a few erogenous zones of his own. She could touch him back if she wanted, and she wanted to touch him everywhere. She wanted to feel him next to her in a way that had become suddenly urgent.

She shoved her hand up into his hair and the hard contours of his skull, and then she let her fingers travel back down across his powerful shoulders. He was trembling.

She had made Tulane tremble? How had she done that?

Just as that thought registered in her brain, Tulane moved off in search of yet another one of her zones. His right hand traveled over her shoulder and down to her rib cage, and then back up to her breast. Even through her T-shirt, things were starting to heat up.

Suddenly, Tulane wasn't nearly close enough. She wanted to feel *him,* not just his hands and his lips. She wanted his . . .

She didn't know what she wanted. She just knew that she wanted something more.

She sagged back a little and managed to look up into his face. What she saw there sent her up in a column of flame. He appeared drugged, aroused, and excited. Somewhere in the back of her brain, she registered Norah on the stereo singing about "the nearness of you." Tulane wasn't anywhere close enough.

"What?" he asked, stroking her hair back from her face. "Tell me."

"I want to get closer," she whispered.

His gaze did a slow circuit of her face. "You want to get naked?"

Yes, that was precisely what she wanted.

She wanted his skin on hers. She nodded, biting her lip. "Don't you?" she said hoarsely.

"Honey, I wanted to get naked when I kissed you out in the parking lot, but I'm a simple guy."

Only that wasn't true at all. Tulane was a lot of things. Simple wasn't one of them. Easy maybe. Easy to arouse. Easy to be with. She had no idea what she had done to put the fire in his eyes.

"I want to feel your skin," she said.

"Okay." He reached over his head and pulled off his old T-shirt. He tossed it on the couch. "Your turn."

She stared at him.

He smiled.

"You don't have to if you don't want to," he said. But she wanted to lose her T-shirt, and she wanted to lose her inner Puritan, who at that very moment was trying to take control of this situation.

So Sarah reached for the hem of her shirt and pulled it off.

She tossed it next to his. He inspected her then, and what she saw reflected in his gaze made something hitch in her chest. No man had ever gazed at her like that, not that there had been all that many men in her life. He stared down at her as if he thought she was beautiful and desirable.

He had her bra unfastened in the next few seconds. No fuss, no muss, no fumbling. He knew what he was doing, thank goodness, because she was out of her element, out of her depth, clueless, and completely out of control.

In the next moment, Tulane had backed her up to the couch. She fell back into it, and he came after her, kneeling on the carpet in front of her.

He came at her once again. His mouth found hers and he nibbled her lips for a little moment and then trailed his tongue over her jaw and down her nape and finally to her breast.

Her hands found the warm skin of his shoulders and then went on an expedition of their own, trailing down over the hard planes of his back. She scratched him without exactly meaning to.

He groaned.

The noise came from down deep in his throat, and he shuddered at the same time. In the next moment, something changed in his approach. Polite went right out the door.

In the next five minutes, he had her completely undressed, and for the first time in her life, she wasn't embarrassed. She was too busy experiencing a wide range of sensations that Tulane seemed to have a real talent for creating.

His hands and his mouth seemed to be everywhere at once on every part of her body, until her little mainspring coiled up again, much faster and much tighter than it had on Saturday morning.

And then something snapped, and the world exploded, and there wasn't anything she could do about it but scream her head off as her body took her on a wild ride.

When it was over, it occurred to her that Tulane still had most of his clothes on, and she had not exactly gotten completely intimate with him. In fact, she hadn't even gotten into the bedroom yet.

Wow!

Okay, he could relax now. Only that didn't seem possible. Holding Sarah in his arms was about the best thing he'd ever experienced in his life.

It felt way too good. And it didn't feel mature either. In fact, he felt like a teenager watching his first-ever X-rated flick. Sarah gazed up at him just like a porno star, a little sweaty, her hair messed up, her lips red and plump, her hazel eyes dark, her nipples . . .

He wanted to pull her right down onto the carpet. By the little self-satisfied grin on her lips, he had this uncanny notion that she might actually let him do it.

He'd seen that look in her eyes once before. Right after he'd fed her that first weak margarita down at Dot's Spot. Right before they started dancing. That look said she had just figured out that orgasms were like potato chips. You couldn't have just one.

Which was a good thing. He could build on that. He had a few additional things he wanted to teach her, but he needed to get her into the bedroom.

On the other hand, she was staring up at him like she might be ready for something advanced, like doing it on the rug. Or on the dining room table, or any place he decided to do it. A million depraved ideas marched right through his head. Damn, but his sweet little church lady was as hot as they came.

"Tulane," Sarah said in a husky voice, pulling him back from his fantasies.

"Uh-huh."

"You're still wearing your pants."

"You noticed."

"I want you to take them off."

"I thought you would never ask, but uh . . ."

"What?"

"Uh . . . I think we need to go into the

bedroom. We could stay here, but . . . uh . . ."

She grinned at him. "Okay. You're the coach."

Tulane got up and pulled her into his arms and carried her across the living room. She sank her head down on his shoulder and that made him feel manly in a way that confused the crap out of him, because she didn't weigh more than a hundred pounds. He regularly bench-pressed twice that.

It was dark in the bedroom, which was probably just as well. Luckily it wasn't a real large bedroom, so finding the bed proved no difficulty.

He put her down on the edge of the bed, and was about to reach for his belt buckle, when she popped up on the bed and beat him to it.

He stood there and let her undress him. It was probably the most erotic thing he'd ever experienced in his life.

When she finally had him all the way out of his jeans, she giggled and said, "So, um, you're going to tell me if I do anything wrong, right?"

"You're doing just fine so far," he assured her. In fact, Sarah found more erogenous zones on his body in fifteen minutes than anyone had discovered in the last fifteen *years.* By the time she found the rubber he kept in his wallet for emergencies like this one, he was lying on his back, gasping for breath, and hardly able to even form the words: "Ride me, baby."

And just like that, the woman up and straddled him.

Man-oh-man, she wound him up tight and then she let him go. His engine kicked in, and it felt like he was riding a jet, going 800 miles an hour without any steering wheel. And when he hit the wall, it felt sooooo . . . gooood.

CHAPTER 17

Sarah cracked open her right eye. The sun poured in through the venetian blinds, making bars of shadow and light across the rumpled sheets. She rolled to her side, and charley-horsed muscles complained. She ran her palm across the pima cotton, the sun heating the back of her hand.

It was late, but Tuesday was an off day.

Tulane had left the bed a few minutes ago. The sound of water running in the bathroom confirmed that he was taking a shower. The digital clock on the bedside table read 10:30. She was kind of surprised that Tulane was still there.

Didn't secret lovers usually make off in the middle of the night?

She drew in a deep breath, redolent of Tulane and the two of them together. It made her want him all over again. This must mean that her inner Puritan had finally been laid to rest. Hallelujah! She would not be mourned.

Although, to be completely honest, the death of her inner Puritan didn't presage a complete fall into depravity. Sarah had no desire to become a harlot. She just wanted more of Tulane Rhodes.

Oh boy.

That was a problem.

What had happened last night was a onetime thing. She had asked him to help, and he'd done what she'd asked. They had agreed on the rules.

Her throat closed up, and she fought her emotions. She had no reason to be sad about what had happened, because he had given her something wonderful and precious and unforgettable. He had been sweet and patient and loving, as well as hot and wicked and amazing. She could ask no more of him. She decided she wouldn't. She would be brave and live by their agreement.

She got up, padded to her closet, and pulled on her big terrycloth robe. At a moment like this, a woman needed an occupation to keep her mind off difficult, emotional things. Making coffee seemed appropriate. She headed for the kitchen and her electric coffeemaker.

Five minutes later, her doorbell rang with the urgency of a fire alarm. The visitor leaned on that thing, making it ding and dong several times in succession. This was followed by hearty pounding.

Maybe the apartment was on fire, although she didn't smell smoke. She headed to the door and opened it.

And there, standing on the other side, was her worst nightmare, wearing a thunderous expression and a Roman collar. Dad didn't ask permission before he marched right into her apartment as if he owned the place.

"What on earth are you doing here?" Sarah asked, trying not to sound panicked.

Her father turned and inspected her out of a pair of flashing brown eyes. He stabbed one of his hands through his silvery red hair. "Where have you been? I've been trying to reach you since yesterday afternoon."

"Uh . . ." Her voice faded and her mind seized up like one of Tulane's motors when it broke. Somehow she didn't think it would be a good move to tell her Bible-toting father the truth.

So she stood there staring up at him as he stared down at her. After thirty seconds of close inspection of her disheveled appearance, the expression on his face softened. "Good heavens, Sarah, are you sick?"

She almost groaned aloud. "What on

earth are you doing here, Dad?" she asked again.

"Jan Applegate fell and broke her ankle yesterday. I'm filling in for her at an ecumenical meeting in Columbia that starts tomorrow. I decided to come early in the hope that maybe I could treat you to lunch, since you don't work on Tuesdays. I've been crazy with worry. I couldn't get you on your cell phone or your work phone, and no one knew where you were. You look awful. What is it, the flu?"

Great. She'd just had the best sex of her life, and she looked awful.

"Well, as a matter of —"

She never finished the sentence, which was a good thing, since she was about to tell a lie. But Providence and Tulane rescued her.

The good ol' boy wandered out of the bedroom wearing a towel and a sexy spattering of water droplets. "Hey, Sarah, have you seen my Braves shirt any . . ." His voice faded out the minute he realized there was a minister standing in the living room. His smile disappeared, and a whole range of new expressions marched across his features, starting with surprise, moving to shock, and ending up with embarrassment.

"Uh . . . sorry . . ." He turned on his bare

heel and went straight back into the bedroom, closing the door behind him.

Dad turned in her direction. "Was that who I think it was?" His words had a measured quality to them, as if he were struggling to remain calm.

"You know, Dad, this may come as a big shock to you, but I'm almost twenty-six years old, and I —"

"I asked you a simple question."

"Depends on who you think that was."

"Don't get smart with me, Sarah. I may not have time on Sundays to watch stock car racing, but I know who that was."

"Then you didn't have to ask, did you?" She said the words and immediately regretted the sarcasm. Her father's lips pressed together, and he gave her his own version of the Look.

She met his stare with defiance. After about a minute of this, Dad blinked and turned away, strolling deeper into her temporary abode, taking in the run-of-the-mill furnishings and the little piles of her clothing scattered over the living room rug.

"Well," he said at long last. It was amazing how much censure the man could invest in a single word. He turned around, his dark eyes intensely bright. "I'd still like to take you to lunch." He nodded toward the bedroom door. "He's invited."

She wet her suddenly dry lips. This was hardly an invitation. Dad was notorious for giving potential boyfriends the third degree, and technically Tulane wasn't even a potential boyfriend. He was her onetime fling, and she suddenly wished he had played by those rules.

Onetime flings were supposed to sneak out in the wee hours. They were not supposed to hang around in the morning.

How on earth was she going to get Tulane out of the apartment before Dad ate him for lunch?

Tulane stepped into his jeans and cursed. He needed the intrusion of a preacher like he needed a hole in the head. He'd had all these plans to drive to Dunkin' Donuts and Walgreens and bring back coffee and food and condoms. And then awaken Sarah with breakfast in bed.

He didn't need the sudden, unexplained appearance of the God Squad. He was buckling his belt when Sarah slipped through the door.

She looked like a little mouse caught in a trap. What the heck was going on?

"Who was that?" Tulane asked, his voice telegraphing his annoyance at having his romantic plans interrupted. "I hope it was just someone collecting for the widows and orphans. I mean, the last person on the face of the planet I expected to see this morning was a preacher."

Her warm hazel eyes filled with unshed tears and Tulane went on guard. "What is it, honey? Something bad?"

"Um . . ." A tear leaked out the corner of her eye. Damn, this was not going well.

"Hey, honey, it's okay." He pulled her into a hug. She felt warm against him, and she smelled sexy as hell. He wanted to hold her there forever.

She pulled away before he was ready to let her go. "The man in the living room isn't exactly a stranger."

Wariness prickled his skin. "No?" he asked carefully.

"Uh . . . no. You see . . . um . . ." Her jaw tightened.

"Spit it out, honey."

She tried to unclench her jaws. "Well, you know how your father's occupation embarrasses you?"

Adrenaline hit his bloodstream. Oh, holy crap. This wasn't happening. "Are you telling me that man is your daddy?" Tulane managed to say around the knot in his throat.

She nodded.

"Sarah, you told me he was a bull rider. You lied to me."

"He was a bull rider, once," she whispered. "I don't think I ever told you his occupation."

"Why not?" Anger started to boil in his gut.

"I'm sorry. I didn't think it was an issue. I never planned for you to meet him. Ever."

His fists balled up. "You never meant for me to meet him?"

"No. Why would I? Tulane, this is not a serious thing between us, you know. And well, Dad can be kind of straitlaced."

All Tulane's plans for the morning went up in smoke. He was a class-A fool. "Shit."

Her eyes widened just a little bit. "Look, Tulane, I'm a grown-up woman. You don't have to treat me with kid gloves. We set very clear ground rules. And besides, if I'd told you the truth, you wouldn't have come up here last night. Would you?"

"No," Tulane said through the haze of anger. Why did he feel so used? "I reckon I can understand that, especially when all you wanted was to go out slumming with a bad boy." His voice dripped with sarcasm.

"Uh, well, that's kind of true, but —"

"I had a good time, Sarah," he said as he

headed for the bedroom door. "I hope I taught you what you needed to know. But I swear, all that crap about how I should be honest about my daddy while you were lying about yours? Honey, that was not nice."

Sarah's daddy hovered in the living room like a bird of prey. The man even resembled a bird, with his dark eyes, bushy brown eyebrows, and hawkish nose. There wasn't a soft thing about him.

This was not your ordinary Boston patriot or preacher of the Word. In fact, on closer inspection, the man seemed more Wyoming bull rider. Thank goodness he didn't have a shotgun like Old Man Nelson that time.

Nope, he did not look like a preacher, but then appearances could be deceiving. Sarah, it turned out, was hardly a nice girl.

Well, the joke was on Tulane, wasn't it? He didn't really know Sarah after all. How could he be falling in love with a woman he didn't even know?

That scared the crap out of him. He needed to hit the brakes. Hard.

The minister put out his hand as if he expected Tulane to shake it. "Thomas Murray," he said.

Tulane shook the preacher's hand. Sarah's father had a firm and honest grip. "Tulane

Rhodes."

Tulane sidled toward the door. "I'm . . . uh . . . sorry I don't have time to visit, but —"

"Hold on one second there, son. You aren't getting away that easy."

Damn. "No, sir."

"You can call me Tom."

"Tom."

"Have a seat." Tom gestured toward the couch.

"No, sir, I think I'd rather stand."

An enigmatic smile crossed Tom's face. "Well then, I'll be brief."

"That would be appreciated."

"I'll bet. Just one question."

"Uh-huh."

"What, precisely, are your intentions toward my daughter?"

Tulane let go of a bark of laughter.

Tom gave him a strange look. "Son, I don't think that was a funny question."

Tulane sucked it up. "Ah, no, sir, it wasn't. Look, I like your daughter. A lot. But Sarah just made it clear to me that she's not serious about what happened last night."

"She's not?"

"No, sir, she's not. She was just looking for a bad-boy experience, and it's amazing how often I get nominated to play that role.

So, if ya'll don't mind, I'll just be leaving you two to catch up on old times."

And with that, Tulane turned and ran from the apartment like it was a house afire.

CHAPTER 18

At eight o'clock on Friday morning, Steve Phelps straightened his tie and made a quick assessment of himself in the mirror of the National Brands executive washroom. He looked cool, competent, and in control.

He squared his shoulders and headed off toward David Ahearn's office. The summons to the CEO's office was not entirely unexpected.

Steve stepped into the executive suite and was ushered into the inner sanctum, an area on the seventieth floor that commanded an amazing view of midtown Manhattan.

The old man stood up and smiled a cadaverous smile. Boy, the guy needed to give it a break and spend some time on the golf course. He looked like a bald troll, with a pair of reading glasses perched on his forehead, held up by a pair of dark, bushy eyebrows.

"Steve, please, sit, I have something difficult I need to speak with you about." Ahearn gestured toward a genuine black leather Bauhaus chair.

Steve sat. The chair was surprisingly uncomfortable. No doubt that's why Ahearn's interior designer had put it there.

The CEO of National Brands took his seat behind a chrome-and-glass desk the size of an aircraft carrier. He leaned back in his chair.

"Steve, we have a problem."

"Sir?"

"I'm sure you're aware of this negotiation Deidre has been involved with."

"With Penny Farthing Productions?"

"Yes. I'd like to know what you think about it."

Steve clamped down on the smile that wanted to come out. This was not the time to gloat. "Well, I don't know much about it, David. Deidre has been pretty tight-lipped about things. I gather the negotiation is at a delicate phase. That Arnold Simons blog had Deidre in a total snit on Monday, I can tell you that. She's been acting a little erratically, if you want to know. I figure it must be stress."

"Well, that article was a valid concern. But I don't think it was entirely accurate. It seemed to be based in large part on a bunch of local gossip. Besides, Rhodes has an amazingly positive image with our core customer. That blog hasn't dented his positives."

"Exactly my point, sir. Deidre made a mountain out of what was basically a molehill."

"So what do you think about this idea to change the Cottontail Disposables logo?" Ahearn asked.

"It's something of a gamble, isn't it? And it's not as if we haven't been gaining market share in the disposables sector. Have you seen the mail we've been getting about those baby-changing races?"

"Yes, I have. Very positive. Rhodes may be eccentric, but apparently he has a real touch with the kiddies." David's mouth twitched, but he didn't exactly smile. "Which brings me to why I asked you up here so early. Your ideas for the baby-changing races and the entire Cuppa Java campaign have caught just about everyone's attention. We're very pleased."

"Thanks."

"So I need you to take on a difficult and sensitive assignment."

The CEO leaned forward and picked up a small stack of papers stapled at the corner. "Someone in the research department . . ."

He wiggled his eyebrows, and his glasses fell down onto his nose. He leaned back in his chair again and tilted his head to read the name on the memo. "A person named Sarah Murray. You know her?" He looked up from the papers.

"Yes, I do. She's a competent researcher."

"Well, Sarah Murray from the research department has written a very interesting memo. Unfortunately, she e-mailed it to the entire Board. The Board is not used to getting e-mails from the research department. That's not exactly how we do things around here, you know?"

"I understand. Do you want me to fire her? She's in —"

Ahearn threw up a hand. "Oh, no, I wouldn't fire this woman. I think she probably needs a promotion. I gather she's in South Carolina serving as sponsor liaison to Ferguson Racing."

"She is. That was Deidre's idea."

"I see."

"To be honest, David, I don't think Sarah is all that happy living in South Carolina."

"Of course she isn't. Who would be? And I'm sure that explains her memo, which, I might add, is very insightful."

"What memo is that, sir? I don't think she copied me on it."

Ahearn looked over the tops of his reading glasses. "No? Hmmm. She's playing a very high-stakes game, isn't she? I like a person who does that. Deidre is much the same way. Unfortunately, this researcher has not learned the finer points of how the game is played, I think. It's an excellent memo, but it has not made me a happy man."

"Sir, what exactly has Sarah done?" Steve played the innocent.

Ahearn leaned forward, handing Steve the papers he'd been waving around. Steve took the papers, looked down at them, and pretended to study them. He knew exactly what was in that memo. It had Sarah's name on it, and it had been sent from Sarah's old workstation in the research department, but Sarah had not written the memo.

Steve finally looked up. "This is terrible," he said.

"Yes, it is. And unfortunately the entire Board knows about it. And that's bad. I can only assume that this researcher has a serious bone to pick with Deidre."

"It would appear so." Steve nodded his head like a good yes-man.

Ahearn continued, "And you know, if her research wasn't so good, I would have this Sarah Murray woman fired on the spot. But unfortunately, everything in that memo has been verified. It paints a very unflattering picture."

The CEO sighed and leaned back. "I'm disappointed in Deidre. She appears to have lost her focus. I understand her reasons for pushing this Racer Rabbit logo deal, but I can't allow her to commit so much of the company's resources on what is basically a gamble motivated by her own personal tragedy."

"No, I can see that," Steve agreed. "Especially not in this economy. It wouldn't be prudent. And with the Board breathing down your neck . . ." In his head, Steve could almost hear the nails being hammered into Deidre's professional coffin.

"So, Steve, I need your help," Ahearn said.

"What can I do?"

"Well, the Penny Farthing people are meeting with Deidre this noontime at Ferguson Racing in South Carolina. I need you to go down there and put the brakes on this deal. The corporate jet is waiting for you at LaGuardia."

"Okay. I take it Deidre doesn't know I'm coming?"

"No. I haven't been able to reach Deidre by phone this morning. I can't imagine why she's not checking her messages, unless she's avoiding me. But I've got my secretary trying to reach her every fifteen minutes. I'm sure we'll connect with her before you get there, so be prepared.

"Now, about Penny Farthing Productions — we certainly don't want to pay their asking price for the licensing fees, but we don't want to burn any bridges either. You never know what the future will bring, and the idea of Tulane Rhodes and Racer Rabbit teaming up in television commercials is very intriguing."

"It is, sir." And it was probably a winner, because Sarah Murray had dreamed it up, and she had the Midas touch. If Steve could figure out a way to get rid of Deidre but keep Sarah around, he'd be made in the shade.

Ahearn stood up. Steve followed suit. "Steve, I'll need you to tell Deidre to get her butt on the plane. I want her in my office on Monday morning to explain all this."

"Yes, sir."

"And finally, I want you to reassure the Ferguson group. I don't want them thinking this has anything to do with that ridiculous article on OnlyLeftTurns.com. Tulane Rhodes is still a hit with our core customer and our diaper sales are going through the roof. I want you to let them know we want to renegotiate our sponsorship package with them for another year. We're very happy with Tulane Rhodes."

"Okay."

"When you get back on Monday, I want to sit down with you. I'm a firm believer in promoting from within. I think we can probably find you a position that will better suit your talents. Let's talk next week. Set up an appointment with Nancy on your way out."

They shook hands. "Keep in touch this weekend. I need to be able to tell the Board I've got the situation under control."

"I'll handle it, sir. And thanks for this opportunity."

At 8:30 Deidre summoned Sarah to the small conference room on Ferguson Racing's ground floor. Because this weekend's race was scheduled for Darlington, South Carolina, a short distance from the Ferguson Racing headquarters, Sarah wasn't planning to head out to the racetrack until right before qualifying laps started later that afternoon.

In the meantime, Deidre was borrowing space at Ferguson HQ for a working lunch with the Penny Farthing people, and Sarah was on standby while she finished details for the weekend's hospitality events.

Sarah wasn't sure how she was going to

feel when she saw Tulane later in the day. She had not seen him since the debacle on Tuesday morning. He'd been off testing car setups in Las Vegas on Wednesday and Thursday. She was glad of that. Stressing about seeing him again had been keeping her awake at night.

She needed to grow up and accept the fact that Tulane had only given her what she'd asked for.

She should have asked for more.

Sarah pushed through the beechwood doors of the conference room, where Deidre was camping out in advance of her meeting. The room had windows overlooking one of the garage floors. Because it was Friday, things were quiet. Everyone who mattered was out at the racetrack.

The minute Sarah stepped inside the conference room, she knew something was wrong. Deidre was pacing the room, dressed to kill in a cream-colored Chanel suit and Christian Louboutin shoes.

"Sit down." Deidre pointed to a chair on the opposite side of the conference table.

Sarah sat and tried to slow her runaway heart rate. Deidre remained standing. She leaned on the table, towering over Sarah. "You really fooled me. And I'm not easily fooled," Deidre said.

"What's wrong? What happened?"

"Your memo is what happened."

Sarah's body went cold. She thought about several choice curse words, but she didn't say them aloud. Instead, she tried to explain the unexplainable. "Uh, you see, that memo was just a joke, and I —"

"A joke? You think this is a joke? You little conniving b—" Deidre cut off the word she'd been about to say and started pacing the little conference room. She waved her arms around like a crazy person. She was raving mad and, if Sarah could believe her eyes, on the point of tears.

Why would Deidre be so angry about the bunny memo? It might have been a joke, and it certainly humiliated Tulane, but it was selling diapers like crazy.

On the other hand, her memo had backfired spectacularly. It had made Steve Phelps look like a marketing genius. That probably wasn't good for Deidre's career advancement.

Especially since Deidre hadn't actually gotten the joke.

Sarah decided that there was absolutely nothing she could say that would calm Deidre down. So she braced for the tongue-lashing she knew was coming. She had lots of practice doing this. Grandmother Howland had been known for her sudden tempers, too.

Deidre turned and shook a finger at Sarah as if she were actually channeling Grandmother. "That memo is going to cost me my job. You do realize that?"

"Uh . . ."

"Of course you realize it. You set out to get me out of the way from the very start, didn't you?"

"Um, Deidre, really, I'm sorry, but I —"

"Get out of my sight."

"But —"

"You heard me. I should never have trusted you, knowing all the things you've done, all the lies you've told. Get your purse and leave. There's a guard outside the door, waiting to escort you from the building. And I'm telling you, Sarah, if you speak with any of the employees of Ferguson Racing, I will personally get a restraining order out on you." Deidre leaned in on the table.

"Um, Deidre, don't you think you're over —"

"I have never been so wrong about a person in all my life," Deidre ranted over Sarah's feeble attempts to calm her. "You're nothing but a little liar. Get out of here." Deidre waved her arms and looked like she might actually breathe fire. There was no point arguing. So Sarah got up and left the room, only to find one of the Ferguson Racing security guards standing there waiting for her.

He escorted her to her third-floor cubby, allowing her to get her purse but making her leave her laptop and BlackBerry, both of which were National Brands property, behind. She was cut off from the rest of humanity, standing in the middle of South Carolina.

The guard saw her to the front door and suggested, in a polite Southern drawl, that she should leave the premises as quickly as possible.

Sarah crossed the large parking lot in a complete daze. She got into her rental car and shut the door. The heat grew. She had nowhere to go. No one she could turn to.

Except Tulane.

Every cell in her body longed to go find him so she could cry on his shoulder like she had done on Monday morning. Tulane had defended her from Deidre on Monday like a big, gallant dragon slayer. But he wasn't going to defend her this time.

Not when he learned the truth. When Tulane learned the truth, he'd react just like he had on Tuesday morning when he'd learned the truth about her father.

She rested her head on the steering wheel. Her world was caving in on her.

She really had lost her job this time. National Brands wasn't going to rehire a person who wrote memos and put other people's names on them.

But even worse than losing her job was the fact that she'd lost Tulane.

Not that she'd ever actually had him. But in her silly heart she had hoped.

Now even the hope was gone.

On Friday afternoon, Tulane stood beside his pink car at the tail end of a long line of brightly painted race cars, awaiting his turn to qualify for the weekend's main event.

He should have been thinking about car setups and all the stuff Doc had been talking about, like tire pressure and forward grip on a track that the sun was heating up with every passing minute.

But he wasn't thinking about cars or track conditions.

He was thinking about Sarah.

He hadn't seen her since Tuesday morning when he'd escaped from her apartment. Looking back on that moment, he was completely ashamed.

He should have stood his ground and staked his claim. He'd had all those romantic plans for the morning, but somehow when faced with her father's question about his intentions, he'd clutched.

Like a moron. Or a not very mature person.

He needed to find Sarah as quickly as possible and apologize. He needed to explain that he never wanted a one-night stand. He should have explained that before they went to bed in the first place. He had really screwed up.

So as soon as he was finished qualifying, he was going to find her and clear the air. He'd been wanting to do this for a couple of days, but he'd been off in Vegas testing car setups. He could have called her, but the conversation he wanted to have with Sarah needed to take place face-to-face. Talking about a serious relationship with a woman was not something a guy did over the phone or in an e-mail.

While he waited for his turn to qualify, Tulane scanned the crowd, searching for her. Jim had mentioned something about her working at headquarters until later in the afternoon. Everyone had expected her to show up in time for qualifying.

She was probably hiding from him. That must explain why he hadn't seen her all day. And it was just his rotten luck that he'd drawn the last spot for qualifying.

"Okay, you ready?" Doc said, breaking into his thoughts.

"Uh, yeah."

Tulane climbed into his car and took off.

Fifteen minutes later, he was sitting on cloud nine, having just turned in a lap that not only put him on the pole for Sunday's race, but also destroyed the track record by a full two-tenths of a second.

He pulled the car back into the pits, disconnected his safety harness and head restraint, and hoisted himself through the window. He scanned the immediate area.

Sarah had to be here somewhere. It was almost three o'clock. He set out to find her, only he didn't get very far.

He was tackled almost immediately by a scrum of reporters from Fox, TNT, and the Speed Channel who wanted comments because he'd just won the pole for Sunday's race. He put on his "aw shucks" demeanor and talked about his car and his team and his sponsor.

A blonde reporter for the Speed Channel shoved a microphone in his face, and he prepared for the inevitable question about how it felt to win the pole wearing a pink suit.

"Do you have any comment about the apparent shake-up at National Brands? And do you think this is because of what Arnold Simons wrote on his blog this week?"

Tulane should have expected this question. But he'd been too busy thinking about Sarah.

"I'm not aware of any shake-up at National Brands, and I have no comment about Arnold Simons's blog." Tulane clamped down on his back teeth so he wouldn't do something stupid like tell the reporter where she could shove her microphone.

In the next instant, Jim Ferguson materialized beside him, his face grim. "Ladies and gentlemen," he said in his slow Texas drawl, "I can assure you our relationship with National Brands has not changed. The decision to recall their sponsor liaison is a staffing decision and nothing more."

Every nerve ending in Tulane's body jangled. Sarah had been recalled? What the hell.

Five new questions were hurled in Jim's direction, but he smiled and said, "I have no further comment." Then he grabbed Tulane by the upper arm and pointed him in the direction of the team hauler. Five minutes later, Tulane found himself in the hauler's cramped sitting room, facing the serious faces of Jim Ferguson, Sam Sterling, and Doc Jackson.

"What's all this crap about Sarah being recalled?"

Jim cleared his throat. "This morning, Deidre asked to have one of our security people escort Sarah from our building. I gather Deidre was upset about something Sarah wrote, but I don't know all the details. A little later Steve Phelps showed up and sent Deidre back to New York on the company jet. Steve has assured me that our sponsorship with National Brands is going to be extended another year. But the car seat safety program has been canceled."

"But —" Tulane started to get up and Sam pushed him down in his seat. "You need to keep calm, boy. You just won the pole. The best thing is to just ignore the crap and focus on driving."

"Jim, can I borrow your phone? I need to talk with Deidre."

"Are you sure?" Jim asked.

Tulane nodded. "I need to know the truth."

Jim pulled his cell phone from his pocket. "Before you call her, I want you to remember one thing — in this business you have to roll with the corporate punches."

"Right." Tulane found Deidre in the

contacts list and pushed the call button.

"Jim?" Deidre answered.

"No, it's Tulane Rhodes. Why was Sarah fired?"

"Because she's a lying, conniving, heartless person."

This described Deidre, not Sarah. "What did she do, aside from keeping my secrets from you for the last few months?"

"Kept your secrets? Ha, that's a laugh. She kept secrets *from* you. Like the fact that she wrote the memo that put you in the pink car."

"What?"

"Everything was her idea — even the baby-changing races. I'll send you the memo. In fact, I'll send you all the memos — even the one that explains why you're more valuable to National Brands wearing pink than any other color."

His body went numb.

Deidre continued, "She put Steve Phelps's name on her first memo. I was fooled by that. I thought she wanted revenge, but now I'm certain that she and Steve are in it together."

"In what together?"

"They set us both up. We fell for their car seat safety gambit like a couple of rubes."

"The car seat, what?" Tulane asked.

406

"Sarah knows how to research. She discovered you and I have something in common. And she used it."

"Used what?"

There was a long pause on the other end of the phone before Deidre spoke again. "Fifteen years ago, I was in a car accident. My two-year-old daughter's car seat wasn't compatible with the car's restraint system, and she died in the crash. Sarah found out about that. And she found out about your niece. She played us, Tulane."

Tulane connected with the sudden emotion in Deidre's voice. "Oh, God. I'm so sorry."

"She and Steve Phelps used our interest in starting a car seat program to undermine me with the Board of Directors. First she suggested the program; then she made me look like a crazy woman for pursuing it. I'm going to lose my job over this."

The cold that seized Tulane turned lethal. He didn't think he would ever feel warm again. Anger was not the word for this. It was something else. Something he had no name for.

The bullies had just struck again.

But Sarah couldn't be a bully, could she? He wanted to trust her. But he also knew that Sarah was a capable and devious liar.

She had lied to Deidre for weeks. She had lied about her father.

He'd been free-falling without knowing it. But he knew it now. Hitting the ground hurt. Bad.

He said good-bye and handed Jim the cell phone. Sam slapped him across the shoulders. "Son, take my advice. Find yourself a nice little Southern girl next time."

After that, Sam, Doc, and Jim didn't give Tulane any time to think. They escorted him to his mobile home, where the No. 57 Team had organized a party to celebrate winning the pole position for Sunday's race.

Thank goodness Lori Sterling had brought plenty of rum punch.

CHAPTER 19

When Sarah finally walked into her temporary apartment, the immensity of what had
happened hit her like a slap across the face.

She was a failure. They had even taken
away her corporate-issued BlackBerry and
laptop, which meant she had no one's
contact information. She couldn't even
make travel arrangements without finding a
pay phone.

Even if she had been able to contact an
airline, where was she going to go?

Back to New York? Her apartment in
Brooklyn was sublet through November, the
end of the racing season.

Back to Boston? Her parents were not cur-
rently speaking with her, since they hadn't
forgiven her for behaving like a slut.

So without a laptop, phone, or future, she
sat on her couch like a zombie until around
five o'clock, when her doorbell rang.

She experienced a moment of wild hope,

which was utterly dashed when she opened the door to find Steve Phelps standing on the other side.

He was handsome, in a preppie, frat-boy kind of way, with his blond hair hanging over one of his half-mast blue eyes. He looked all Madison Avenue in his buttoned-down, Polo-logo oxford shirt and gray slacks. He'd ditched his jacket and tie, but he appeared to be carrying Sarah's laptop case.

"I've come to take you back," he said.

"Back where?"

He snorted a laugh and sauntered into her apartment. "Back into the fold, Sarah." He stopped and gave the living room the once-over. "I see National Brands spared no expense with their housing allowance." As usual Steve's sarcasm was dripping all over the place.

He settled onto the couch, leaned back, and cocked one leg over the other. "So, you got anything worth drinking in this place?"

Did he expect her to be his servant? Or was he trying to make her feel small because she didn't keep beer in her refrigerator?

"I have water," she said with all the puritanical dignity she could muster.

He let go of a sigh. "Look, Sarah, you're a smart woman, so lose the attitude and sit down." He pointed to the facing easy chair.

He was kidding, right? *She* had attitude? Maybe she should actually display some and employ the profanity Tulane had taught her. It was an enticing thought. On the other hand, the quickest way to get the jerk out of her apartment was to play by his rules.

And after he left, she could shower off the slime.

She sank into the easy chair.

He smiled like the proverbial evil nemesis. "David Ahearn disapproves of your methods, but he's very impressed with your research abilities and your hardhearted business sense. David thinks you're a player."

"What?" A frisson of surprise and shock shuddered through her. "David Ahearn doesn't have the slightest idea that I exist. I'm a peon."

"Not anymore, thanks to me. In fact, your memo on the Penny Farthing negotiations has definitely improved your cachet. I'm sorry David wasn't more amused by it, but he was very impressed. And in my experience, impressing a CEO is way better than amusing one of them."

"What memo on the Penny Farthing negotiations?"

Steve cocked his head. "Deidre didn't

explain why she fired you? You didn't ask?"

"She said she was angry about the memo. I assumed she was angry about the pink car memo. Although, to be honest, I couldn't quite understand why she would be *that* angry about a memo that has been selling diapers like mad."

The snarky smile remained plastered on Steve's face as he unzipped the computer case and pulled out some papers stapled at the corner. "You need to read this."

She took the papers and began to read, her heart rate climbing right into the stratosphere with every word.

When she finished, she felt like she might be sick. "Deidre had a kid who died in a car wreck? How did you find that out? And how did you get these numbers about the Penny Farthing deal?" The numbers were accurate, but they were dated. Deidre had done a masterful job in negotiating down the license fees for use of the cartoon character. That memo with Sarah's name on it was misleading — and completely nasty.

Steve shrugged. "I have friends in the IT department. I hacked Deidre's computer."

"Deidre really believes I wrote this crap?"

Steve leaned back into the couch pillows. "Oh, yes. She does. Don't you think that's fabulous? I mean, no one gets the drop on the Dragon Lady. But you did."

"I did nothing of the kind."

"Hmm, that's true. But then again, I'm not the one who dreamed up those baby races. Kind of evens up the score and puts us back into the same boat, doesn't it?"

Sarah shot him her best dirty look.

"Oh, c'mon, Sarah, quit looking at me that way," Steve said. "David Ahearn thinks you rock. He thinks you have the potential to be another Dragon Lady. And since the old Dragon Lady is . . . well . . . a little off her rocker . . ."

"David Ahearn thinks I'm a Dragon Lady?" Her voice sounded small and insignificant.

"Well, not yet, but you have potential. He told me that you needed to get out of the library."

She stood up and paced to the window and looked out onto the parking lot and the suburban scene beyond. "You came to give me my job back?"

"Yes. And no. I don't want to give you a job in the research department or as the sponsor liaison to Ferguson Racing. I want you on my marketing team. But there are rules."

"Ah, rules." Weren't there always.

"Your job is to make me look brilliant.

You've already done a good job of that. And in return for making me look brilliant, I will take care of you and make people afraid of you. Oh, and you'll get a lot more money."

"You trust me that far?" She turned around and stared at him.

He gave her one of his phony innocent-me looks. "Sarah, please don't make me laugh. We both know you have no talent for nasty corporate games. But you do have a talent for marketing. Together, we're a team made in Heaven."

"No."

She turned and stalked into the kitchen. She yanked open the refrigerator because she needed something to do with her restless hands, and she was afraid to open the drawer where she kept her knives. Murder seemed like a fitting reward for Steve Phelps, but Sarah wasn't ready to break any more commandments.

The fridge was practically empty. Boy, she could use a beer right at the moment. Or a margarita. Or something stronger that would make her numb.

Steve followed her and leaned in the kitchen doorway. "Well, okay, you can choose not to take this offer. But if you're thinking that you have any kind of future down here with Ferguson Racing or any other NASCAR team, you can forget it. Deidre has pretty much told everyone you're dishonest, and the yokels around here seem to value honesty. It's kind of funny, actually."

Anger of a kind Sarah had never known hit her bloodstream. She felt hot all over. Her hands shook. Her head throbbed. She slammed the refrigerator door closed and almost launched herself at Steve.

"You bastard."

Steve shrugged. "Me? I don't think so. C'mon, Sarah, I've done you a favor. I've created an impression that you are cool and driven — just the kind of go-getter David Ahearn admires. I've just given you everything you ever wanted."

Sarah stood rooted to the cheap vinyl flooring and tried to keep from throwing up. Steve was right. Ever since that Cuppa Java thing had happened, Sarah had been working diligently to lose her niceness.

So diligently, in fact, that she'd done a few heinous things she wasn't proud of. She might not have written the memo that wrecked Deidre's life, but she *had* written the pink car memo and put someone else's name on it. That memo had hurt and humiliated Tulane and his pit crew. She had lied about that memo.

All of that might be forgivable, except that she'd also used Tulane. She'd even slept with him, after going on about how all she wanted was a sex coach and a one-night stand.

Mother and Dad were right to be disappointed in her.

She was disappointed in herself.

Sarah took two steps toward Steve, her fists balling up. "I don't want your job. I don't want to be a player. I want to be a nice girl from Boston."

"Sarah, are you crazy? I'm offering you everything."

"Maybe you are, but I value my soul. I've lost my way these last few weeks, but I've found it again. Now get out of here."

He pointed a long finger at her. "You'll regret this."

"No, I don't think so. Many other things, yes, but not this."

"Look, Sarah, I need you."

Was he whining? Oh yeah, maybe a little. "I'm sure you need me, Steve. I heard they gave you the Rice Doodles account. Good luck with that."

"Sarah, please, listen, I can get you everything you want."

"You mean everything I *wanted*. Past tense. I've grown. I don't want what you're offering. Now leave."

His shoulders slumped as Steve turned. He picked up the computer bag and headed for the door. He turned back right before he left. "You can kiss your relationship good-bye with the people at Ferguson, especially with that yokel of a driver."

Steve's poison dart hit her heart, but Sarah stoically resisted the urge to cry out. She loved Tulane, but she hadn't told him how she felt. And by not telling him the truth, she had hurt him — terribly. She saw that now. He was never going to forgive her. Not in a million years.

After Steve left, the real crying jag hit. Sarah bawled herself to sleep. And when she awakened at nine o'clock on Saturday morning, even a hot shower couldn't undo the damage she'd done to her nose and eyes.

Her reality was so not good. She was alone in Florence, South Carolina without a friend, or a cell phone, or a computer. And Miriam Randall's prediction loomed large in Sarah's mind, as she imagined a boring new life in Boston, dating a seminary student.

Well, there was nothing to be done about it. So, with a stoicism she had inherited from her New England ancestors, she set about making that future a reality.

She made a to-do list. The first two items were:

1. Get a phone.
2. Call Tulane and apologize.

She pondered these items. She had a problem, because Tulane's telephone number had been stored in her BlackBerry. She had not bothered to memorize it. She added a new #2 to her list: Call Ruby and get Tulane's number.

She studied this new item for a long moment. The number of the Cut 'n Curl would be listed, but this to-do item seemed fraught with pitfalls.

Ruby could hang up on her. And then where would she be?

She crossed out "Call Ruby" and wrote "Drive to Last Chance and speak with Ruby."

Tulane's head hurt. He cracked an eye and blessed whoever it was who had put him to bed the night before. They'd had the foresight to shut the blinds and put a bottle of Excedrin and a glass of water on the bedside table.

He took his medicine and swore that he

would never, ever again touch Lori Sterling's rum punch.

He checked his watch. It was nine in the morning. He should have been up and about an hour ago, checking in at the garage and going over the schedule for Saturday's hospitality and sponsor events with Sarah. He squeezed his eyes shut. Thinking about Sarah made his heart hurt worse than his head.

But last night, after he'd read the various corporate memos that Sarah had penned, he'd forgotten his rule about Lori's punch.

Boy, Sarah sure had a head for business. But her heart was missing.

He hauled his butt out of bed. Even though Sarah was gone, sooner or later someone was going to show up and give him something to occupy his time. Usually, on a Saturday, his time was spent making the sponsor happy.

And, the aftereffects of the rum punch notwithstanding, his sponsor had left a real sour taste in his mouth.

He dragged himself into the shower and stood there until he ran out of hot water. That wasn't very long, this being a mobile home. His hands weren't steady enough to shave, so he just toweled off, threw on a pair of old jeans and a T-shirt, and declared himself dressed.

It was almost ten by then, and Tulane had decided that he didn't want to be found. So he jammed his old Braves ball cap on his still-wet head and snuck out of his mobile home. Without his pink bunny shirt and khakis, he looked like just another NASCAR fan. He was able to make it all the way to the parking lot without being asked for a single autograph.

He found his Mustang and escaped. He turned onto one of South Carolina's more obscure two-lane roads, punched the gas, and let the miles roll by.

He needed to try to do what Daddy said and toss out all the garbage that had been cluttering up his mind. Sarah Murray was the first piece of trash he needed to get rid of.

It was a little after ten when the old-fashioned bell at the front of the beauty parlor announced Sarah's arrival at the Cut 'n Curl. The aroma of shampoo and body wave hit her like a slap to the face.

And maybe the ammonia smell of the permanent solution woke up a few of Sarah's sleeping brain cells. Or maybe it was the six pairs of eyes that suddenly aimed in her direction. The leadership of the Committee to Resurrect Golfing for God appeared to be all present and accounted for.

The president, Hettie Marshall, was getting a manicure. The secretary, Thelma Hanks, was under a dryer. The treasurer, Millie Polk, was getting a body wave. The vice president, Miriam Randall, was enjoying the company of the others, and the ex officio members of the board, Jane and Ruby Rhodes, were hard at work.

"Good Lord, sugar, what happened to you?" Ruby said.

"Shouldn't you be at the track?" Jane asked with a frown.

Thelma ducked out of the dryer and said, "I knew what we saw down at the golf course on Monday was going to be a problem."

"Hush up, Thelma; you should have more faith." Millie rolled her eyes in Miriam's direction.

"Cried yourself to sleep, huh?" Miriam asked.

Hettie looked down and said nothing. She was wearing Ralph Lauren casual today.

Sarah hesitated. These ladies were going to run her out of town on a rail when they discovered the truth. Even if Sarah hadn't written the memo that trashed Deidre's career and the car seat safety program, she

421

had still written the pink car memo and lied about it. She'd lied about Dad. She'd lied about her feelings. She'd even lied about those stupid ground rules she'd made up last Monday night.

She was ashamed of herself.

When she made huge mistakes like this as a little girl, she had been required to make a full and accurate accounting of herself in front of Grandmother Howland. Grandmother may have been from good Puritan stock, but she believed in the concept of penance.

So facing Ruby and the rest of the members of the committee was nothing more or less than Sarah's chance to make a full confession. Maybe if she accounted for all her actions, Ruby would take pity on her and give her Tulane's telephone number.

"Uh," she said as the tears gathered in her eyes. "See, I lost my job and Tulane hates me and it's all my fault because, see, I wrote the memo that put him in a pink car . . ." She couldn't finish, because two things happened.

She started bawling like a little kid.

And Ruby Rhodes put down the permanent roller she'd been holding, stepped across the room, and pulled her into a big, motherly hug.

"Now, you hush, sugar, because I'm sure Tulane doesn't hate you. After all, you're a minister's daughter, aren't you?"

Sarah pushed back, wiping tears away. "Uh, yeah, how did you know that?" Tulane wouldn't have told his mother about Tuesday morning, would he?

"I'm to blame," Jane said, getting up and coming to join in what was becoming a group hug. "You told me the night Pete died, and I know I said I would keep it a secret, but I told Clay and Clay mentioned it to Ruby. Clay couldn't keep a secret if his life depended upon it."

"Now, Sarah, you just calm down, because everything will work out. You'll see." Ruby gave her another big squeeze.

"You're a preacher's daughter?" Thelma asked. "I don't believe it — really?"

"Yeah, I know, I really haven't been behaving like one, have I?"

Ruby rubbed Sarah's backbone. "Never you mind, sugar. Just dry your eyes and I'll get you some sweet tea and you can tell us what happened." She gave Sarah a critical look and then pulled the banana clip from her hair. "I told you to stop wearing these things. I think after you tell us what's wrong, we'll just fix you up with some highlights."

"And a French manicure," Jane added.

"But you won't like me after I tell you what happened." Tears began to leak from Sarah's eyes and Jane pressed a tissue into her hand.

"Oh, I doubt that," Ruby said.

It was almost noon when Tulane topped a hill and spied Last Chance's watermelon-striped water tower through the windshield of his Ford.

He had driven himself home.

Again.

Irritation prickled his skin. What was he doing here? Pete was dead.

But Daddy was alive, and Tulane felt the sudden need to let Daddy in on the truth about Sarah.

He drove by Momma and Daddy's house, but Elbert's truck wasn't in the driveway, so he headed south toward Golfing for God.

Tulane pulled his Mustang into the parking lot, right next to Daddy's old pickup. The sound of a weed-whacker split the serenity of the summer day as Tulane opened his car door.

Daddy was cutting weeds, like he always did every summer. For some reason, knowing that Daddy wasn't moping around the house made Tulane feel a little better. He tried hard to push that positive thought out of his mind, because he wasn't here for anything positive.

He was here to make Daddy see the truth. Finally.

He got out of his Mustang and slammed the door. He strode down the gravel walk, the midsummer sun casting short shadows in the middle of a hot, humid day.

Tulane found Elbert trimming the main walkway. Beyond Daddy the ark baked in the noonday sun, its peeling paint giving the place a seedy feel. Even so, the grounds at Golfing for God had been tidied. The place looked better than it had on Monday morning.

"Hey, Daddy," Tulane called, his voice tight, even to his own ears.

Elbert killed the motor on the weed-whacker and turned with a slow grin. "What brings you to Golfing for God this morning? Aren't you supposed to be up in Darlington?" Elbert leaned the whacker against a pine tree. His T-shirt today said "Enlighten Up!"

"I've come to set you straight."

"Set *me* straight? About what?"

"About Sarah. Daddy, she used you. And she made a fool out of both of us. She's a liar and —" Tulane bit off his own words.

He couldn't manage to say the rest, because the emotions he'd tamped down suddenly bubbled up and caught in the back of his throat.

Daddy seemed unaffected. He stood with his feet planted wide, the noonday sun glinting on his gray hair like a halo.

"Did you hear what I said?" Tulane raged, his voice ragged.

"Well, you don't have to shout. I don't believe Sarah's a liar or that she used me, son."

"Well, you should believe it. She set me up. She set all of us up."

"Uh-huh. And what makes you think this?"

"Oh, crap, it's a big complicated mess." With that Tulane started to pace the walkway as he described every one of Sarah's underhanded, no-account, dishonest actions. When he finished his detailed indictment, Tulane didn't feel any better. Especially since Daddy didn't seem very impressed with it.

Elbert stood with his hands planted on his hips and said, "Let me get this straight. You think that Sarah put Hettie up to forming the Committee to Resurrect Golfing for God for some cockeyed scheme to advance her career. And then, once we got the com-

426

mittee rolling, Sarah turned on us and made us look like fools by talking to that idiot Arnold Simons?"

Tulane stopped pacing and gave his father a dirty look. "Daddy, this is not about Golfing for God. It's about the stupid pink car, and the car seat program, and all those nasty interviews they did of me, and then that vicious article about Haley." He took a couple of steps toward his father. "Are you even listening?"

"Oh, I can hear you. But you're wrong. This is not about a pink car or that nasty blog. This is, actually, about the golf course."

"You're crazy." Tulane turned and took two steps. He wanted to scream out so loud that the angels would hear him.

"You can think what you like," Daddy said.

Tulane heard the disappointment in his father's voice. He took several deep breaths and tugged hard at the anger that was about to pull him out of control. When he'd managed to center himself again, he turned around.

"I'm sorry I said that."

"I accept your apology. Besides, I didn't take it literally."

"Daddy, don't you see, she used me."

"Well, that might be true, son. But Sarah didn't use me. And she didn't use Haley, or Hettie, or your mother or any of the ladies that formed that committee. I don't think she talked to Arnold Simons at all, although Lillian Bray sure did run her mouth off to that man when he came through town looking for background."

"He came here?"

"Yeah. He came. I didn't talk to him. And near as I could tell, he didn't have any inside information when he arrived. Whatever nastiness he printed in that online blog of his came from Lillian. Lord knows that woman could poison the sweetest well on earth."

"But, Daddy —"

Daddy put up a hand and gave Tulane his scary father look. "No, son, you listen now. Did you know that Sarah came down here on her day off and worked with the church ladies to help them organize their nonprofit committee? She wrote up a whole list of instructions about what they needed to set it up, legal like. She spent a lot of time on that. Ruby and Hettie were so grateful. Sarah didn't have to do that, you know? And I don't see where a person who does a thing like that is evil or nasty. And I sure can't figure out how helping the committee get started was part of some crazy master plan designed to advance her career. So, I'm sorry, Tulane, but I don't think I'm crazy or deluded when it comes to Sarah. I like that girl. A lot."

"But —"

"And lemme tell you one more thing. You going off and listening to the ugly things those people from New York had to say and then rushing over here to spread that filth makes you just the same as them. Good Lord, Tulane, you should know better than anyone that just because someone says something ugly don't mean it's true. When did you become a bully, like Lillian and those New York people?"

Tulane backed up a step. The sun beat down on him, but all the heat inside him suddenly froze. Everything froze except his brain.

His brain, on the other hand, started to add things up, but it ran into some serious inconsistencies in the data.

"But if it's not true, why didn't she defend herself? Daddy, I saw the memos with my own eyes. She wrote one that said it didn't matter if I won any races, because just having someone like me in a pink car would sell diapers."

"Well, I reckon she was right about that.

It did sell diapers. And it's her job to sell diapers. You can't hold that against her, Tulane."

"But she wrote the memo about the pink car."

"Well, I reckon that sold a lot of diapers, too."

"But she wrote this awful nasty memo about Deidre and her child, Daddy. I just couldn't believe that Sarah would do a thing like that. And if she was capable of doing that, well, then she was capable of playing us all like fools. Me included."

Daddy smiled. "And how did she play you for a fool?"

Tulane wasn't going to explain about the one night he'd spent in Sarah's bed. He just said, "She broke my heart." The words came out husky.

It was hard to admit the truth. But the way his chest felt right at that moment, he knew for a fact that his heart was not just broken, it was shattered. He wanted Sarah like nothing else, but the Sarah he wanted didn't really exist.

"Oh, I see." Daddy sounded concerned now. The humor had left his voice. "A broken heart is an awful thing. You just have to look at what a broken heart has done to your oldest brother. I can't help you with a

430

thing like that either. On the other hand, I'm sincerely glad to hear you have a heart to break. It shows maturity on your part."

Tulane closed his eyes and kind of sagged where he stood. His head hurt. His heart hurt. He was confused.

"Did you ever tell Sarah that you love her?" Daddy asked.

Tulane opened his eyes. "I was going to."

"You were *going to?* Son, that's not the same as actually telling a woman you love her, you know. It's hard to be brokenhearted if you never actually say the words."

"I was *going to.* I had it all planned out for yesterday. I planned to have a serious conversation with her about a relationship."

"Well, that sounds grown-up of you, I guess."

"But then the shit hit the fan, you know? And then everyone was telling me that she wasn't worth it."

"And you didn't come to her defense when the bullies attacked? Boy, that's a change in your usual MO. I can't remember how many fights you got into over me. And I know you love me."

Tulane blinked. "Daddy, last Monday you told me I should ignore the bullies, not fight them."

"Well, yeah, you could have ignored them

431

and gone and found Sarah and had that serious conversation. But you didn't do that either. From the purple bags under your eyes, I'd be willing to bet you did something stupid instead, like getting drunk."

"Oh, crap." An emotion that was both wonderful and awful gnawed at Tulane's insides. Was this how Racer Rabbit felt every Saturday morning when the clueless bunny finally figured out the lesson he was supposed to learn?

"I *am* an idiot," Tulane said.

"Yup. You are," Daddy agreed. "But you wouldn't be the first Rhodes male to stake a claim to that title. Clay behaved pretty idiotically when Jane crossed his path, too. You missed that last October when you were off testing cars. It was right entertaining there for a while watching that boy squirm."

"I gotta go, Daddy. I gotta find her. You think she's already gone home to Boston?"

"Uh, no. I don't think so."

"No?"

"Absolutely not." Daddy grinned like the proverbial cat who had lunched on the canary.

"Daddy? What's going on?"

"Well," Elbert said, "the truth is that Sarah's at the Cut 'n Curl, having her hair and nails done. Now, mind you, she didn't exactly come to get her hair and nails done, that's just a by-product of the real reason she came, which was to get your phone number."

"But she has my phone number."

"No, I guess it was in her corporate-issue BlackBerry, which National Brands took away from her when they fired her. And if you ask me, that is truly tragic, when you think about the way Sarah used that thing to manage Pete's funeral."

"She came to get my phone number?"

"Uh-huh, something about needing to apologize to you for something she wrote. Anyways, your momma called and told me I should send you to the Cut 'n Curl just as soon as you showed up."

"When I showed up?"

"Uh-huh, see, Miriam and your momma have been waiting on you since about ten this morning, on account of the fact that Miriam Randall is never wrong."

"What are you talking about?"

"Son, Miriam told your momma that you would marry a preacher's daughter back when you were about fifteen years old. None of us really believed it until Sarah showed up. So anyway, Sarah came to your mother this morning, full of apologies for things that weren't really her fault. And

Ruby's been keeping Sarah on ice, so to speak, until you showed up. Apparently, Miriam was certain you would show up before lunch. You're running a little late."

"Miriam said I would marry a preacher's daughter? Really?" Something eased in Tulane's chest. "Hey, wait, how did ya'll know Sarah was a preacher's daughter? I didn't even know that until last Tuesday."

"Well, I guess she told Jane. And Jane told Clay, and you know how that works. Once Clay knows a thing, it's not a secret anymore."

"So when did ya'll know this?"

"Oh, well, I think Clay told me on the day Pete was buried. That's why your momma has been working so hard to match you two up."

"Momma's been what?"

Elbert put up his hand. "Son, I try not to pay attention to details when it comes to stuff like that, but Ruby and Jane were laughing about some kind of pointy-toed boots or something. Look, if you want my advice, you should just give up. Sarah was made for you. You have Miriam's word on that. If I were you, I'd get my butt over to the Cut 'n Curl and start apologizing. Take it from me, there ain't nothing a woman loves more than a man who knows how to grovel and beg forgiveness."

CHAPTER 20

Sarah hadn't managed to get Tulane's phone number from Ruby. She'd confessed all her sins, and the members of the Committee to Resurrect Golfing for God had absolved her of all wrongdoing. Except for the pink car memo, which they all agreed was an idiotic way to wreak revenge but which had, nevertheless, turned out to be a brilliant piece of marketing.

Sarah had lost count of the glasses of sweet tea she'd consumed while Jane did her nails and Ruby added highlights to her hair. But she had failed in her mission.

Sarah firmed her resolve. When Ruby finished blow-drying her hair, she would make a stand. She *would* get Tulane's phone number.

And just then, the bell above the Cut 'n Curl's door jangled.

Sarah looked into the mirror, which reflected the door, to see what new denizen of

Last Chance had come by to gossip. The shop seemed to be overflowing with ladies this morning. Most of them weren't even getting their hair done.

But it wasn't one of the female residents of Last Chance. No, this visitor was definitely male. And the minute Tulane walked into that shop, Sarah's autonomic nervous system went haywire.

He wore his favorite Alabama T-shirt and looked like he'd rolled right out of bed this morning. A cowlick stood straight up in the back of his head that would have made him look about twelve — except for the day-old beard darkening his cheeks. Sarah's fingers itched to push that little tuft of hair back into its place. God, she loved the feel of his hair against her palm.

She ached with the thought that she would never touch him that way again. It was over between them.

She needed to apologize and then go home to Boston.

Ruby shut off the blow-dryer, and Sarah hopped down from the chair, still wearing her beauty shop drape. She turned and met him face-to-face.

"Tulane. This is a surprise."

"Not as big a surprise as finding you here." His drawl was deep and did some-

437

thing wicked to her insides. She loved him. She wanted to fall into him. But he was angry. The little muscle along his jaw was working. And when his muscle twitched like that, it was a warning sign.

"I was going to call you. Just as soon as your mother gave me your phone number."

Tulane's sober gaze flicked over the gallery of Last Chance ladies, who were following the conversation like spectators of a close tennis match. Sarah was suddenly glad for the audience. She was going to prostrate herself, and having witnesses was probably part of the penance she needed to serve before she could clear her conscience and move on with her life.

So she reached deep for that quiet authority that Grandmother Howland always possessed when faced with a difficult situation.

"I need to apolo—" They spoke in unison.

"What do *you* need to apologize for?" Sarah said.

"For believing that crap Deidre told me yesterday. I read that memo you wrote, Sarah. I'm still trying to understand how a person like you could write a thing like that."

Despite Sarah's efforts to remain quiet, logical, and formidable, her hands began to shake and heat crawled up her cheeks. "I know. It was really stupid. And my explanation is equally lame. Steve stole one of my ideas, and I thought if I wrote something silly, put his name on it, and then put it on Deidre's desk, it would take his reputation down a little. I never gave one thought to what might happen if Deidre took the memo seriously. And I never even considered what putting a man in a pink car and driver's suit would do to him. You've been incredibly patient. Really. I admire that about you."

"Thanks, but —" She held up her hand to stop him.

"No, let me finish. I've learned my lesson. If I hadn't been so set on getting revenge, or trying to be something that I'm not, then none of this would have happened. So see, I'm really, really sorry for the pain I caused you. And I can assure you that I'm going back to Boston and I'm not ever going to break any rules again."

She ran out of breath.

Defeat curled around her insides when she saw the expression on Tulane's face. She wasn't sure what that vulnerable look was all about. He might be about to explode in a profanity bomb, or he might be about to laugh at her.

"I wasn't talking about the baby-changing

memo," he said.

"Oh."

"I want to understand why you used the death of Deidre's baby the way you did. I want to believe that you couldn't write a thing like that. But it has your name on it. I don't want to doubt you. But doubt is eating me alive."

"Oh. You read *all* the memos?" Her voice came out in a whisper.

"Deidre sent them to me yesterday. I have to tell you that the one you wrote where you said I didn't have to win a race to sell diapers really stung. But not as bad as the one where you trashed Deidre. The Sarah I've come to know would never do a thing like that."

Sarah twisted her fingers together. "I don't expect you to believe me, but I didn't even know Deidre had lost a child in a car wreck. Honestly. I didn't write that memo. Steve wrote it. He wrote it to get rid of Deidre. He offered me a job last night, but I told him to go to hell."

Tulane's lips twitched, and he shoved his hands into his pockets. He looked emotional. Unshed tears glittered in his eyes.

"Look," Sarah said, "I'm not trying to get out of the blame for what happened. I may not have written that awful, hurtful memo, but everything that happened is still my fault. I'm so, so sorry about everything that's happened. And now that I've apologized, I'll just get out of your life."

Sarah pulled the beauty shop drape from around her neck and handed it to Ruby, who was standing there with tears in her eyes, too. A quick inspection of the other women in the shop showed that half of them had their hankies out. Mascara was running all over the place.

"Thanks for the haircut," Sarah said. "How much do I owe you?"

Ruby gave her a little hug and kind of pushed her forward, toward Tulane. "Sugar, you owe me a grandbaby when the time is right."

Sarah didn't have a chance to examine that comment, because the next thing she knew, she was enveloped in Tulane's arms. He pulled her right in to his chest, the way he'd done on Monday, and he pressed his lips to the top of her head. He smelled great, like himself, and his breath feathered over her skin. She sagged against him.

"I accept your apology," he whispered. "And I'm really sorry that for about ten hours I believed what Deidre said about you. I should have listened to my heart instead of the bullies. I'm so sorry I didn't come find you last night. I was stupid. I let Lori Sterling feed me her rum punch, and you know how deadly that stuff is."

Sarah closed her eyes and drank in the sensation of coming home.

"Uh, Sarah, we need to go someplace private, 'cause there's something else I have to say."

She looked up at him. "I don't think so. The ladies are here as witnesses, I think." Tears of relief were starting to smear her vision.

"Yes we are, Tulane, so get on with it," Ruby said.

"Yes, ma'am." His smile broke out in earnest as he looked down at Sarah. "I have something else I need to apologize for."

"You do? What?" Sarah asked.

"For not being honest with you on Monday."

"But you were honest, right from the start. You were clear about everything."

Tulane grunted a little laugh. "No, honey, you were clear. But maybe not so honest. See, you could say that —" He bit off the words and looked around at the ladies.

"Momma, this is really private stuff."

"Uh-huh, we haven't had such fun since all of Clay's ex-girlfriends came to town and confused the living daylights out of him.

Now, you get on with it, you hear."

"Yes, ma'am."

Tulane looked back down at Sarah. "I'm really sorry about this. I should take you out into the alley and say this, but Momma would kill me, so I'm going to say it here."

"I don't mind."

"I figured, since you're basically one of them."

"I am?"

"Oh, yes, you are. So see, the thing is, you were clear on Monday, but I knew you were lying. You were lying to yourself. And I knew it, going in. I let you believe it was all just a casual thing because that was what you wanted, but I always wanted more."

"You wanted more?"

"Yeah, and if I'd been a man instead of an idiot on Tuesday morning, I would have stayed and told your father that I loved you and that my intentions were honest. He asked me, by the way, and I was so angry at being blindsided that I said something stupid."

"You love me?"

"Yeah, I do. But the question is, do you love me?"

She wrapped her arms around his neck. "You love me? Really?"

"Yeah, Sarah, I do."

"I love you back. I've loved you for a long time."

He gave her a less than erotic kiss on the lips, then linked a trail of semi-chaste kisses to her earlobe.

Sarah wanted him to do something wicked with her ear, but instead he whispered, "Sarah, honey, I know you say you've given up breaking the rules, but I'm feeling a little constrained here with this audience. And I thought, since I'm already AWOL from the track, that it might be real fun to go on over to the Peach Blossom Motor Court for a long, serious conversation about our future, followed by a little hanky-panky. I'm sure Lillian Bray would enjoy the show, and since we've already got an audience, I'll bet we don't even get into too much trouble."

Her whole body flushed and she looked up into his beautiful green eyes. "You want to take me to a no-tell motel? Really?"

"Oh, yeah."

EPILOGUE

Two weeks later, the blazing sun beat down on the top of Sarah's head as she walked down a row of soybeans. Not that she was an expert in South Carolina agriculture, but Tulane called them soybeans, and she figured he probably knew.

This particular soybean field belonged to a person named Old Man Nelson.

"It's over here," Tulane said, taking Sarah's hand like a little kid and pulling her down the row toward a giant live oak that stood smack-dab in the middle of the field.

Sarah was dressed for the outing in a pair of sneakers and shorts and a sleeveless T-shirt. Her skin reeked of sunblock. Ruby had been sure to hand her a large tube of the stuff when they stopped by the Cut 'n Curl earlier in the day to say hi. Ruby had given her a whole lecture on the Southern sun and what it was likely to do to her fair skin and freckled face.

Sunblock notwithstanding, Sarah was glad when they reached the shade of the tree. Its gnarled roots and spreading branches made it a great climbing tree. It had to be very old, and its bark was marked with hundreds of carved initials.

"Shoot," Tulane said as he ducked under the oak's branches. "There isn't any space left, is there?"

He sounded so disappointed. This business of coming out here and carving their names was very important to him. His parents' names were somewhere on that tree, and so were Stony's and Sharon's, and Clay's and Jane's, and from the looks of it, most of the couples who lived in Last Chance.

"I guess we'll have to bypass the graffiti," she said gently. "I'm sure you're relieved. I've heard all about Clay's tree house and how you fell out of it when you were twelve and almost died. Your mother explained that you've been afraid of heights ever since."

Tulane turned around and stared at her. "You don't understand. We have to do this. It's a tradition."

She glanced over at the tree. The trunk was easily eight feet in diameter, and every inch of it was covered with carvings. The carvings ran from the roots all the way past the first branches, which forked from the trunk about seven feet from the ground. It looked as if lovers had been forced up to those first branches to find pristine bark to destroy. The carvings wound around the trunk at least fifteen feet up.

"I'm amazed there are that many lovers in Last Chance," she said.

"Generations of folks have carved their names in this tree. Look yonder." He pointed to an old carving bearing the initials CR and EA. "That's Chance Rhodes's carving."

"You mean the guy who lost the plantation in that card game and condemned your family to generations of poverty and the occasional angel sighting?"

"Yeah, him. He started the tradition. And we're going to continue it, but before I have to man up and go climb that tree, there's something we need to discuss."

"What?"

"I want to move back to Last Chance. I want to make my home here. I want to be part of Hettie's committee, and I want to do more. I want to help this town rebuild itself. Shoot, Sarah, all this land used to belong to my kin, but my stupid ancestor lost it all in a card game. I want to get it back."

"Because you don't want people to laugh at you?"

He shook his head. "No. I just want to do the right thing. And, honey, that's what I love the most about you. You make me feel like a grown-up man, and you make me want to be worthy of that feeling. And, also, you're on the side of the angels, which in my family doesn't exactly hurt."

She laughed.

"So you wouldn't mind living here?" he asked.

She shook her head. "Oh, Tulane, I can't think of another place I'd rather call home. I love this place."

"That's good, because we have an appointment with a realtor after I finish with carving our names. And after that, we've got a meeting with Reverend Ellis. I figure we better get married quick, especially since everyone knows we spent that afternoon at the Peach Blossom Motor Court."

"Well, I'm not worried about the Last Chance ladies. And I'm okay with a quick wedding, before my mother decides to plan it for us."

"Good," Tulane said. "So, there's only one more detail I need to clear up, and then I guess I've got to go climb that tree."

"Are you stalling?"

"Maybe a little." He reached into his jeans and pulled out a little red leather box. "You need a ring."

"Oh!"

He handed her the box. "Look, if you don't like it, I'm sure we can —"

"I'm sure I'll like it." She opened the top of the box and found an old-fashioned ring of rose gold with a fiery opal in its center. "It's beautiful. Wherever did you find it?"

"It belonged to her." He nodded toward the tree and the initials EA. "Elizabeth Ames. It's been handed down for years. It was the one thing Chance Rhodes didn't lose in that card game. Momma wore it for a long time, and so did Sharon, but . . ." His voice faded out.

"Oh, Tulane, did Stone give you this?"

He nodded. "I told him I was going down to the jewelers to look for a ring, and he insisted that I have this one."

"I can't —"

"Stony wants someone to wear it. He hates the fact that it's been sitting in a box, gathering dust. It's important to him that you have it. He thinks you're good for me, which probably explains why he didn't give the ring to Clay for Jane. I'm afraid that Stone and Jane got off on the wrong foot with each other. But I bet he eventually comes around. Stone moves like a glacier on a lot of things."

Sarah nodded. Poor, brokenhearted Stone. She understood. Stone didn't intend to ever marry again.

She took the ring out of the box and slipped it on her left hand. It fit perfectly. "The green in this opal is the same color as your eyes," she whispered.

The next moment she was in his arms, being thoroughly kissed. The kiss was heading in an entirely predictable direction when Tulane gently pushed back.

"Uh, I would love to get sidetracked, honey, but we have appointments this afternoon. I think I need to screw my courage up and go climb that tree."

"You know you don't have to do that. We could pretend we did it."

"Honey, we're not going to lie about this, okay? And besides, it's important."

He turned and studied the oak. "Man, it looks like Clay had to climb all the way up that branch. Look, up there, there's Clay's and Jane's initials." He pointed to a spot about fourteen feet up, where the initials WJC and CPR had been carved.

"All right, if we have to do it, you could lift me up and I could —"

"*I* am climbing this tree, Sarah, even

though it scares the crap out of me. I need to fly." He said this with a firm nod of his head. Then he gave her an adorable look and asked, "Got any fairy dust, Tinkerbell?"

"No," she said. "No fairy dust. But I promise you, I'll be here to catch you if you fall."

The employees of Thorndike Press hope you have enjoyed this Large Print book. All our Thorndike, Wheeler, and Kennebec Large Print titles are designed for easy reading, and all our books are made to last. Other Thorndike Press Large Print books are available at your library, through selected bookstores, or directly from us.

For information about titles, please call:
(800) 223-1244

or visit our Web site at:
http://gale.cengage.com/thorndike

To share your comments, please write:
Publisher
Thorndike Press
10 Water St., Suite 310
Waterville, ME 04901

L